THE
BRIDE
WORE
BLUE

Other Books by Mona Hodgson

Historical Fiction

Two Brides Too Many
Too Rich for a Bride

Children's Books

Real Girls of the Bible: A 31-Day Devotional (Zonderkidz)
The Princess Twins and the Kitty (Zonderkidz I Can Read)
The Princess Twins Play in the Garden (Zonderkidz I Can Read)
The Princess Twins and the Tea Party (Zonderkidz I Can Read)
The Princess Twins and the Birthday Party (Zonderkidz I Can Read)
The Best Breakfast (Zonderkidz I Can Read)
Thank You, God, for Rain (Zonderkidz I Can Read)
Bedtime in the Southwest (Northland Publishing)

THE
BRIDE
WORE
BLUE

A Novel

MONA
HODGSON

Book Three

The Sinclair Sisters of Cripple Creek

WATERBROOK
PRESS

THE BRIDE WORE BLUE
PUBLISHED BY WATERBROOK PRESS
12265 Oracle Boulevard, Suite 200
Colorado Springs, Colorado 80921

All Scripture quotations or paraphrases are taken from the King James Version.

This is a work of fiction. Apart from well-known people, events, and locales that figure into the narrative, all names, characters, places, and incidents are the products of the author's imagination or are used fictitiously.

ISBN 978-0-307-73030-5
ISBN 978-0-307-73031-2 (electronic)

Copyright © 2012 by Mona Hodgson

Cover design by Kelly Howard; cover photo by Richard Jenkins

Published in association with the literary agency of Janet Kobobel Grant, Books & Such, 52 Mission Circle, Suite 122, PMB 170, Santa Rosa, CA 95409-5370.

Published in the United States by WaterBrook Multnomah, an imprint of the Crown Publishing Group, a division of Random House Inc., New York.

WATERBROOK and its deer colophon are registered trademarks of Random House Inc.

The Cataloging in Publication data is on file with the Library of Congress.

Printed in the United States of America

2012—First Edition

10 9 8 7 6 5 4 3 2 1

For my mother, Stella June Shindlebower Gansberg, and her sisters,
my Aunt Marion, Aunt Pauline, Aunt Alma, and Aunt Nellie

Therefore being justified by faith, we have peace with God through our Lord Jesus Christ: by whom also we have access by faith into this grace wherein we stand, and rejoice in hope of the glory of God.

ROMANS 5:1–2

ONE

1 June 1897

See that man over there?"

Vivian had no trouble hearing Aunt Alma over the *clickety-clack* of the train wheels. She poised her pencil over her sketch pad and followed her aunt's gaze to the man who slouched in the seat two rows ahead of them.

"He's been chewing and spitting most all the way from Colorado Springs." Aunt Alma, Vivian's chaperone, shook her head, causing the penny-colored braid encircling it to rock back and forth. "That's the kind of man you need to watch out for," she said. "You're not in Maine anymore, child."

The label stung Vivian's ears. Why did everyone think of her as a child? It didn't help that she was four or five inches shorter than all three of her sisters. Straightening, she pressed her back against the seat. "I'm not a child. Aunt Alma, I hardly think one can determine which man to watch out for by what he wears or how he looks."

Nothing in Gregory's debonair style of dressing indicated he was a cad.

"You can't be so trusting of men out here in the West. They're, well…" Blushing, her aunt cupped her mouth with a gloved hand. "They're quite lonely."

Vivian tugged the sleeves straight on her percale travel dress. She might be the baby in her family, but she wasn't a child. She'd lost her mother before she'd lost her first tooth. Her father had left home before she did. So had her sisters, Kat and Nell first and then Ida.

Plus she'd had to leave Sassy in Maine. Her poor cat didn't understand being left behind any more than Vivian did. And her familiarity with growing up too fast had to remain her secret.

Moving to Cripple Creek hadn't been her choice. But any plans for a future with Gregory were history, and Father had made it clear as rainwater in his last letter that she wasn't welcome to join him in France. Even New York's latest fashions couldn't measure up to the costume prowess of Paris. There she would have had the opportunity to secure her future as a fashion designer.

But instead Father insisted she reunite with her sisters in Colorado. That would have suited her fine before Gregory. At least the move to Cripple Creek ushered her away from Portland, if not her past. She did miss her sisters and wanted to see them, but she couldn't bear the thought of them seeing her for what she was.

She returned her attention to the opera gown she'd been sketching. Too much flouncing at the waist. She pulled a pink eraser from her reticule and brushed away the last lines she'd drawn. If only mistakes in life were that easy to erase.

Vivian drew in a fortifying breath. She had to hope her new home could offer her the fresh start she needed. Nell had written more than once about the wondrous growth taking place in Cripple Creek. While an opera house or two did not a thriving metropolis make, perhaps the move to Colorado wouldn't be as bleak as she had expected. Surely the town was big enough now to host a clothing designer who would value Vivian's eastern fashion sense.

"I'm sorry if I upset you." Her aunt punctuated her whisper with a frown.

Vivian dropped the eraser into her bag. It wasn't Aunt Alma's fault her youngest niece wasn't lovable enough to make anyone want to stay with her. "You needn't worry about me, Aunt Alma."

Aunt Alma patted Vivian's knee. "But you know I do."

Vivian offered her aunt the best smile she could rally. Would her prim and proper aunt care so much if she knew the truth? But she couldn't know. Neither could her sisters. Enough had changed for Vivian already, and she couldn't bear the blame she deserved. Especially if it meant seeing her guilt reflected back to her in the virtuous eyes of her sisters.

While the train's steel wheels screeched and howled, slowing it down for what Vivian hoped was its final descent, her mind stalled on thoughts of her sisters. Ida would be so relieved things didn't work out with Gregory that she probably wouldn't even mention him. Nell would want to match her up with a suitable beau. When she just wanted to forget.

A sharp clanging noise drew their attention to the glass-paned door at the back of the train car. Vivian twisted in her narrow seat in time to watch two men dash up the aisle toward her, their faces covered by bandannas. Both wore soiled dusters. The shorter man in front clutched a large metal box. The man behind him ran bent but still nearly brushed the hanging lights with his straw hat. He wielded a pistol.

"Bandits!" Vivian wanted to turn away from them and slide to the floorboard, but her legs refused to move.

"Remain calm." The bandit carrying the box sounded as if his mouth harbored marbles. "Everybody mind your own business, and nobody'll get hurt."

Vivian intended to do just that, but Aunt Alma's arms encircled her, knocking her off balance. Her sketch pad and pencil fell to the floorboard. She had no idea her foot lay in the aisle until the first man tripped on it.

He lunged forward, snarling as the box crashed into the seat two rows ahead of her, narrowly missing the shoulder of the kind of man she needed to watch out for. The hem of the bandit's coat snagged on the arm of the seat, revealing a large belt buckle at his waist. Quickly regaining his composure, he turned and glared at Vivian over the filthy blue bandanna tied across his mouth and nose that did little to mask the pungent scent of licorice-root candy.

Vivian clasped her trembling hands and swallowed hard against the lump forming in her throat. "I'm sorry."

"You tryin' to be a hero, are you?" His beady eyes narrowed. "Think you're smarter than us?"

Before Vivian could manage a response, the conductor charged through the door, carrying a shotgun. "Stop those thieves!"

When men in the back of the car began to stand, the taller bandit waved his gun, and the shorter man jerked open the door at the front of the car. He tossed the metal box into the passing brush, and both men jumped from the train. The conductor stopped just short of leaping off the train himself. Vivian watched out the window as the two bandits tumbled down a hill, then disappeared into the scrub and short trees.

The conductor retrieved his shiny black cap from the floor and straightened his vest. His forehead sported a lump the color of a pome-granate. "The danger has passed, folks, and we'll arrive at the Cripple

Creek station shortly." He traced the curls on either end of his thin mustache. "Please do all you can to remember what you've seen and heard, so the law can bring these criminals to justice."

Aunt Alma laid a quaking hand on Vivian's arm. "Now do you understand what I mean about judging by a man's costume out here?"

Vivian nodded. "I'll do my best to stay away from men who wear dusters and bandannas." And gaudy belt buckles.

Carter Alwyn pinched the bridge of his nose. Tuesday was his least favorite day of the week. The *other women* usually created a stir on their designated morning in town. Not that they set out to do much more than shop for baubles and bustles, but the activity never failed to provoke at least one citizen's self-righteous indignation and drive him—or her—to Carter's office with his chin in the air. This week's upstanding representative of the moral community scowled at him from the other side of his desk.

"It's scandalous." Mr. Updike stiffened to his full five feet five inches. "And we want to know when you're going to do something about it, Deputy Alwyn."

Carter leaned forward. If only he had a nickel for every time he had engaged in this same conversation. He had his own reasons for avoiding the *other women,* besides the obvious moral ones, but as long as they paid their fees and checked in with a doctor regularly, their services were a legal and accepted practice in Cripple Creek—an enterprise welcomed by many influential people here.

Mr. Updike tugged on the lapels of his oversized herringbone suit jacket and glared at Carter. "I'm here as a representative of the business community, and we want change. We insist you outlaw such depravity."

If the *business community* really was making such demands, a large segment of the *business* owners were shooting themselves in the foot. A lot of money flowed between Bennett and Myers Avenues. And Carter knew the banker would be the first to whine about the shortfall created by losing that breed of businesswoman. No doubt the man's zealous campaign was on his wife's insistence. It wouldn't surprise Carter to see Mrs. Updike waiting outside the door with her hands planted on her hips, but he resisted the temptation to stand and look out the window.

He opened the top drawer of his desk and pulled out a file folder, then looked up. "Mr. Updike, you know about the recent rash of bank robberies this side of the divide. I've been more concerned with protecting your bank and the money that belongs to the fine people of Cripple Creek than with what our citizens choose to do with their money in the moonlight."

"Yes, well, I do appreciate that, but—" The whistle on the incoming train blew, and Updike jumped.

It took all the self-control Carter could muster to stifle the laughter camped in his throat. He swallowed hard against it. "Mr. Updike, I suggest you raise your concerns at the next city council meeting." He opened the folder full of wanted posters.

The banker huffed. "I can see I'm getting nowhere with you."

Carter looked up. "By the very nature of my job, sir, I am a man with a measure of authority to enforce laws, but little say in the creation of those laws."

Updike spun on his heels. The force of the door slamming behind him rattled the window and Carter's nerves. The man was a weasel and probably just as nocturnal as the others.

Carter's energy needed to go into keeping his town safe. He thumbed through the stack of posters. Robert LeRoy Parker, also known as Butch Cassidy. Clean shaven, square jaw. Rounded chin. Harry "Sundance Kid" Longabaugh. Narrow oval face. Dark eyes. And a guy known only as Pickett. Six foot two. Lean and lanky.

Carter tipped back in his chair and scrubbed his face, already stubbled by this time of day. Witnesses to the bank robberies over in Divide had described one of the three robbers as lean and lanky.

As soon as Jon, one of two deputies under the authority given to Carter by the El Paso County Sheriff, returned to the office, Carter would ride to Victor for a chat with Gilbert about the bank robbery there yesterday. None of the criminals pictured on these posters would spend any time in his town. He had to make sure of it.

Carter had just closed the folder when the telephone on his desk jangled. He lifted the earpiece from the hook and spoke into the cone.

"Deputy Alwyn speaking."

"Yes, good afternoon." As usual, the young woman's voice sounded too sweet. "Deputy Alwyn, you have a call from Mr. Wilbert Ratcliff."

"Yes, thank you." Why would the agent at the Midland Terminal Railroad be calling him?

A click followed, then a sentence that made no sense to Carter, but its fevered pitch burned his ears and set his heart racing.

"Mr. Ratcliff, you need to slow down."

"The train's in. Bandits got the cash box. Jumped off just north of town."

Carter leaped from his chair, knocking it against the wall. "Anyone harmed? You need a doctor down there?"

"I sent for one. But except for a nasty lump on the conductor's head, no one was hurt."

"Good." Carter slapped the folder on his desk. "No one else steps foot off the train. I'll be right there."

On his way to the depot, Carter saw Jon walk out of the boot shop and waved him over. While they took long strides to the depot at the far end of Bennett Avenue, Carter briefed his fellow deputy on what little he knew from the station agent. Jon went inside the depot to let the agent know they'd arrived while Carter made his way through the crowd gathered on the wooden platform.

"Deputy Alwyn?"

Carter recognized the woman's voice that rang loud and clear. He turned to see Mrs. Raines—his friend Tucker's wife—standing in front of him, flanked by her two sisters, one holding a baby.

"Ladies." He touched the brim of his Stetson and then glanced at the folder in his hands. "I have duties to attend to."

They fell in step with him as he walked toward the train's passenger car. "We have family on that train," Mrs. Raines said. "No one will tell us anything. What has happened? We need to know if they're all right."

Carter climbed the metal stairs to the deck of the train car. Turning, he faced the impatient throng. "There's been a robbery." The murmurs rose to a hum, and he raised his hand for quiet. "No passengers were harmed. We need your full cooperation while we try to gain pertinent information from those on board. We'll release the passengers and ready the train for its continuance as soon as possible." He turned and pushed open the heavy steel door.

In contrast to the charged anticipation on the platform, the atmosphere inside the smoky car was solemn. He could have heard a feather drop on the hardwood flooring.

"Folks, I'm the sheriff's senior deputy stationed here in Cripple Creek, Deputy Carter Alwyn. I need to speak to any of you who saw or heard something that may be useful in capturing the bandits."

"Sir." From a window seat several rows back, a matronly woman waved a gloved hand. "My niece here…" She glanced at the young woman sitting beside her. "She tripped one of the outlaws."

Carter's jaw tensed. "You did what?" He didn't care that he'd shouted. This girl who had tried to play the hero couldn't be a day over sixteen. He'd seen similar circumstances, and being reminded of their outcome soured his stomach. "Young lady, do you have any idea—"

"First of all, Deputy Alwyn…" She squared her shoulders and glared at him, her eyes a fiery brown. "I am not stupid. Nor am I heroic. I didn't trip the man on purpose, so you can save your lecture. I haven't the time or the patience for it."

Perhaps she was older than she looked. Sassy, no matter her age.

"Secondly, bandannas covered the two men's faces, and they wore long coats. None of us saw very much, so this is clearly a waste of time."

Carter choked down his frustration. "Miss—"

"Sinclair."

He met her defiant gaze. "Miss Sinclair, I am the professional here, and I'll be the judge of what *very much* includes." He had outlaws to track down. He didn't have time to bicker with a petulant female.

Jon stepped into the train car, and Carter rested a hand on his partner's shoulder. "Folks, this is Deputy Jon Ondersma. He'll accompany those of you going on to Victor to hear your statements concerning the matter. The conductor will get the names and contact information from those of you planning to depart the train here." Carter looked at the young woman sitting in the aisle seat five rows back. "And I'll speak to any of you who may have critical information. Miss Sinclair, if Cripple Creek is your destination, I'll begin with you."

"It is."

Shifting his attention to the others, Carter walked toward the door. "Deputy Ondersma and the conductor will direct the rest of you. Please meet me inside the depot, ladies. Directly."

His mother had taught him to get the most unpleasant tasks out of the way first, and he'd learned his lesson well.

Two

oung lady!

Were all lawmen in the West this cocky and sarcastic, or was this just her unlucky day and Deputy Alwyn happened to be part of its ill will? Vivian retrieved her satchel from the floorboard and followed the snappish deputy down the narrow aisle.

They made their way to the back of the car, and the deputy stepped out onto the platform and offered his hand to Aunt Alma. "Ma'am."

Once her aunt had both feet on the platform, he held out his hand to Vivian. She didn't need the man's help but accepted it anyway. His firm grip matched the stern expression on his face.

"Thank you," she said.

"You're welcome." He let go of her hand and tugged his leather vest straight. Taking their satchels from them, Deputy Alwyn glanced to ward a small brick building about two train-car lengths ahead of them. "We need to be quick about this. I'll only detain you a few minutes."

The promise had no sooner left his mouth when the crowd began closing in on them, her three sisters in the lead. Vivian waved.

"You're Reverend Raines's sister-in-law?" Placing far too much emphasis on the first word, the deputy quirked a dark eyebrow.

"Yes, one of three."

Nell reached them first. "Are you all right?" She wrapped Vivian in a tight embrace, transporting her to a time and place that was familiar and freeing.

"They're well, Mrs. Archer."

The deputy was apparently acquainted with at least two of her sisters. It made sense that a lawman would know the preachers and mining officials in town. Probably the doctors too.

He brushed a midnight black curl under his hat and looked at her sisters. "I just have a few questions, and I'll be quick about it. I have outlaws to track." The deputy met Vivian's gaze and motioned for them to make haste to the depot.

She hurried to keep up with him. Yet another instance in which a height greater than five feet two inches would prove useful.

The crowd around the depot hummed like a beehive. Inside, a man with deeply hooded eyes waved them toward an open door behind the ticket counter. "You can use my office, deputy."

"Thank you, Wilbert."

The office felt more like an oversized wardrobe. A small desk, one file cabinet, and two spindle-back chairs in front of the desk.

"Please have a seat, ladies." Deputy Alwyn set their satchels on the floor between the chairs and pulled a notepad and pencil from his shirt pocket. Settling into the desk chair, he looked at Vivian. "Miss Sinclair, did you notice anything else about the two men, besides the bandannas?"

"They both wore soiled dusters. The taller man wore a flat-top straw hat and waved a pistol. I didn't hear him say anything. The shorter man came through first, carrying a large metal box."

Aunt Alma squared her shoulders. "Which narrowly missed hitting a man in the head when my niece tripped the thief."

The deputy smoothed his mustache as if he were trying to hide a smile and met Vivian's gaze. "Unintentionally, if I remember correctly."

Her cheeks grew warm. "That's correct." Sitting a little straighter, Vivian forced herself to remember as many details as she could. "The surly one carrying the box was thick in the middle, spoke as if he had something in his mouth, and smelled of licorice root."

The deputy flipped a page in his notepad and wrote feverishly before looking up at her. "Good details. Was he wearing a hat?"

Aunt Alma straightened. "A dusty derby."

"I apologize, ma'am. I didn't get your name."

"Alma Shindlebower."

His pencil snapped as he wrote her name.

Vivian pulled a pencil from her satchel and handed it to him.

"Thank you." He busied himself writing the results of his questions and then regarded Vivian with a sideways glance. "Where will you be staying while you're in town, ma'am?"

"Miss Hattie's Boardinghouse on Golden Avenue."

"I know the place." Another notation. "Should I need anything further, I'll contact you there."

Vivian nodded, hoping that wouldn't be necessary. She'd just as soon toss the whole trip behind her, especially this last leg of it. Starting now. She stood and retrieved their valises from the floor. "Good day, deputy."

Standing, he pinched the brim of his hat. "Ladies."

As she and Aunt Alma stepped out of the office, a woman with a small child, the next person in a line of weary travelers from their train, brushed past them through the open doorway. Deputy Alwyn had a busy day ahead of him.

Finally, the Sinclair sisters' reunion. If only Father were here too. If only…

Ida waved from where Vivian's sisters waited near the depot door. Her baby niece bounced in Kat's arms, and she couldn't wait to get a good look at her. How was it possible that all three of her sisters were married and one had a baby? Where had the time gone?

To Gregory.

Her oldest sister wore the blue serge skirt and embroidered jacket Vivian had designed especially for Ida's job interview with Mollie O'Bryan last year here in Cripple Creek. Nell swiped at the tears streaming down her cheeks and offered Vivian a smile that would brighten the darkest night. The snood at Kat's neck added to her motherly appearance, a role in which she seemed quite comfortable.

All her sisters looked good. Healthy and happy. Cripple Creek and marriage seemed to agree with them. As Vivian closed the gap between them, she hoped Cripple Creek would be enough for her. At least until she'd earned enough money to be able to move on to somewhere she could truly make a name for herself.

"Let me take those." Ida took the bags from Vivian. "I made arrangements to have your trunk and Aunt Alma's second valise delivered to the boardinghouse."

"Then we don't have to go back to the platform to search out our bags. Thank you." Vivian could always count on Ida to tend to any details. And, although she wanted to be able to take care of herself, the help felt mighty good right now.

"My carriage is right out front, but first, Auntie Viv, I'd like to introduce you to your niece." Kat held the baby out to her. "This is Miss Hope Joyce Cutshaw. Hope, this is your Aunt Vivian Dee Sinclair."

Vivian stared at the pink knit bundle. "It's wonderful to meet you, little Miss Hope."

Kat raised an eyebrow and lifted baby Hope closer. "Take her."

A shiver scampered up Vivian's spine. "I've never held a baby."

"Well, you're not getting any younger." With far too much ease, Kat placed Hope's head in the crook of Vivian's right arm.

Vivian's breath caught. Life felt especially fragile wrapped up in this little one, and she felt inadequate to tend it. The infant began to fuss and squirm.

"Just hold her tight, and she'll feel safe," Kat said.

Her insides quivering, Vivian pressed Hope to her bodice, then sealed the baby's bootie-clad feet in her left hand. The infant instantly relaxed and began to peep like a baby chick.

"Isn't she delectable?" Nell's blue eyes shone like sapphires as she trailed her fingers across Hope's rounded cheeks.

Vivian gazed at her niece. Wide brown eyes like her mama. Dark lashes. Auburn peach fuzz on her soft head. Vivian blinked back tears. "She's adorable." It came out a reverent whisper.

"I cried too when I first held her," Kat said. "I felt as if I'd just unwrapped a most precious gift."

Vivian felt her tears spill over. Tears of wonderment in response to the thrill of being an aunt. But that wasn't all that caused her heart to cry. Her sisters' babies were as close as Vivian would ever come to having one of her own to hold. Not so long ago she'd been lovable like this little one, but her imprudence had swept it away forever. And along with it, any hope of experiencing the joy she glimpsed in her sister's eyes.

Nell glanced toward the office that contained Deputy Alwyn, then leaned toward Vivian's ear. "He isn't married."

That was bad news. "Ever the matchmaker, you are. But I'll have you know that the man is incorrigible." She turned toward the others before Nell could respond. She'd just gotten into town, and Nell was already at work on her. This wasn't going to be easy.

Kat opened the depot door. "Aunt Alma, you get to sit up front with me, and you can hold Hope all the way to the boardinghouse."

"Fair enough." Aunt Alma led the way out the door. "As long as you drive real slow to give me more time with her."

In mere minutes, Aunt Alma was seated in the front of a white carriage and reaching for Hope. Vivian breathed in the powdery scent of her niece, then handed her off to Aunt Alma before climbing into the carriage. The train whistle blew, and the locomotive chugged up the hill away from town.

Vivian planted her feet on the floorboard. Mule-drawn carts, horses carrying a rider or pulling a wagon, and men on foot created a maze outside the depot and up the street lined with brick buildings. Kat sat directly in front of her, guiding a mare full of brio around a corner and up a steep hill. In sharp contrast to Portland's flat oceanfront property, this place sat nestled amongst hills and mountains of varying size and stature.

As far as Vivian was concerned, they couldn't arrive at the boardinghouse soon enough. She'd spent the better part of a week on one *clickety-clacking* train after another with far too many ups and downs. Aunt Alma's callow warnings about men. Clumsy train robbers. A deputy as intense as a summer thunderstorm. So far, her introduction to Cripple Creek left much to be desired. She'd best work on lowering her expectations if she didn't wish to be endlessly disappointed.

Kat gave the reins a tug, and the mare smoothed out her cadence. Ida leaned forward to catch Vivian's attention. "We planned a family welcome dinner at the parsonage for tonight, but you and Aunt Alma are probably all in but your shoestrings. If you need to rest this evening, we can have the big supper tomorrow night."

They *had* been delayed, and she did have some unpacking to do, but now that she was here, she was more anxious to catch up with her family. Many of them she hadn't even met. "Aunt Alma?"

Her aunt sat beside Kat, chattering to baby Hope. She twisted in the carriage seat. "Visiting with all of you and this precious baby is my idea of restful." A smile warmed her hazel eyes.

Vivian nodded. "I agree."

"Tonight it is then," Nell said. "I'm bringing a big bowl of my peanut cabbage salad."

Vivian's mouth watered. "Perhaps we should go straight to supper."

"We don't dare." Kat wagged a finger. "Your new landlady would chide us all something awful."

"The boardinghouse is right up there." Ida waved toward the top of the hill. "Besides, Hattie loves to bake while she waits and is sure to serve a tasty morsel or two that will tide you over."

At the end of the next block, Kat made another turn. "This is Golden Avenue." Flower beds in full bloom skirted the yards of bright, neat houses. She pulled the carriage up in front of a springtime-yellow house with a crisp white trimming. "Here we are."

Ida climbed down first and reached for Hope. "Come on, little one. Let's go see Nannie Hattie." She watched Vivian climb down. "Hattie Adams is practically family, you'll see."

"Why, this boardinghouse has become a Sinclair sister tradition. Now we all will have stayed here." Kat tapped Hope's dainty nose and reached for her. "Viv, you're going to love Miss Hattie."

Wanting to make a good first impression, Vivian smoothed her sleeves and skirt and took her satchel from Nell. Right now, she loved the idea of having her feet planted on solid ground again. Kat tied the mare to the hitching rail, and the five of them made their way up a brick walkway. Vivian surveyed the lush yard and colorful window boxes. Her eyes and her spirit feasted on the white and lavender flowers. By the time she arrived at the porch, lively music reached her ears, and she slowed her steps toward her new home.

Nell raised a thin, blond eyebrow, her eyes a slightly darker shade of blue than the late afternoon sky. "We didn't warn you about that?"

"Warn me?" In their letters, her sisters had written of the woman's kindnesses, but she'd not received any warnings. Vivian shook her head.

"About Miss Hattie's phonograph. Her music is one of her many endearing qualities." Ida reached for an electric doorbell. "Just be thankful I bought her new cylinders this last Christmas. Now she has five songs in her repertoire."

Kat giggled. "You don't know how lucky you are, Viv. We only had three songs."

When Hope began to fuss, Kat pushed the doorbell again. This time the music shut off.

"On my way, dears." The words puffed out just before the door swept open. A wide smile filled the face of a woman of ample portions, top and bottom. Her friendly gaze locked on Vivian. "I'm Hattie, and you must be our Vivian."

Before Vivian could answer or even nod, the woman enveloped her in a robust hug. She smelled of cinnamon and vanilla. Welcoming. Comforting. So undeserved.

Sighing, Miss Hattie stepped back as if she sensed Vivian's unworthiness, then gripped her shoulders at arm's length. "You're a smaller version, for sure. But right adorable. And so fashionable in your travel dress. I love the straighter lines and full-length jacket."

Vivian nodded. "Yes ma'am. Thank you." The woman had an eye for fashion. Vivian already liked her.

Miss Hattie released Vivian's shoulders. "The Sinclair sisters are at long last together again."

Together, but for how long? They'd only been apart for two years, but it was long enough for her to do something stupid, something that would place an immovable wedge between them. Vivian looked at her sisters. How long they would be together depended upon her ability to keep her sordid history a secret. Her sisters were good girls and now upstanding women, married to pillars in the community, revered by the deputy and her landlady. Why couldn't she have been more like them?

Aunt Alma stepped around them. "Miss Hattie, I'm Alma Shindlebower. And I'm most pleased to make—"

"Aunt Alma!" After embracing their aunt, Miss Hattie waved them all inside. "Land sakes if I haven't heard a boatload about you."

"And I about you. I understand you've taken real good care of our girls."

"I try." Miss Hattie's wink deepened the webbing at the corners of her blue-gray eyes.

"And a fine job you've done. Even found first-rate husbands for them, from what I hear."

Vivian could abide hearing the same five songs again and again, but matchmaking was an entirely different matter. A complete waste of the woman's time.

"Can't take much credit," Miss Hattie said. "They have the good Lord to thank for those matches."

Vivian's stomach clenched. She'd frustrated the Lord's match for her.

Miss Hattie offered Vivian a warm smile. "I say we rest and visit for a spell in the parlor while we wait for your trunk to arrive."

Vivian followed her new landlady into an inviting room with flocked wallpaper and a polished mantel. A hint of lemon oil tickled her nose. The Edison phonograph she'd heard about posed in the corner. A teacart stood at the end of the sofa, complete with a teapot puffing steam and a full platter of cookies. Ida poured tea for each of them while Kat handed everyone a plate.

Miss Hattie set her teacup and cookies on a side table near the window and settled into the Queen Anne chair beside it. She pulled a footstool in line with her chair and propped up her feet, shoes and all. "Was your train late?"

Breathing in the scent of peppermint tea, Vivian carried her dishes to the sofa table and joined Nell and Aunt Alma on the sofa. She expected her aunt to respond to the woman's question, but apparently she was just as weary of the recounting as Vivian was. "I apologize for the delay, ma'am. We were late disembarking due to bandits."

"On the train?" Miss Hattie shoved the footstool away and planted her feet on the ground.

"Yes ma'am." Vivian reached for her plate. "Two men wearing bandannas."

"At Cripple Creek?" Her brow pinched, Miss Hattie glanced from Vivian to Aunt Alma. "And you two are all right?"

"'Twas an ordeal, for sure." Aunt Alma pressed her collar. "Our Vivian tripped one of the hoodlums."

The landlady's eyes widened. "You don't say. They were apprehended, then?"

"They jumped from the train before the conductor could catch them. They hit him on the head before fleeing to our car." Vivian bit into a cookie. Perfectly warm. Chewy. Lemony. Her favorite.

"That long ole ride from the East, and then bandits. Of all the things." Miss Hattie shook her gray head. "Here I was baking sweets while you were facing down hoodlums."

And a snappish deputy.

Kat held Hope against her shoulder and patted the baby's back. "To think I considered mine and Nell's introduction to Cripple Creek dramatic."

"I'm thankful I wasn't in your situation—two missing misters." Vivian folded her hands in her lap. "At least I had Aunt Alma with me and three sisters waiting for us."

"Well, thank you, dear." Her aunt turned and winked at her. "And here I figured myself for a mere tagalong."

Vivian offered her aunt a crooked smile. "I may not have been keen on having company at first, but I'm glad you came." Although she would've gladly forfeited the lectures on wily men.

"Well, I for one am delighted you're both here." Miss Hattie lifted her teacup off the table. "Vivian, dear, your sisters tell me you design clothing." She raised her cup to her mouth. "And wedding gowns too, I'm told."

"I do." Vivian nearly choked on the words she'd expected to say at the front of a church, face to face with Gregory. "I aspire to have my own shop one day, but..."

"Perhaps you could work with the fashion designer we have here in the valley."

Vivian sat straighter. "You do? I mean, there's a designer here?"

"Indeed, there is. Etta Ondersma."

"Ondersma? On the train, at the depot, I met—"

"Deputy Jon Ondersma?"

"Yes."

"His mother owns Etta's Fashions in Victor."

She glanced at her sisters. "Victor?"

"The train ride takes nearly an hour, with stops in Anaconda and Elkton." Ida's teacup clinked against the saucer. "Too far for you to go every day to work."

Leave it to Ida to disapprove. Vivian wanted to ask if Victor had lodging available, but since staying with Miss Hattie was a Sinclair sister tradition, the question might not set well on her first day in town.

She'd wait until next week to ask.

THREE

Carter patted his shirt pocket. *Good.* He still had his notepad. And Miss Sinclair's pencil. Which gave him at least one excuse to see her again. The spirited young woman possessed a captivating mix of vim and charm.

He settled his boots into the stirrups and slapped Liberty's rump. As his bay stallion lunged forward, Carter motioned for his makeshift posse to follow him north, up and over Tenderfoot Hill. He had assembled three others to ride along—Jesse from the livery, Otis from the Raines Ice Company, and the banker. He couldn't say what good pursuit would do at this point, but he had to do something while praying for a lead. He needed clues as to who might be responsible for the terror on the train.

They rode hard toward Ute Pass, to the area witnesses described as the place the two men had jumped. Carter's thoughts returned to the wanted posters and the image of Pickett: six foot two, tall and lanky. He definitely fit the description Miss Sinclair had given of one of the bandits. And the Schofield six-shooter matched the pistol described in the Divide bank robbery.

Thunder crashing in the distance drew Carter's attention to the clouds rolling through the pass from the north.

"Deputy Alwyn."

The banker's voice managed to overpower the slapping of horse hooves against the dirt-packed road. Stopping for a conversation would negate any hope he had of picking up a trail. Maintaining his steady pace, Carter glanced at Updike, who looked like a frog on a horse.

"I still don't think this is the best idea, deputy."

Of course he didn't. Antagonism had etched deep lines at the man's gray eyes and his toady mouth. "I didn't insist that you join us." In fact, he'd tried to talk the banker out of it.

"Someone needs to be the voice of reason. Otherwise, you could end up like your father."

Time healed all wounds? Ten years hadn't been enough. Carter swallowed hard, fighting down the memories. He was chasing train bandits. Not a souse and a prostitute.

"I think telephoning the deputies in the surrounding towns and sending out sketches would be more effective. And less dangerous." Updike put slack in his reins, and thankfully his horse dropped back behind Carter.

Carter hated the route Updike had taken to make his point, but his logic held water. It would be harder for the bandits to outrun the telephone. He hadn't thought of that before they left. Hopefully Jon would telephone the surrounding towns when he returned from Victor on the train. Still, one or both of the bandits could have been injured in their fall. And if they were on foot, there was still a chance Carter could find them.

The men rode in silence for the last mile until they reached the area of scrub oak the conductor had described as the robbers' jumping-off point.

Carter pulled up on Liberty's reins. The other men came to a stop directly in front of him. "This is the general area where the two thieves jumped. Conductor said they took a tumble into a clump of trees and scrub brush." Pointing toward the likely spot, he noted the clouds looming closer. "Best find what we can in a hurry. Look for any evidence of blood, horses, the cash box—anything out of the ordinary."

Carter and the others spread out over the hill and at the bottom of it, examining the ground and the surrounding area.

"Over here!" Jesse's shout had them all scrambling around a shaggy-barked juniper about a quarter of a mile from the train tracks. "They're on horseback."

Carter dismounted and stepped around the still-steaming evidence that at least one horse had been present. He also found freshly rubbed stripes on the tree trunk where the horse had been secured by a rope.

"They had another horse tied over here." Otis waved his hat from a sycamore several yards away, no doubt trying to fend off the flies.

Carter studied the area. "Both horses were shod." Unfortunately, there was nothing special about the tracks in the dust.

"Looks like they headed farther north, away from Cripple Creek." Updike pointed at the gray sky. "No sign of any injuries. On horses, with a three-hour lead, they'll be long gone by now and the coming rain'll wash out any tracks." He pinned Carter's gaze. "I say we head back." A thunder crack served as punctuation.

Carter blew out a deep breath. The banker was right—the bandits could be anywhere by now, but... "They wouldn't have hauled the cash box with them. Has to be somewhere close."

Otis Bernard straightened his floppy canvas hat. "Real quick-like, I can go check around those outcroppings." He pointed out about another half a mile.

"Does seem like a good place to empty a cash box." Carter

considered Otis. He was as big as a bear. Lifting blocks of ice had added brawn to his bones. Otis could easily take either of the outlaws down. Unarmed. Carter nodded. "Take Jesse with you, and be careful. We'll"—he looked at Updike—"follow the brush line this other way."

They split up to finish their search. A raindrop the size of a healthy grape plopped on the horn of Carter's saddle. Another one thumped his hat. Carter was about to turn back when he saw Updike heel his horse toward a stand of pine. He rode up beside the banker.

"Find somethin'?"

The banker dismounted and tugged a steel box out from under a sage bush. "I saw the lock on the ground and followed the drag marks."

Sure enough, the rocky soil was smoothed where the bandits had dragged or pushed the box. Carter followed the marks back to the lock, stuck it in his jacket pocket, and slapped Harry Updike on the back. "Good eye."

The portly man smiled—something Carter had never seen him do. "Glad I could help."

They bent over the empty box. Not a single stock certificate, receipt, or bill remained inside. By the time they'd loaded the box onto Liberty's back and mounted their horses, Otis and Jesse were headed their way.

Once Carter returned, he'd get on the telephone to Divide, Florissant, and Colorado Springs. And then he'd return Miss Sinclair's pencil.

❧

Vivian pulled the last shirtwaist from her trunk and hung it over a yarn-wrapped clothes hanger. She added it to the wardrobe and looked around her new bedchamber. A fourposter bed with a sunbonnet quilt served as the centerpiece on the back wall. An oak chest of drawers stood on one side, a matching washstand on the other. A small lamp table sat beside a rocking chair in the corner opposite the wardrobe. Her trunk fit nicely under the second-story window.

A mansion suite compared to the bed and slight wardrobe she had in Aunt Alma's sewing room. Admittedly, the location was handy for designing costumes, but hardly private.

For now, this was her home. And Cripple Creek, her proving ground.

She knelt in front of her open trunk and unfolded her mother's lap quilt. The large family Bible lay neglected, nestled in the bittersweet memories of her mother's life and death. Tears stung Vivian's eyes as she ran her fingers over the gold leaf decorations and the embossed lettering as if they were priceless jewels. *HOLY BIBLE.*

I'm so deeply sorry, Mother.

Teardrops escaped her clenched eyes, and she brushed them away. After she wiped her wet hand on her chemise, Vivian lifted God's Word out of the trunk and carried it to the rocker in the corner. Seated, she laid the Bible on her lap and stared at the inscription at the bottom right corner: "The Harlan Sinclair Family."

Would her sisters have accepted her so freely, their hearts and arms open wide, if they knew the truth? Would Hattie Adams? How could they feel anything but disgust and disdain? She and her sisters had received the same teaching. They'd all been raised to be respectable and to revere God's Word and His laws. None of her sisters had broken His commands.

She alone.

Cupping her face in her hands, Vivian let her silent tears pool and stream down her wrists. She'd placed a man's word above God's Word. She'd given her heart to Gregory. Then she'd given him more.

When her tears subsided, she snuffled and trailed her finger over the brass clasp that sealed the leather-bound Holman. She hadn't opened the family Bible since that day last December. Dare she open it now?

Vivian wiped her hands on the skirt of her dressing gown and gently pinched the sides of the clasp, releasing its hold. She choked back her shame and opened the cover. Taking in the colorful illustrations, she turned the gilt-edged pages until she came to the Family Records.

MARRIAGES
Harlan Sinclair and Elizabeth "Betsy" Shindlebower wed
1872, 5 August

Her mother's handwriting.

Katherine Joyce Sinclair and Morgan Cutshaw wed
1896, 30 May
Nellie Jean Sinclair and Judson Archer wed 1896, 30 May

Written in Ida's confident penmanship, her *S*'s regal and her *T*'s controlled.

The next line, where Ida's name belonged, was blank. Vivian looked at the fountain pen and the pencil that lay on the round oak table beside her. When Ida packed her trunk to leave for Colorado last year, she'd left the Bible in Vivian's charge. Grasping the fountain pen between her fingers, Vivian drew a deep breath and began writing.

Ida Marie Sinclair and Reverend Tucker Raines wed 1897,
31 January

Vivian stared at the empty space below her untamed penmanship. That line would've held her name and…

She longed to do the right thing, remain detached. To gracefully accept her life as a spinster as Aunt Alma had. Her aunt lived in a comfortable house and owned a small dry goods and sewing-supply store in Portland, Maine. Her ever-expanding family loved her, and she loved them. Aunt Alma had a good life.

Feeling a slight lift in her chin, Vivian carefully turned to the next gold-trimmed page.

BIRTHS

Ida Marie 1874, 15 July to Harlan and Elizabeth "Betsy" Sinclair

Katherine Joyce 1875, 18 December to Harlan and Elizabeth Sinclair

Nellie Jean 1877, 20 March to Harlan and Elizabeth Sinclair

Vivian Dee 1879, 17 April to Harlan and Elizabeth Sinclair

Vivian ran her finger over the blank line that belonged to her sweet-faced niece. Yes, she was blessed with the love of a family she held dear. And she wouldn't…*couldn't* risk jeopardizing that love, no matter how badly she wanted to step out of the lie she was living.

She sighed and began to write.

Hope Joyce 1897, 21 April to Dr. Morgan and Katherine "Kat" Cutshaw

Finished with the updates, Vivian closed the Bible. She held it to her chest and leaned back in the chair. While she rocked back and forth in a gentle rhythm, her thoughts ran away with her. Aunt Alma had provided her room and board for nearly a year and a half. Her father had sent the money for her train ticket. Her sisters had let her room from Miss Hattie for the first three weeks of June.

After that, she was no longer their charge. Her aunt would board the train Monday to return to Portland. If Vivian ever expected to alter her reputation as the baby of the family, she must first prove she was capable of providing for herself.

FOUR

ivian followed her brother-in-law Morgan up a floral-lined walk to the front door of Ida's home. He cradled his infant daughter in his arms. Kat and Aunt Alma trailed them, talking about Cripple Creek's ups and downs with the fires last year and the rebuilding of the business district.

A district that didn't yet house a costume-design shop. But at least nearby Victor did.

White paint trimmed the red brick parsonage that sat behind the First Congregational Church, just up the hill from the center of town. Cheery columbines and primrose swayed in the building breeze. Clouds grayed the sky above.

Standing in the shadow of the church, Vivian stared at the white steeple as if pardon and some measure of faith might rub off in the viewing. She and God hadn't always been at odds.

The front door whooshed open. The man who stepped out onto the small front porch had to be Tucker Raines. Nell had described her Judson's blue eyes in nauseating detail in her first letter after their wedding. The man smiling at them from the porch better fit Ida's description of her husband—broad-shouldered and brown-eyed.

"Vivian, I presume." He gave her a warm smile and wrapped her in a welcoming embrace. "We're so glad you're finally here with us. Ida has told me much about you."

"It's good to meet you. She's told me a fair amount about you too, Reverend Raines."

His eyes widened. "We're family. Call me Tucker."

The ostrich feather in Aunt Alma's hat swayed as she moved up the steps. "By the looks of things, Tucker, I'd say you're still lifting big blocks of ice. No preacher I know has arm muscles like that."

Ida, wrapped in a crocheted lavender shawl, stepped out onto the porch and squeezed her husband's upper arm. Vivian recognized the tomfoolery sparking her sister's blue eyes. "Tucker's strapping physique has nothing to do with delivering ice, Aunt Alma. We can attribute it to his many attempts to push me back into line."

Aunt Alma tittered. "I needn't ask how he's faring in that regard."

Ida wagged a finger at her husband. He pretended to seal his lips.

Vivian laughed with them, fighting the knot in her midsection. The two brothers-in-law she'd met were wonderful. Attentive. Good-humored. Charming. And knowing Nell, Judson Archer was certain to be just as grand a husband.

Vivian took a big swallow of regret and pressed her hand to her throat. She would never forgive herself for destroying her chances for such a spellbinding love and marriage. How could she? Her married sisters would unknowingly serve as a constant reminder of what she'd given up.

Ida finished the introductions, glanced up at the dark clouds gathering overhead, and waved them inside. On the other side of the threshold, Ida took their summer wraps and hung them on a coat tree. "You still have one more brother-in-law to meet, Vivian. Judson and Nell are in the kitchen. I'll give you the full tour of our home after the meal."

Vivian nodded and followed her oldest sister into a small kitchen that smelled like Sunday suppers back in Maine. Before Father left for Paris. When life was right.

At the cupboard, a trim man sliced a ham. Nell lifted a salad bowl out of an oak icebox. When she saw Vivian, she stopped and stared at her. "You're really here in Cripple Creek." The Edison bulb hanging in the center of the room lit the smile that widened Nell's freckled face. "I was sure I'd imagined the whole afternoon—the carriage ride...tea at Hattie's with you. All of it."

"I know. While I hung my clothes in the wardrobe I pinched myself." Vivian squeezed the sleeve on her red plaid shirtwaist. "But it's true. I'm finally here."

The man laid the knife on the platter and extended both hands to Vivian. "I'm Judson." Nell was right about his vivid blue eyes. "Good to finally meet you, baby sister."

Vivian bristled but accepted his hands. He'd meant it as a term of endearment, she told herself.

He studied her from shoe-tip to the curls atop her head. "A bit of a pipsqueak, but a solid grip and toes that can frustrate a bandit, from what I hear."

Her timing perfect, Aunt Alma stepped into the kitchen and extended her hand to him. "I bumped against poor Vivian in all the excitement and knocked her off balance."

"Aunt Alma. A pleasure to meet you, ma'am." Judson slicked his wavy blond hair back from his broad forehead. "Your braids are every bit as bright as Nell described them. Like the cinnamon atop Kat's applesauce."

Ida had mentioned Judson's tendency to be straightforward and outspoken, and he was true to the description. As well as attentive and good-humored.

"I say we eat while the food's hot." Ida poured a pan of peas into a fluted serving bowl.

They moved into the dining room. As soon as Tucker finished saying grace, Ida started the platter of ham around the table. Tucker plopped two thick slices onto his plate just as someone knocked on the door. "My apologies, but duty calls. Knocks, rather." Standing, he laid his napkin on the chair.

Vivian had just sprinkled a pinch of salt over the vegetables on her plate when Tucker returned to the room. Whoever was at the door hadn't followed him in.

"That didn't take long." Ida added peas to Tucker's full plate.

"Deputy Alwyn came to speak with Vivian. He's waiting in the parlor."

Vivian glanced at the food on her plate, and then up at her brother-in-law. "Right now?"

"He said it has to do with the train robbery business."

"Did you tell him we were eating our supper?"

Tucker nodded. "Said he wouldn't keep you long."

Sighing, Vivian pulled the napkin from her lap and dabbed her mouth. She reluctantly rose from her chair.

"I'll show you the way to the parlor," Tucker said.

"Thank you."

Vivian followed him on the same path she'd taken with Ida, but it seemed a greater distance to the entryway knowing Deputy Alwyn awaited her. Water dripped onto the pine flooring beneath a light overcoat and a black cowboy hat that hung on the hall tree. Worn, wet boots slouched on the floor beside the puddle.

Tucker stopped at an open doorway, motioning for Vivian to enter a small sitting room off the entryway.

Deputy Alwyn gazed at her from where he stood in front of a brick hearth. "Miss Sinclair."

"Deputy." She dipped her chin in greeting, trying not to stare at his stocking feet.

He ran a hand through his hair, the color of a wet pine cone. A limp towel lay on the bricks behind him. Had he been drying his hair?

Her brother-in-law slid his hands into his trouser pockets. "I can remain, if you like."

"That won't be necessary," Vivian said.

A deep breath swelled Carter's chest tight against a black shirt.

Tucker's brown eyes glimmered with amusement. "Very well, then, I'll leave you two to your business." He turned, then looked back over his shoulder. "You've had a long day, Carter. Can we set a plate for you?"

"Been too busy to think about food. That is, until I walked through your door and got a whiff of fine cooking." The deputy glanced at her, an eyebrow cocked, as though seeking permission.

"'The more the merrier,' my father used to say," Vivian said.

"Yes, thank you." The deputy seemed to be answering Tucker's question, but he didn't shift his gaze from her.

When Tucker left the room, Vivian walked to the sofa and sat at the end closest to the fireplace. The deputy with the distracting wet hair pushed the soggy towel to one side and lowered himself to the raised brick hearth.

"I heard you and a posse went looking for the men responsible for the robbery," Vivian said.

"We did. Didn't find them, but before the storm hit we did find their trail and the cash box."

"Good." Any conversation skills she'd learned in Miss Brighton's School for Girls seemed to have vanished. Vivian folded her hands in her lap.

"I apologize for interrupting your family meal," Deputy Alwyn said. "I went to the boardinghouse to speak with you, and Miss Hattie told me you were here."

Rain pelted the window behind the sofa, and flames snapped and popped behind the deputy, ticking off awkward moments of silence. Vivian tucked an errant curl behind her ear.

He cleared his throat. "You said the man with the cash box glared at you, growled at you."

Vivian nodded. Gooseflesh shimmied up her arms and neck at the memory.

"That had to be frightening."

She hadn't let herself think about it. She'd managed to keep busy visiting with her sisters and unpacking her trunk. But now that he had labeled the experience what it was—frightening—she recalled the image of the bandit glaring at her, and tears pricked her eyes. Blinking them away, she offered the deputy another nod.

His dark eyes transformed into pools of pure compassion that made her thankful she was seated.

"I didn't expect such a rugged welcome to Colorado," she said.

"You're safe now."

She hoped so. At least her feet were firmly planted on the ground. A train car left her with nowhere to run.

He suddenly straightened and pulled a pencil out of his pocket. Her pencil, freshly sharpened. "Thank you, again, for the loan."

"Of course." Accepting the pencil, Vivian couldn't help staring at the drop of water poised on the tip of a curl at his forehead. "Did you have more questions for me?"

"Uh, yes. One. I know you've had a long day yourself, and several of them on the train, but would you be willing to meet with a sketch artist tomorrow in my office?"

"That's what I do."

His mouth dropped open, revealing a row of straight teeth. "You're a sketch artist for wanted posters?"

Vivian giggled. "No. I mostly sketch costumes."

He glanced down at his sodden denims and stocking feet.

She forced herself to suppress another round of giggles. "I sketched the men's coats and hats and such. The ones from the train."

"You did?"

"I have them at the boardinghouse."

"I think we'll focus on the facial features for now." He stood, and Vivian rose from the sofa. "Say ten o'clock tomorrow in my office on Bennett Avenue?"

"Aunt Alma and I will be there."

"Are you sure you don't mind me joining your family for supper?"

"I don't mind."

A different fact she did mind. Disliked, actually. She'd glimpsed a certain charm just beneath the lawman's gruff exterior. Even a bit of attentiveness and good humor. All of which made him likable.

Not that it mattered. Given her track record with men, it would be in her best interest to avoid him. And she would…after tomorrow's appointment.

FIVE

dmiring the snowcapped peaks that towered over the valley, Vivian drew in a deep breath of fresh air. A meadow-
lark warbled a sunny song as she passed another street lined with houses
boasting lush flower gardens. Savoring the sun's warmth on her back,
she strolled down the hill from Golden Avenue with Aunt Alma at her
side.

Aunt Alma snagged Vivian's hand and gave it a squeeze. "Monday
will be here too soon, and, well, I'm going to miss you."

"I know. I'll miss you too." And she would, just not to the same
degree. "I'm not alone here."

Her aunt nodded and dabbed her eyes with an embroidered
handkerchief.

Following Miss Hattie's directions, Vivian turned right at Bennett
Avenue, away from the depot, and stepped up onto the wooden boardwalk. She was thankful Aunt Alma had turned down Miss Hattie's
offer of her carriage so she could enjoy her new surroundings and give
her limbs a good stretching.

While crossing Third Street, Vivian dodged a mud puddle, a rem-
nant of last evening's downpour. The unbidden image of Carter Alwyn
standing in front of the fireplace, his hair wet and his smile wide, sprang

to her mind. That image and the one of him sitting on the raised brick hearth, looking at her with eyes full of compassion and concern, were ones she'd best not withdraw from her bank of memories again. Better that she recall his condescending tone when he referred to her as "young lady."

Vivian and her aunt returned the smiles and greetings of passersby. The people were friendly and the mountains glorious. This place may suit her just fine while she worked to make a name for herself.

They passed several shops on the main thoroughfare through town, including a barbershop, a cobbler, a grocer, a confectionary, and a butcher. The El Paso County Sheriff's Office sat on their right, a narrow storefront in a brick building just up the block from the Cripple Creek Police Department.

Vivian opened the door and looked around the modest room. A kerosene cookstove to her left. A file cabinet in that corner, and a closed door in the other. A picture of President William McKinley hung above a plain oak desk.

The man sitting below the portrait didn't resemble Carter Alwyn in the least. Springing to his feet, the small gentleman with a receding hairline waved them inside. The black bow tie hanging crooked on his crisp white collar further abbreviated his short neck. A bold hiccup escaped his thinned lips, and he hooked his thumb on a button on his red vest, but it was the white apron over black trousers that surprised Vivian the most.

Aunt Alma raised a gloved hand to her mouth and whispered behind it. "He looks more like a bartender than an artist."

"Miss Sinclair." He turned his attention to Aunt Alma, a smile revealing a cleft in his pointed chin. "Miss Alma Shindlebower, I presume."

"Yes." They answered him at the same time.

"I once had a flame named Alma." Another smile for Aunt Alma and another hiccup. "Beg your pardon, ma'am. Gotta get me a bottle of bitters when we're done here."

Straight-faced, her aunt nodded. The ostrich feather on her summer hat bobbed.

He removed his apron and flung it over a side table, then pointed to the two wooden chairs on their side of the desk. "The deputy is out."

Vivian seated herself in the chair with the best view of the door. Just as well that Carter Alwyn was absent.

She followed the bartender's gaze to a wall clock behind them. "You ladies were spot on the dot of ten o'clock."

"If you're going to bother to be somewhere, bother to be on time." Aunt Alma lowered herself into the chair beside Vivian and stared up at the man. "And, sir, who might you be?"

"Edgar Hamilton, ma'am, the proprietor of the Cripple Creek Barroom." Another hiccup. This time he covered his mouth. "I'm also a humble sketch artist." He seated himself behind the desk and pointed to a pencil and a pad of drawing paper. He sealed his lips and tapped his chest, swallowing a quieted hiccup.

For the next thirty minutes, Vivian and her aunt recounted the shapes and colors of the outlaws' eyes. The sizes and shapes of their bandanna-shielded noses. The approximate length and shape of each face. And any other details they recalled.

When they stood to leave, Mr. Hamilton rose and walked to the side of the desk. "Deputy Alwyn said to thank you for your time, if he wasn't back to do so himself." He glanced toward the door. "So thank you. I'll tidy up my sketches and hand them over to the deputy."

Aunt Alma inserted her arm through the handle of her reticule.

"Tell him he's welcome to contact us should he have any additional questions."

The bartender sketch artist had just opened the door for them to leave when Deputy Alwyn practically skidded to a stop in front of them. His black hat lurched forward, and he scrambled to catch it before it hit the ground. If Vivian hadn't been swift in her back step, he would have snagged her arm in the process.

When he'd righted himself, Deputy Alwyn pressed his hat to his leather vest and met Vivian's gaze, his eyes as warm as the sunlight slanting in through the open doorway. "I was called away. Tried to make it back before you left." A shy smile tipped his lips. "As you can see, I did. My apologies for the ham-fisted entrance."

"Apology accepted." He needed to quit looking at her as if she were something other than an irritating young woman and as if he were pleased to see her. He wouldn't so much as share the same side of the street with her if he knew what she'd done. "We were just leaving."

He worried the brim of his hat with his fingers, turning it in a circle. "Did Mr. Hamilton thank you for taking the time to—"

"He did." She took a step toward the door.

He scrubbed the trim goatee that framed his chin. "Very well, then. I won't keep you."

"Thank you." Vivian looked back at the shorter man. "Good day, Mr. Hamilton."

Out on the boardwalk, Vivian's thoughts raced to keep up with the rapid tapping of her heels. Carter Alwyn the lawman was unnervingly charming when he was eager. Hopefully, it was a one-time occurrence brought on by his dedication to solving a crime.

SIX

෧෧෩

$\mathcal{S}$eated in the backseat of Miss Hattie's surrey, Vivian admired the folks dressed in their Sunday best. From a young age, she had considered Sunday her favorite day of the week. A day of fashion, family, worship, and rest. Perhaps here, in a new place and in the company of her sisters, she could once again enjoy the experience. Even if God wouldn't accept her, hearing the old, familiar songs lifted on her sisters' voices might bring her the comfort she'd once enjoyed in God's house.

She and Aunt Alma had spent the past three days touring the town with her sisters—Nell and Judson's modest home for lunch, the icehouse and icebox showroom, the Sisters of Mercy hospital where Morgan worked as a doctor, the mine office where Judson worked as an accountant, the mercantile, the telegraph office, the Butte Opera House. A day of rest sounded wonderful.

Aunt Alma twisted on the front seat next to Miss Hattie, beaming a smile as bright as the sunshine lighting the white ostrich feather on her hat. "I'm over the moon to think of sitting in church with all my girls again."

As if on cue, Miss Hattie pulled up on the reins, directing her mare to stop at a hitching rail across the street from the First Congregational

Church. The white steeple atop the brick building was first to draw
Vivian's attention, but then she caught sight of all three of her sisters
waving from the steps. Yes, Sundays could easily be her favorite day
again. At least it seemed possible from this side of the door.

By the time Vivian climbed down from the wagon, Judson had
taken the reins from Miss Hattie and stood at the hitching rail. "Morning, sis." Smiling, he wrapped the reins around the wooden post.

"Morning."

Judson moved to the side of the wagon and extended his hand to
her aunt. "Good day, Aunt Alma." He was as charming as Nell pur-
ported him to be.

Her sisters had been lucky in love. While all three of her brothers-
in-law were distinctly different, they all seemed like hard workers and
attentive family men. She swallowed hard against the ache in her heart
and smoothed her skirt.

Aunt Alma clutched her Bible in one hand and accepted Judson's
help with the other. Once her aunt's feet touched the ground, Judson
bowed and offered his help to Miss Hattie.

Her landlady patted his cheek in a motherly way, and then turned
to Aunt Alma. "Are you sure you must leave tomorrow?"

"I'm afraid so." Aunt Alma sighed. "I have my store to think of."

By the time they had crossed the road, Ida was down the steps and
reaching for Vivian's hand. "At long last, another Sunday together."

Vivian squeezed her sister's hand. "I just hope your husband is as
good at preaching as you are at playing checkers."

"That's right," Ida said. "I owe you a long overdue rematch."

Vivian exaggerated her nod.

"You and I have the first game this afternoon. But first, we'd better
go inside before my husband starts without us."

Vivian stepped into hugs from Kat and Nell and then followed them into the warm foyer. A tall vase of lilacs stood on a mahogany table, an open Bible beside it. But for a few soft greetings, the building held a hushed reverence.

Judson opened the door into the sanctuary and, like a shepherd, ushered them all inside. At the back row, Kat lifted baby Hope from the arms of an elderly woman and led the way to an empty row near the front. Stained-glass windows lined the walls on either side. A rough-hewn cross stood at the back of the raised platform, where Morgan sat at a square grand piano.

Vivian followed Aunt Alma into the row with Nell at her heels and seated herself. On her way up the aisle, she'd gotten a good enough view of the congregation to see that Deputy Alwyn was nowhere in sight. She relaxed against the pew.

❧

Carter had made a habit of arriving at the church early to pray with the reverend and the other elders before the Sunday morning service.

He'd been chatting with Tucker for about five minutes when his friend glanced at his office door. "I guess it's just you and me praying this morning. You lead out and I'll close."

Carter nodded and bowed his head. He'd become a church elder a month ago, and his prayer was much the same every week. He prayed that God would bless his friend with a clear message, boldness in the delivery, and people with hearts to receive it. When he'd finished, he waited in the silence.

"*Lord God, I'm in agreement, and I add my own request,*" Tucker prayed. "*I ask, Lord, that You would add grace and give strength to my friend here for the formidable task You've set before him. Please protect him in his calling."*

An added measure of humility suddenly poured into Carter. He had been praying for God to help him protect his town and to help him bring the outlaws to justice, but he hadn't specifically sought God's grace and strength in the doing.

"Lord God, it is our privilege to pray these things in the name of Your Son, Jesus the Christ. Amen."

"Amen." Carter opened his eyes and met his friend's warm gaze. "Thank you."

Tucker gave him a knowing nod and stood. "We best get in there before they start without us."

Carter followed his friend up the center aisle as Morgan Cutshaw played the first bars of "It Is Well with My Soul."

Before he reached his seat, Carter caught sight of an especially fashionable young woman in the middle of the third row on the right. When her eyes widened at the sight of him, he couldn't help but smile.

❧

Of course the deputy would attend this church.

Vivian shifted her gaze to the pulpit where her brother-in-law stood, welcoming his parishioners. Carter Alwyn and Tucker were good friends. She didn't have a problem with that, or at least she shouldn't.

Ida leaned toward her. "He's an elder," she whispered. "They pray together every Sunday before the service."

Vivian nodded. It'd be a waste of breath to try to convince her sister she hadn't been wondering about the deputy. Ida had apparently observed Vivian watching Carter walk up the aisle.

Vivian focused her gaze on Morgan's piano prelude. Unfortunately, her mind wasn't so easily redirected. She needed to be more careful in her attentions. Better yet, she needed to avoid giving any man undue notice. Even though she had no romantic intentions, those around her weren't likely to let go of their fondness for matchmaking.

Tucker had just uttered the last word of the benediction when Deputy Alwyn stepped out into the aisle and walked toward Vivian and her family. A wide smile on his face, he greeted her first.

"Miss Sinclair, it was good to see you in the congregation this morning."

"It was good to see you here…to be seen here." Vivian looked away. Nell's crooked grin told her she needed to do a better job of pretending the man wasn't a distraction.

Morgan shook the deputy's hand. "Supper's at our house today. Can you join us?"

Carter looked at Vivian, then back at Morgan. "I appreciate the invitation, but I need to decline."

"Another time, then," Morgan said. He chucked Hope under the chin, causing the baby to giggle.

"Yes, another time." Deputy Alwyn waved his hat. "Miss Sinclair. Ladies."

Vivian didn't watch him walk away. Instead, she tapped Hope on the nose.

Avoidance was best. So why was she disappointed that he had other plans?

An hour later, Vivian sat in Kat and Morgan's parlor, staring at the checkerboard.

"Just admit it." Ida assumed a regal pose, her nose in the air. "I'm still the reigning champion."

Vivian raised her index finger without looking away from Ida's neat row of kings. She was tired of settling for second best. Pressing her lips together, she studied every piece on the board.

Why hadn't she seen it before? Vivian moved her checker, capturing two of her sister's recently crowned pieces and gaining a new king. She couldn't contain her giggle.

Ida was clearly not as amused and could only stare at the board in obvious disbelief.

Morgan sauntered into the parlor. "Kat says supper is nearly ready." He joined the crowd encircling the octagonal game table. "Who's winning?"

"I am." Vivian's assertion came out almost in perfect harmony with Ida's reply.

"You can't both win." Aunt Alma had been observing the match from an armchair near the window.

"I can't believe I didn't see it coming." Ida glanced at Tucker, who sat backward in a chair. "This is your fault."

"Of course it is." A coy grin dimpled his chin. "Why is it my fault this time?"

"Same humdrum reason—you're such a charming distraction."

He snatched Ida's hand, and she giggled like a schoolgirl.

Vivian longed for such a house, where love and laughter filled the rooms.

If only she were lovable.

SEVEN

❧

On her tiptoes in front of her open wardrobe, Vivian pulled her purple sateen hat from the top shelf.

Monday. She'd been gone from Maine for nearly two weeks and had arrived in Cripple Creek almost a week ago, but in many ways, today felt like the beginning of her new life. Since Father left her in Portland, Aunt Alma had served as her guardian. This morning, her aunt would board the train to return home, leaving Vivian here to sink or swim. She'd been sinking since her father left for Paris.

At her dressing table, Vivian looked in the mirror. She tugged the collar of her purple serge jacket straight. She'd pin her hat on after breakfast.

Today she'd strike out on her own and swim. She had plenty of ideas for costumes but no real experience with the business side of clothing design. Working at the shop in Victor would give her the know-how she needed to succeed in bigger cities like San Francisco or New York or Paris. Perhaps her father had done her a favor in telling her not to come to France. She wasn't ready. Not yet.

Vivian pulled back the curtains on her second-story window and looked down on the center of town. Banks. The stock exchange. Hotels.

All represented people who might appreciate her eastern-inspired de-signs. The possibilities for success were endless.

Satisfied she'd done all she could to prepare for the day, Vivian wrapped her shawl about her shoulders. She fairly floated as she made her way down the pine staircase, her steps made light by a newfound confidence. No music wafted from the phonograph this morning. In-stead, Miss Hattie warbled, "Blessed assurance, Jesus is mine...praising my Savior all the day long." Vivian peeked inside the parlor.

Miss Hattie sat in a rocker in front of the fireplace with a Bible on her lap. She quieted and motioned for Vivian to join her. "Come in, dear."

Vivian took a slow step through the doorway. "I didn't mean to disturb you."

"The Lord would probably welcome a respite." The laugh lines that framed Miss Hattie's blue-gray eyes crinkled like lace.

Before Vivian could respond to the warm-hearted landlady, the front door opened and all three of her sisters and her niece swept into the parlor on a wave of chatter. Vivian wanted to hold baby Hope but didn't dare take the chance of spoiling her dress before meeting Mrs. Ondersma.

Kat looked around the room. "Where's Aunt Alma?"

Miss Hattie rose from her chair. "She insisted on cooking us break-fast her last morning here."

"Well, it smells wonderful." Kat kissed Hope on the cheek and laid her in Miss Hattie's open arms.

Nell sniffed the air. "Skillet-egg-pileup. That pungent aroma is as recognizable as the scent of a pine forest after a good rain."

"My specialty." Aunt Alma sashayed into the room wearing a well-floured apron.

"I'm tired of hearing my stomach growl." Miss Hattie patted her generous belly. "Is this mystery specialty of yours ready for consumption yet?"

"Indeed it is."

They all fell into line behind Aunt Alma. Except for the butterflies flitting about Vivian's midsection, breakfast was delightful.

An hour later, she stood on the Midland Terminal Railroad platform with her sisters and Aunt Alma. A sharp whistle drew their attention to the top of the grade where the train puffed its way down the hill from Ute Pass.

"In one of his infrequent letters, Father mentioned plans to—" Kat shouted as the train pulled into the station and the last loud puff of steam blew out from somewhere under the iron monster. The contraption then went eerily silent except for a faint hiss. "Ahem, as I was saying," Kat continued, "Father mentioned plans to come to Cripple Creek next year. You could join him, Aunt Alma."

"We'll see." Their aunt swept a curl of copper hair behind her ear. "Oh, but I'm going to miss this little one." She looked at Vivian. "And all my girls—young women now."

Finally, her aunt had accepted the fact that Vivian had grown up. Now all Vivian had to do was prove it to herself.

Vivian boarded the train with Aunt Alma and sat on the aisle. She'd get off in Victor.

Shortly after the noon hour, Vivian settled her lavender lace shawl over her shoulders, then tucked her sketch pad under the arm that held her reticule. She lifted her skirts with her free hand and stepped off the platform onto the packed-dirt road beside the depot in Victor. The short ride on the Florence and Cripple Creek Railway had been uneventful.

Drawing in a deep breath, Vivian studied one mountain and hillock after another—all of them covered with metal miniatures of the Eiffel Tower, evidence of the mines that dotted this valley like a polka-dot print. Unlike the mines at Cripple Creek, Victor's mines spilled over into the town itself. The Strong Mine stood like a sentry just across the road from the depot. Coal smoke layered the air, punctuated by the constant drone of the stamp mill. Not the most pleasant of environments, but she could adapt if it drew her closer to her dream of becoming a sought-after dress designer.

She pulled Miss Hattie's note from the seam pocket in her skirt.

South down Second Street to Victor Avenue. Turn right, then left on Third Street. Etta's Fashions sits on the left side of the street.

Miss Hattie's directions looked easy enough to follow. Vivian adjusted her sateen summer hat to the proper angle and started down Second Street. Weathered pine fronted the shops and stores that lined the wide streets in contrast to Cripple Creek's more modern brick faces.

Vivian turned left onto Third Street and began studying the signs that hung from the facades on the left side of the street. Painted in crisp white letters on a lavender sign, ETTA'S FASHIONS stood out, the fourth storefront. Vivian glanced down at her lavender shawl. She'd chosen the right color to wear; apparently it was the proprietor's favorite.

Several felt-covered forms stood in the windows on either side of the door displaying a variety of outfits. One such figure was dressed in a Sunday dress made of taffeta. Another was clad in a plaid skirt and a bibbed shirtwaist. The window on the other side of the door featured a brocade ball gown and a sateen-lined mantle. All the fashions mirrored the small-town feel of the Cripple Creek District, which excited Vivian. She'd been studying the latest from Paris in magazines such as *Godey's Lady's Book, Frank Leslie's Gazette of Fashion,* and *Harper's Bazar* and was certain she could reproduce the latest fashions. Maybe even improve upon them for life in the West, more durable yet still fashionable.

Drawing in a fortifying breath, Vivian reached for the brass door latch. A bell jingled as she stepped inside.

"Good day!" A woman's voice came from a back room, puffed out on ragged breaths as if she'd been running. "I'll be with you straightaway."

"Thank you." Vivian raised her voice to be heard over the clatter behind a closed curtain. "No need to rush on my account."

She studied the store, which was barely twice the size of the sheriff's office in Cripple Creek. A round oak breakfast table sat in a front corner, framed by two spindle-back chairs. Outdated issues of women's magazines covered its top. A smaller side table held a stack of drawings of men's suits and coats.

A stately looking woman stepped out from behind a curtain, wearing wheeling regalia—bloomers and all. Graying tufts of blond hair framed her lined, narrow face beneath a yellow straw hat that sat askew atop her head. The woman did a slow turn like the ballerina on Vivian's mother's music box. "How do you like the wheeling outfit, Miss?"

The knickerbockers were too ballooned and unshapely for Vivian's taste, but the woman was clearly proud of them. "It's quite sporting, ma'am. And yellows and greens are especially fashionable colors this summer."

"They are." She clutched the seams on the bicycle bloomers and pulled on the abundance of fabric. "It's not for me." She peeked at her bare feet, a smile adding fullness to her cheeks. "If it were mine, I'd have the button boots to complete the outfit."

"Of course."

"It's for a schoolmarm, but seeing as we're of similar size and shape—close enough, anyway—I decided to see what a cycling getup felt like."

Vivian studied the ruffled hems. "And what do you think?"

"Well, I feel quite sporting in it. A bit of a spring chicken." Another twirl. "Do you ride?"

"I haven't, but I have a sister who has, and she rather enjoyed it." Ida seemed game to try most anything. Anything respectable, anyway. Although in some circles women wheelers were still considered indecent and definitely eccentric. Vivian looked from the full-length gilded mirror on one wall to the teakettle atop a small potbelly stove on the other. "You have a lovely shop."

"Thank you." The woman extended her hand to Vivian. "I'm Etta Ondersma, the owner."

Vivian accepted her hand and glanced at the costumes adorning the windows. "You made all of these?"

Mrs. Ondersma laughed. "I'm afraid my expertise lies in the design and procurement of materials. My sewing skills are fairly limited— camisoles and dressing gowns. Three very gifted seamstresses do the stitching for me." A thick line creased her generous forehead as she assessed Vivian from her pointy-toed shoes to her summer hat. "You're obviously working with a gifted designer. From the East?"

Vivian straightened her shoulders. "Thank you, ma'am. I am from the East Coast—Maine."

Mrs. Ondersma's thick eyebrows formed an arch. "And your designer?"

Time to get down to business. Vivian removed her sketch pad from beneath her elbow and smiled. "I designed the suit myself."

"You did? And the hat?"

Vivian nodded. "Yes ma'am."

Mrs. Ondersma walked around Vivian, then stopped directly in front of her. "But you're so...young."

Vivian swallowed her frustration, willing her face not to betray her. "I'm eighteen. Young to some, I'm sure." She laid her sketch pad flat on her hands as an offering. "I've had what my father calls an 'obsessive fascination with fashion' since I was old enough to attend school. I've been studying design for many years. Hattie Adams in Cripple Creek told me about your shop."

"Hattie, you say?"

"Yes ma'am. I'm a resident in her boardinghouse."

She reached for the pad. "I presume these are sketches of your designs."

"A sampling. I have dozens more back in my room."

Etta Ondersma carried the sketches to the round table. Vivian seated herself in the second chair as the shop owner perused page after page and outfit after outfit. "You favor the Gibson girl influence. The narrower, wasp waist. Gigot sleeves. Straighter lines. Laced collars. Braiding at the hems. Flouncing."

Vivian nodded. "My other samples include tea aprons. Capes and cloaks. I can design fashions from travel frocks to wedding gowns and pieces with calico prints or satin in mind."

"Your designs are a bit more modern than mine, but lovely. I'm sure your flair for eastern fashion would be well received, particularly in Cripple Creek, which is becoming the cat's meow when it comes to culture and refinement."

Hope welled in Vivian. Perhaps Mrs. Ondersma would pay her to do most of the designing and patterns from the boardinghouse in Cripple Creek. If not, she'd gladly ride the train to Victor every day for the opportunity to gain experience. She sat straighter, her hands folded at the table's edge. "I'd like to think that you and I could form a good team. You know the local women and their needs, and I—"

"I agree. You and your designs have much to offer the women of Colorado." Etta Ondersma's frown defied her enthusiastic statement. She rubbed the gold wedding band on her left hand. "My husband passed this winter, and money has been tight without his income." Closing the sketch pad, she slowly raised her head. "I'm sorry, dear. Right now, there isn't enough business to hire a second designer or even another seamstress."

If the woman hired a younger, more relevant designer, she'd gain new clients, which would build the business. Keeping her argument to herself, Vivian lifted her sketch pad off the table. She knew not to spoil her chances in case Etta Ondersma changed her mind. "Thank you for your time, Mrs. Ondersma. And my condolences."

Nodding, the widow stood, and Vivian followed suit. "The town is still growing. We can pray that my business will expand as well."

Vivian wanted to take comfort in the woman's compliments and assurances, but marriage wasn't an option for her. She had to find work. Granted, she didn't deserve the career of her dreams. But if not dress designing, then what? That was all she'd ever thought about doing. She tucked her sketch pad under her arm.

"Rest assured, you'll be the first I contact should I need a designer," Mrs. Ondersma said.

As Vivian left the shop, she didn't have the faintest idea what she would do in the meantime.

EIGHT

⚘

Carter's bay stallion snorted at a passing wagon team and yanked the reins tight at the hitching rail. Carter pushed his hat back on his head and studied his friend, Gilbert Neilson, the chief of police for Victor. The two of them shared a ten-year history, having both lived in the silver camp of Leadville before moving south to the Cripple Creek District. They sat in front of Gilbert's office, swapping stories over mugs of coffee strong enough to grow hair on a baby's chest.

Just last week, the Bank of Victor had succumbed to a robbery, the third Colorado bank hit in less than two months. Carter suspected the men who robbed the banks were connected to the train bandits, if not the same. "There were three guys in on the robbery at the bank in Divide too."

"Yup." Gilbert sat slouched with his legs extended, leaving plenty of room for passersby on the boardwalk. "Older one clanged the sawed-off barrel of a scattergun between the bars at the teller window."

"Second fellow a tall one, carry a nickel Schofield?"

Gilbert nodded. "Held the revolver on the guard by the door. Third one, younger, stood just outside with a wide-brim cowboy hat pulled down over his whiskered face. Told folks the banker was holding a meeting for his tellers and would reopen soon. A shopkeeper said the kid had a southern accent."

Carter took a long swig of black coffee. The robbery pattern was as distinct as the tea roses on his mother's English dinnerware. Gilbert raked his hair, the color of a cooked carrot. "Did either of the train robbers have an accent?"

"Witnesses didn't hear the tall one say anything. The second one sounded like he had something in his mouth and smelled of licorice root. Witness said it sounded like he was chewing on marbles." Miss Vivian Sinclair had said it, to be precise.

Gilbert straightened. "Sounds like the same guys hittin' the banks took the cash box Tuesday."

Carter set his mug of steaming coffee at his feet. "Only two men involved on the train, but they didn't need a lookout."

"Could've been waitin' for them with mounts."

"We only found evidence of two horses."

"Three banks. Whoever's doing the robbing should have had enough by now. That first haul in Manitou Springs should've satisfied them for a month of Sundays." Gilbert peered into his cup and gave the contents a swirl. "Dealin' with a real greedy bunch."

"Especially if they're responsible for the escapade on the train too." Carter picked up his folder and pulled out the sketch Edgar Hamilton had made of the two men. "Here's a drawing based on the information one of the witnesses gave."

Gilbert stared at him, his eyes narrowing as he tipped his head. "Miss Vivian Sinclair?" His tone carried more than a hint of teasing.

"How did you know?"

"Small county."

"It's about the biggest county in the state." Carter paused. "You talked to Jon."

Gilbert's exaggerated nod set his hat to flopping. "Said you and Miss Sinclair threw off enough sparks to light the train car."

"She'd been through an ordeal, coming face to face with a bandit and all. So, yes, she was a bit tetchy, and I had a job to do." Keeping the more flattering adjectives to himself, Carter looked away and tugged his vest straight. "Getting back to business—"

"If we must. But a little fun wouldn't hurt you, Mr. All-About-Business."

Ignoring his friend's comment, Carter pulled the wanted poster from the folder. "You think this man, Pickett, could be the one with the Schofield at the bank?"

"Could be." Gilbert pointed to the physical description. "Fits the height of the guy wielding the six-shooter. They pegged him at six feet plus and skinny like an aspen trunk."

"Witnesses described the second man on the train as being tall enough to hit the lamps if he hadn't hunched." Carter handed Gilbert the sketches from his folder.

"Looks like the same guy to me." A frown clouded Gilbert's blue eyes. "This gang is rumored to be moving southwest."

Carter nodded.

"Cripple Creek's bank could be next."

"Won't happen on my watch." Carter shoved the poster back into the folder.

"I said that about Victor."

Heat flooded Carter's face, and he cringed. "Didn't mean to imply—"

Gilbert raised a freckled hand. "I know. You're out to prove something. I might do the same if I was trying to get out from under my dead father's shadow."

Trying to? A vein in Carter's neck throbbed. This wasn't a new conversation for him and Gilbert. Although he had nothing new to say on the subject, Carter looked at his friend and responded anyway. "I don't have any say in the matter."

"Sure, the man's a legend, but—"

"I know." Carter drew in a deep breath. "That was then. This is now. Easy to say, but trying to do the work, knowing what happened to my father, is like going hand to hand with a bear."

"Fair enough." Gilbert gulped coffee. "Just don't go getting yourself killed tryin' to prove something." He paused. "Not when I'm finally gettin' used to having you around."

Carter chuckled. "Point taken."

"Good."

"Except for a knot on the conductor's head, no one's been hurt in any of the robberies."

"Doesn't mean it can't happen. So far all the bankers and customers have cooperated. Given freely. But all it takes is one person resisting."

Even one that accidentally extended her foot at an inopportune time. Carter's gut tightened.

"You okay?" Gilbert asked.

"Nothing that catching a gang of robbers won't cure." Carter lifted his cup from the wooden boardwalk and drained it. "I best head back." He handed Gilbert the mug. "Thanks for the coffee. Watch your back."

Gilbert nodded. "You do the same."

"Telephone the office if you find out anything that might help me keep my end of the valley safe."

"Will do."

When Carter turned back to the road, he noticed a particularly fashionable young woman crossing Fourth Street on the other side of Victor Avenue. He repositioned his hat for a better view. Couldn't be who he thought it was. Not here. Not alone.

Gilbert stood beside him. "Let me guess—Miss Vivian Sinclair?"

"The one and only."

Waving at her, Carter didn't know whether to give thanks that there was only one Vivian Sinclair, or to thank God she existed and had moved to his part of Colorado.

Vivian had taken too long to recognize one of the two men staring at her from across the street. She blinked, hoping the scene was nothing more than a figment of her imagination, but the men were still there, and now Deputy Alwyn was waving at her.

After hearing the bad news from Etta, she was already prone to be rude, and she had vowed to avoid the lawman who wore an inviting smile. Since avoiding Deputy Alwyn was proving to be impossible, ignoring him had to be forgivable. Vivian turned to retreat up Victor Avenue. She'd wait at the depot for her afternoon train.

"Miss Sinclair." The familiar baritone voice sounded much closer than the boardwalk on the other side of the street. Before she could confirm his whereabouts, he stood directly in front of her, his shoulders broad and his jaw set. A folder was tucked under his arm.

"Deputy Alwyn." She considered adding *it is you,* but the darkness in his eyes told her he knew he'd been snubbed.

"I thought we'd put our rough start behind us."

"We had." Vivian matched his stare. "We did. It is."

"Then why are you avoiding me? First you couldn't leave my office fast enough last Wednesday. You darted out of church like a startled rabbit. And now—"

"Now I have a train to catch." Vivian moistened her lips, hoping it would ease her dry throat as well.

"Unless they've changed the schedule, the train isn't due for another hour."

He was relentless. Vivian looked him straight in the eye, a softer brown now. "I do have a little time on my hands. Did you have further robbery business you wished to discuss with me?"

He blew out a long breath.

"If so—"

"Did I do something to offend you?"

He never should have made the switch from exasperating to charming. "It isn't you."

He cocked an eyebrow. "I resemble someone you wish to avoid?"

She couldn't help giggling. Humor and heart. Relentless and respectable. All of which made it impossible for her not to like this man. "My adjustment to Colorado isn't going as smoothly as I'd hoped. I just came from an interview that I was sure would lead to employment."

"It didn't?"

"No. Despite my best effort."

"I'm sorry. Please allow me to walk you to the depot."

She nodded. "That would be fine."

He held up the folder. "Mr. Hamilton's final sketches of the bandits you described. I came to Victor to show them to the chief of police here." Glancing across the street, he returned the police chief's wave.

"I'd be interested in seeing the sketches as well."

"I'd like that too." He pressed his hat onto his head and smiled. "Looks like my friend wants to meet you. Come with me while I retrieve my horse?"

"I can do that." All part of her adventure.

"We can look at the sketches while we wait at the depot."

Vivian nodded. *We wait?* He intended to see her onto the train? Well, that was better than offering her a ride back to town on the back of his horse.

The deputy stepped off the boardwalk first and held his hand out to her. His confident touch did nothing to encourage avoidance, even if it were possible. As soon as her left foot felt solid on the ground, she let go of his hand. "Thank you."

"Yes ma'am."

He repeated the kind gesture at the boardwalk on the other side of the street.

"Gilbert, this is Miss Vivian Sinclair from Cripple Creek."

His friend tugged the brim of a floppy hat that did little to tame his wavy red hair. "Gilbert Neilson, ma'am. It's good to meet you. I've heard favorable things about you."

"Oh?" She glanced at Deputy Alwyn, who suddenly colored as if he'd been in the sun too long.

"Yes. We talked about the train robbery." Deputy Alwyn scrubbed his goatee. "I told Chief Neilson that you've provided important information." He exchanged quiet looks with his friend and stepped to the hitching rail, where the horse nudged his shoulder. "Now if you'll excuse us, Gilbert, I'm going to walk Miss Sinclair to the depot."

"Good to catch up." Mr. Neilson shifted his attention to Vivian. "A pleasure to meet you, Miss Sinclair. I hope you'll visit our fair town again soon."

"Thank you, I'd like that." Especially if it meant Etta Ondersma had called to hire her. Vivian dipped her chin and turned toward the horse. His hand ready, Deputy Alwyn guided her to the rocky street.

He let go of her hand too soon, and not soon enough.

～～

Carter swung up into the saddle and rode away from the depot and Miss Sinclair. The independent Miss Sinclair, who had a passel of sisters and still preferred to venture out on her own. Bold. And beautiful.

While Liberty's shod hooves scraped against the rocks on the road, Carter forced his thoughts away from Miss Sinclair to the facts he had concerning the robberies.

They were dealing with a gang, and he knew of at least two of them, infamous for terrorizing the mining towns of northwestern Colorado. Had one of them ventured to his little corner of the Rockies?

He groaned. "Gilbert's right; it makes sense that they'll eventually target Cripple Creek."

Carter clucked his tongue and shook his head. He was talking to his horse. Pitiful. He did need to socialize more, but he couldn't risk becoming better acquainted with Vivian Sinclair. He couldn't risk that part of his heart. Or that part of any woman's heart.

Carter pushed his Stetson down to shield his eyes from the afternoon sun. He'd just settled back in the saddle, ready for the descent down Battle Mountain, when he heard hooves clambering up the rocky hillside.

"Sheriff!"

Carter pulled up on the reins and sat taller in the saddle. He recognized the crusty old miner who scuffled toward him, waving his worn canvas hat.

"Jon said I'd find you headed back from Victor. We got trouble, Deputy!"

Carter swung to the ground. Liberty followed him over to Boney and his pack-bearing mule. "What kind of trouble, Boney?"

The wiry man slapped his hat on his leg. "It's Peter McHenry. Heard a gunshot. Then yellin' and groanin'. Me and a couple other miners up there found Mac knifed and alone in his cabin. Died before he could say anything." The miner spit into the tall grasses beside them. "They come for his sock of gold and must've found it. It's not there."

Gritting his teeth, Carter stuck a foot into the stirrup. A shiver ran up his spine, and the chilling wind on the mountain wasn't the only culprit. "You said Mac had been knifed, but you heard a gunshot?"

Boney nodded. "Just one."

"See anyone out by his place?"

"Just the backs of two men riding away fast." Boney turned his mule around, and despite Sal's brays, he climbed onto her back. "His cabin's up in the hills by my place. I'll take you there."

After about thirty minutes of hard riding, Carter tied Liberty's reins to a juniper and stepped up onto the stoop of Peter McHenry's wood-shake shanty. Blood marked a path across the plank wood flooring to where a man's body lay at the edge of a straw mat in the corner.

Carter recognized the man known as Mac. He'd come to Cripple Creek last year with gold on his mind but charity in his heart. He'd donated a generous portion of his poke to help the Sisters of Mercy care for widows and orphans. Some men deserved such an end, but Mac wasn't one of them. Carter swallowed hard against the anger that tensed his shoulders. He looked over at Boney, who held a photograph.

Boney rubbed his scraggly beard and shook his head. "Mac was gonna wire for his wife and young'uns to join him here this summer." Turning back toward the body, the old miner made the sign of the cross.

Carter looked around the sparsely furnished shack. What there was—a rough-hewn table, two straight-back chairs, and a supply shelf—lay strewn across the floor. Focused on the light streaming through the open doorway, Carter drew in a fortifying breath. "Tell me about the riders you saw."

"One was sittin' forward. Still had plenty of body left leanin' over the horn."

"His build?"

"Like one of them new telephone poles in town."

"Think Mac got him?"

"The way the fella was clutchin' his head, he could have been hit. But not bad enough to leave a blood trail outside."

"You find a gun?"

Boney shook his head. "Mac's huntin' rifle was still under his bed. Hadn't been fired. Must've shot the interloper with the crook's own gun."

Carter looked up at the whittled cross hanging on the wall. Why hadn't it been enough to protect Mac? His own father? He blinked hard, then returned his attention to Boney. "You notice anything else? Color of the horses? Hats?"

"The stocky man rode a chestnut and wore a derby. The bent man was on a dapple. Wore a big straw hat. Wanted to go after 'em, but…

Turned out I was too late to do Mac any good. And then too late for me and Sal to catch up."

"Wouldn't have done any good for you to get killed too." Frankly, Carter didn't know what Cripple Creek would do without the ever-ready miner and his sassy mule.

"You think maybe this is the same rascals that robbed the train and the banks?"

"Completely different crimes. And nobody was killed at the banks or on the train." Carter wasn't sure if he was trying to convince Boney or himself.

"Been hearin' talk of a gang that come over the Rockies."

Carter nodded. "The police chief over in Victor and I think that gang could be responsible for the other robberies. The two who did this could be part of a gang or just lazy poachers. Whoever they are, if they have the nerve to stay around here, we'll find them."

He had to. He'd been trained by the best, and now it was time he put his father's legendary legacy to the test.

"In the meantime, Mac needs a proper burial." Boney slapped his hat back on his head. "I'll go fetch the undertaker."

Carter watched the miner's bowlegged amble to his mule while dread soured his stomach. He had to wire Peter McHenry's wife and children with the news. First, he and Jon had a killer to track.

NINE

◄━━━◄

Vivian hung her purple suit in the wardrobe. Had it really been just this morning that she'd bid her aunt farewell and taken the train to Victor? She'd had such high hopes, but she'd failed to secure a job with the only fashion designer in the valley. To top it off, she'd encountered Deputy Alwyn—the man she had vowed to avoid.

Her heart had been so full of adventure and hope on her trip to Victor. On her return to Cripple Creek, two images taunted her: Mrs. Etta Ondersma in a cycling getup, telling Vivian she couldn't afford to hire her, and a certain deputy tipping his hat her direction and riding away.

Sighing, Vivian pulled a checkered housedress from the wardrobe. She wiggled into the dress and slid her feet into house slippers. All she wanted to do now was crawl into bed and drift into a numbing sleep, but Miss Hattie was expecting her company at the supper table.

As she made her way down the stairs and into the kitchen, the lively song playing on the phonograph poked fun at her maudlin disposition. Her robust landlady set a dish on the round table in the corner and looked up at her. Sympathy softened Miss Hattie's blue-gray eyes. "If your shoulders were any lower, dear, they'd be resting on your bosom."

Vivian didn't know whether to laugh or cry. Miss Hattie had her own special way with words.

"Either you're sorely missing your aunt, or you didn't fare well in your visit with Etta."

"She didn't hire me."

"That is disappointing news." Miss Hattie removed her apron and hung it on a hook near the pantry. "I'm sorry that didn't work out."

Vivian carried two cups of steaming tea to the table and seated herself. "Mrs. Ondersma doesn't have enough business for a second designer or another seamstress."

Now Miss Hattie's shoulders sagged as she set a basket of biscuits on the table and sank into the chair across from Vivian. "The poor woman is recently widowed. A bad case of influenza got him. Quite the adjustment to make." Miss Hattie's voice faded for a moment. "I feel bad that I raised your hopes, dear." She patted Vivian's hand.

Vivian chided herself. The poor shop owner had lost her husband just months ago, and Miss Hattie had only been trying to help. She forced her shoulders up a notch. It was childish to think only of herself. "I'm glad you told me about Etta's Fashions. I enjoyed meeting Mrs. Ondersma and seeing her store. As a matter of fact, she was wearing a cycling costume when I arrived."

Miss Hattie's eyes rounded. "She wasn't."

"Indeed she was. Bright yellow and green bloomers. Designed it for a school teacher. Said it made her feel quite sporting."

"Good for her. Does a woman good to try something new now and again."

Nodding, Vivian reached for her teacup. "I'll just have to find other work until she has enough business to justify hiring me."

A warm smile widened Miss Hattie's cheeks. "That's the Sinclair spirit I know."

An optimistic spirit that didn't come as naturally to her as it did to her sisters. For now, she'd just have to slap it on like a wig.

Following her landlady's prayer of thanksgiving, Vivian pulled a red and white checked napkin off the table and spread it across her lap.

Miss Hattie stirred sugar into her tea and looked up at Vivian. "The way the Raines Ice Company has been growing, I'm sure Ida would be delighted to have your help."

Work for Ida? The thought hadn't even crossed Vivian's mind. And there was a good reason for that.

"What are sisters for, if not to help one another?" Miss Hattie said.

Vivian set her cup and saucer on the table while trying to form a suitable answer. No matter how noble her intentions, Ida's letter early last winter didn't help matters.

"Iceboxes can be quite fashionable." Grateful for the reprieve, Vivian followed Miss Hattie's gaze to the brass-handled oak icebox on display at the end of her cupboard. "You could sell folks on the finer points while Ida manages the bookkeeping for all the sales you bring in."

Fine points of a box that stored food? That was a leap. Vivian couldn't help grinning. "I'm afraid you're giving me far too much credit as a saleswoman."

"Nonsense. A handsome young woman like you would have but to smile. One look at you, and the town's businessmen would pour into the showroom to purchase an icebox."

"I think the millinery may be my second choice. At least a hat and clothing store relates to being a fashion designer." Working there, she could gain the recognition and contacts she'd need later to start her own business.

"The hat shop is a fine idea too." Miss Hattie leaned forward and pointed to the golden crust on the dish in the center of the table. "In the meantime, my beef and potato pie will give you the nourishment you need to go fishing another day."

❧

Carter swung down from his horse in front of Jesse's Livery. Stretching, he rolled his shoulders and reached for the moonless sky. His back ached, but its soreness was no rival for the ache in his heart.

He looked up Bennett Avenue. Street lamps cast a shaky radiance on the citizens coming and going. The brick-and-stone-front opera houses, eateries, and drinking establishments that lined the street from the depot on one end past the police department on the other teemed with activity. A dozen saloons belched tinny piano music and raucous laughter from both sides of the street.

The bank robbery in Victor had been close enough, and the recent train robbery had a full leg over his property line. But Mac... This was his home. Every morning the miner had enjoyed the same view Carter did of the mountains—a display of God's design and glory. Now the family man was gone.

Those same mountains could be harboring his killer.

Slapping his hat on his pant leg, Carter watched dust particles float on the chilled air. His other hand curled into a fist. His dedication to justice wasn't about setting out to prove something. Neither was it about avenging his father's killer, although he wouldn't have a problem hanging the guy. More than anything, he wanted to keep the peace and protect the innocent.

He'd lost his father to a cold-blooded killer, and now Mac's three children in Missouri had too. Carter pushed his hat back onto his head.

He cupped his hand under Liberty's jaw and led his bay stallion down the dirt path beside the livery barn. "Got more business to tend to, boy. I'll pay to have you brushed down."

Still talking to his horse. At least Liberty didn't go out of his way to avoid Carter and then offer excuses full of holes. Had it really been just this afternoon that he'd seen Vivian Sinclair on the street in Victor?

Jesse met him at the gate with a glowing lantern in one hand and a full pitchfork of hay in the other. "I recognized Liberty's nicker. Figured you'd be late gettin' him in the corral tonight." Jesse was about as tall as Pickett's six foot two description but had a lot more meat on his bones. A frown creased his chin. "Heard about Mac."

Carter nodded and removed the folder from the saddlebag. He didn't have to ask how Jesse already knew about this afternoon's tragedy. Cripple Creek was growing faster than the prairie grasses, but its strong word-of-mouth communication still gave it a small town feel.

"You find out who did it?" Jesse asked.

"Boney saw two men fleeing Mac's cabin. One of them could be Pickett."

"I remember seein' the poster. Tree tall. Skinny as a branch."

"He was bent over on a dapple gray. Mac may have shot him."

Jesse hooked his thumbs on the bib of his greasy overalls. "A dapple gray?"

"Yeah. Jon and I found one with a lead slug in its head while searching for the killers. Looked like it went lame."

"Three white socks and a dark hind leg?"

Carter straightened. "You know the horse?"

"Sounds like one I bought from a miner awhile back. Sold it about five months ago."

"To anyone I might know?"

"Pearl DeVere." Jesse whispered her name as if to avoid embarrassing Liberty or the horses in the surrounding corrals. Pearl was one of the most wealthy and renowned *other women* in town. "He pulled her buggy alongside her chestnut for a while. Haven't seen him for a couple weeks. Maybe a month."

"Thanks. I'll look into it. Could you have Archie pull the saddle and brush Liberty down for me? Gotta go."

"Will do."

Carter walked down the hill behind the corrals. How many times had his dad told him he had to think like criminals if he expected to catch them? Well, if he was a thief who'd been shot and needed immediate attention, he'd avoid the hospital and any doctors who could be considered longtimers. Dr. Cutshaw would likely question the injury. Instead, he'd go see the new woman doctor who'd only been in town for a week.

At the edge of Poverty Gulch, Carter cut toward the creek until he had a good view of the doctor's cabin. Enough light shone through the windows for him to see that no horses stood at the hitching rail. If Pickett and his pal had come here, they'd probably fled town after the doctor patched him up, but a man couldn't be too cautious. Carter had told his mother he wouldn't repeat his father's mistake, and it was a promise he intended to keep. Satisfied that nothing looked out of place, he walked down the rocky path to the doctor's log cabin.

A wooden box with a red cross on the lid hung on one side of the door. A dog barked inside, and the door swung open. The young woman who stood at the threshold, staring at him, stuck a pencil into the bun at the nape of her neck.

"Ma'am." Carter removed his hat. "I'm Deputy Carter Alwyn. I apologize for the late hour."

She snapped her fingers at the small, white fluff ball that yapped and bounced at her heels. "Quiet down, Pooch."

"Dr. Susan Anderson?"

"Folks call me Doc Susie."

Carter glanced down at the closed Bible she held in her hand. "Reading to a patient?"

"To myself." Her sigh caused the strand of hair that dangled at her forehead to shudder. She stepped aside. "Please, come in."

Carter followed her into the two-room cabin. A cot and a washstand lay nestled against the far wall, an island in a sea of clutter. Stacks of books towered on most flat surfaces, save the sofa and one chair. Boxes formed tables around the edges of the room.

"I'm seeing patients here until my office in town is ready." She set her Bible on a side table by the door. "Not too many patients yet. I've only been back in town as a doctor for about a week. It'll take folks some time to warm up to me."

Carter nodded. It didn't make sense to him that people in this town made as much of a fuss over women being engaged in legitimate business and medical practices as they did over women who took money for favors.

The doctor studied him from his dusty boots to his neglected hair. He'd see it cut as soon as things slowed down long enough for him to get to the barber. "You don't look like you need my services." A thin smile brightened her blue eyes.

Carter pulled Pickett's likeness from the folder at his side. "I came on business."

"Of course." The doctor pointed to the sofa beside a crowded bookcase. "Would you care to have a seat?"

When she settled into a bentwood rocker, he sat on the sofa across from her. "Have you seen this man?"

She took the wanted poster from him and the little color in her face turned a pasty white. "This man was here just hours ago with another man. The shorter, stocky one did all the talking." She lifted a medical journal from the table and fanned herself. "The talker never gave his name, but he called the injured man Timothy."

Carter wrote the name in his notebook.

"He said Timothy was chasing a deer when he dropped his rifle, and it went off." She looked down at her trembling hands and then back up at Carter. "It wasn't a hunting trip, was it?"

"No ma'am. Well, hunting for someone else's gold." He glanced at the poster. "The tall one's known moniker is Pickett."

"He'd been shot through the auricle of his rather large right ear." She pointed to her outer ear, about halfway up the length of it. Another sigh.

"A miner named Mac was robbed and killed this afternoon."

She covered her mouth.

"The men who came here fit the description of the two men seen leaving Mac's cabin."

She fanned herself again. "I wiped a lot of dried blood from his face and neck. His floppy straw hat was ruined. I wanted to throw it out, but they took it with them."

The hat matched the description of the one seen on one of the three men at the bank holdups.

"Gunpowder burns also tattooed Timothy's face," she continued, "and there is no known way of removing them."

"I'd say that makes him pretty identifiable."

"Yes, it would. I sterilized the wound and stitched the ear. The bullet came right close to finding its way through his head."

Carter slid the poster back into the folder. "Did either of them have an accent?"

"Couldn't tell. The shorter man's speech was distorted. He smelled like licorice-root candy. Probably had it in his mouth."

Same two that robbed the train. "What about Pickett? You hear him say anything?"

She nodded. "Didn't say much. Mostly groaned, but he did manage a sentence or two in response to a question before the other fellow's stern look quieted him. His voice shook, but not enough to shake the Ozark twang out of it."

Carter's pulse quickened. At least two of them shared the accent. Probably all three of them, since the spokesman favored having something in his mouth when he spoke, which would distort any accent.

The dog collapsed on a braided rug at Carter's feet, and he bent down to scratch the fluff ball's belly.

"Pooch is a spitz," Doc Susie said. "Don't know whether or not it's true, but I remember the stocky man saying that his neighbors in Kentucky had a spitz."

The thought of another good lead dried Carter's throat. He made a mental note to wire some lawmen in Kentucky. He lifted his hat from the stack of books on the table and stood. "You've been quite helpful. Thank you."

"You're welcome."

"You watch yourself, ma'am. We're dealing with hardened criminals here."

"I will." She glanced at the lever-action Winchester propped in the corner behind the door, then reached for the knob.

"You know how to use that thing?" Carter asked.

"I do. And despite my oath to 'never do harm to anyone,' I will use it, if necessary."

"I'm glad to hear it." Carter stepped out onto the stoop and set his hat on his head. "They've probably left the area, but you let me know if you hear from either of them again."

"I will." She tugged her shawl tight against the dropping temperatures. "You be careful too, deputy. I don't want you back as a patient."

TEN

Thursday morning, Vivian was ready to resume her search for a job. She'd spent the past two days laundering clothes, organizing what was left in her trunk, and rearranging her wardrobe. Her summer hats now sat on the shelf in order of color, from light to dark. She pulled a grass-green straw hat from the shelf and carried it to her dressing table.

Etta Ondersma hadn't telephoned with regrets of not having hired her, and Vivian's rent was due in two weeks. She pulled a hatpin from the box. Even though she'd never held a regular job, she knew one didn't get paid for work up front. It would be at least a week or more after she started before she'd see a payout. Hopefully, the folks at the millinery favored the shorter waiting period.

Twenty minutes later, Vivian rounded the corner at Bennett Avenue and stepped up onto the boardwalk. She mailed letters to Aunt Alma and Father at the post office and continued past a cobbler's shop to the millinery. Black lettering swirled across the window above a display of hats and handkerchiefs. Summer shawls and gloves draped a parlor rocker.

This was a new day and a new opportunity. Vivian's knowledge of fashion would serve her well here.

She reached for the door and stepped inside the sparkling store. Shiny metal racks presented menswear on one side of the room and women's on the other. A smartly dressed young woman helped a customer choose a reticule from a basket at the front of the store. While Vivian waited for the clerk to finish, she studied a rack of women's belts.

"May I help you, miss?"

The man's voice startled her. Turning toward a curtained door, Vivian looked up at the spectacles on a man she guessed to be in his early fifties, Father's age.

"Yes, thank you." She moistened her lips. "I've come to speak to the owner about employment."

He pushed his glasses up on his face. "Did you see the new brick front outside?"

"Yes sir, I did."

He glanced around the well-stocked store. "Well, those fires last year wiped us out. Had to start over brick by brick."

"I'm sorry." She knew what starting over felt like. She'd experienced her own raging fire.

"I'm afraid it has made our store a family affair. Any clerks or hatmakers you see are my wife, my son, or my daughter-in-law." He straightened a bowler displayed on a hat rack. "I wish I could oblige you, but I can't."

"I understand. Thank you for your time." Vivian turned to leave.

"I hope you'll come back. You're a stylish girl, and I know you'd fancy some of the fashions we carry."

"I will. Thank you."

Vivian stepped out onto the boardwalk. She looked left and right. Now what? She'd been so sure at least one of the two prospects on her list would employ her.

A family affair. The man at the millinery employed family members.

Perhaps it was time she swallowed her pride and went to her sister for a job.

She turned right and took slow steps toward the depot at the end of Bennett. If she closed her eyes and engaged her imagination, she could attribute fashionable qualities to an icebox. After all, she did admire the oak one with brass latches in Miss Hattie's kitchen. But if she applied for a position at the Raines Ice Company, there was more to consider than iceboxes: Customers. Sales slips. Money exchanges. And, most daunting, she'd be working for her eldest sister. The sister who didn't like Gregory.

Ida hadn't trusted him from the start. Or was it Vivian she didn't trust? Either way, Ida had been right, and Vivian stood little chance of hiding her past from her sister if she worked with her day in and day out. She couldn't take the risk. Surely there had to be something else she could do.

She looked around. A smoke shop and a saloon. Her sisters would think her working at either of those was scandalous. Little did they know. There was always the laundry. She'd done enough of her own washing since Father left for Paris to know she despised it. Besides, it, too, was probably a family operation. A Chinese family. The mercantile across the street caught her eye. Brooms grew like cornstalks out of a crock in front of the brick store. Several barrels crowded the door.

Vivian waited for a team of horses to pass and crossed the street. Then she saw the sign in the window.

Help wanted. See Mr. Heines inside.

It wasn't the job she wanted, but there was rent to be paid. If she wanted to stand on her own two feet, she could certainly scoop beans into a sack or stack apples in a box until something better came along. Working up a smile, she opened the door. A bell jingled, and a man about her height but with added girth, stepped out from behind a stack of pickle barrels.

"Good day, sir. I'm Miss Vivian Sinclair." She glanced back at the window. "I saw the sign, and I'd like to speak to Mr. Heines about a job."

"You're speaking to him, miss, but you're not what I'm looking for."

Vivian raised her chin. "I'm not as young as I look, sir."

"Your youth isn't the problem." He studied her from shoe to hat. "It's your size. Not a muscle on you."

Her cheeks warmed. "Muscles?"

"Yes ma'am." He raked his graying hair. "Not as young as I used to be. Need someone who can shoulder heavy sacks and barrels."

"Very well. Thank you." Vivian retreated.

Perhaps she had no choice but to work for Ida.

⤚⤙

Carter worried the brim of his hat, waiting for Pearl DeVere in the lavish parlor of the Homestead House on Myers Avenue. The tip of his boot bounced on the plush carpet. He'd be more comfortable rolling in a cactus patch. The women here were nothing but trouble.

"Deputy Alwyn?"

Carter spun toward the doorway, nearly dropping his folder. He hadn't heard the infamous madam enter the room, but there she stood in a fancy gown the deep green of piñon pine. "Good afternoon, Miss DeVere."

A slow smile curled her lips, only a shade brighter than her neatly coiffed red hair. "To what do I owe the pleasure of your visit?" Had she just batted her eyelashes? "Is it safe to assume you've come to your senses, deputy? You finally ready for our services?"

"You know me better than that." Carter extended his hand toward two parlor chairs and drew in a deep breath.

The madam walked toward the chair farthest from him, her dress swishing more than necessary. Once he'd positioned the other chair and sat down, she hooked a thumb under her chin. "You know what they say, deputy. 'All work and no play makes Carter Alwyn—'"

"I'm here on business, ma'am." He waved the folder in his hand.

"Not only is that disappointing news for all of us, but an unnecessary waste of your time. Since Ruby left, I only have three girls, and we had our monthly checkups last week." She snapped her fingers.

A blonde resembling a stage star entered the room. "Did you need something, Miss Pearl?"

"The deputy wants to see the medical records from last week."

Carter raised his hand. "No ma'am. This is about a horse."

"Oh." Miss Pearl looked away, and with a wave of her fingers, shooed the girl out of the room. When the door clicked shut, the bejeweled madam met Carter's gaze. "A horse?"

"You bought a dapple gray gelding from Jesse over at the livery."

"I've purchased several horses from him in the past three years."

"It was less than six months ago. A dapple with three white socks to his knees."

She looked past him, squinting as if she were thinking, and then nodded with the enthusiasm of a fly trapped by a spider. "Yes, I remember. I sold the horse."

"When?"

"Three weeks ago."

"To a client?"

She shook her head. "I didn't know him."

"You sold the horse to a stranger?"

"He approached me in town on a Tuesday morning." She stood, turning toward the drawn velvet drapes. "Said he needed transportation to go home to his family."

"Where was home?"

Shrugging, she tilted her head. "He didn't say."

Carter pulled the wanted poster out of the folder and held it out to her. "Could it have been this man who bought the horse?"

She glanced at the poster and handed it back to him. "I've never seen him before."

"The man you did business with wasn't tall and thin?"

She shook her head. So Pickett didn't buy his own horse, which supported the doctor's report that the other fellow ran the show.

Carter slid the poster into the folder and pulled out the sketch of the second man Vivian Sinclair had described. He held it up. "What about this man? Could he be the one who bought the horse from you?"

A quick blink hinted at recognition. "No. Wasn't him either." She sat on the edge of her chair, her lips pressed together. She swept curls back from her temples. Fidgeting. Pearl DeVere knew more about the horse's buyer than she was saying. "Why all this interest in an old horse?"

Women like her were nothing but trouble. A breed of strife and suffering that haunted him. Carter looked straight at her. "I found the horse up in the hills, shot in the head." Not so much as a blink from the madam. "Not long after a miner was robbed and killed."

"And you think one is connected to the other?"

"A witness saw two men matching these descriptions leave the miner's cabin, one of them on your dapple gray."

"That's terrible. I never should've sold the horse."

"Why did you?"

"The buyer really wanted him and offered me a good price." She smiled and winked. "Wouldn't be much of a businesswoman if I started turning down men with a desire and a hand full of cash, now would I?"

He'd have to settle for a hint of recognition for now. "Thank you for your time, Miss Pearl."

"Sorry I couldn't be of more help." The madam stood and smoothed her skirts.

Carter followed her to the front door.

"I hope you find your man," she said. "Men, I suppose it is."

"You can be sure I'll find them." Carter started to step over the threshold and paused. "If you remember anything else, please let me know."

He set his hat on his head and stepped out into the sunlight. If he had expected Pearl DeVere to say or do anything to disprove his prejudice against women in her profession, he was undoubtedly delusional.

ELEVEN

❧

*V*ivian walked up Golden Avenue toward Third Street. She'd been in Cripple Creek only two weeks, and already she'd suffered enough rejection: Etta Ondersma, the millinery, the mercantile.

She needed some sister time. Nell had a way of inspiring her.

Vivian was willing to take the chance that Nell would be home midmorning. If not, she would have given her legs a good stretch and her mind a rest. She'd been in Nell and Judson's home last week during the Sinclair sisters' whirlwind tour of the town. They lived near the base of Mount Pisgah. Vivian decided to go down the hill and head west on Bennett instead of trying to navigate the maze of roads on the hill.

Fifteen minutes later, she turned the corner at B Street. Judson and Nell's log cabin sat on the fourth lot on the left. Colorful flower boxes underlined the open windows, where yellow gingham curtains fluttered in the breeze.

"Vivian!" Nell waved to her from the porch swing. A knitting project filled her lap. That was Nell, always doing something with her hands.

Vivian stepped up onto the porch, which was just big enough for the swing and a wicker armchair. A basket of clothes sat at Nell's feet. A half barrel of geraniums graced the corner on the other side of the door.

"I took a chance you'd be home," Vivian said.

"I'm glad you did." Nell tugged yellow yarn from the ball on her lap and glanced toward the armchair. "Join me. Sitting, I mean. You don't have to knit." She giggled and wove her needles through the yarn.

Vivian seated herself on the swing next to her sister. "It's been two days since I saw you at church, so I thought I should let you see that I haven't headed back to Maine." She set her reticule beside her. "Yet."

Nell straightened, a frown creasing her forehead. "You wouldn't really leave Cripple Creek, would you?"

"I may have to if no one will hire me."

"Etta's Fashions?"

"She doesn't have enough work for another seamstress right now, let alone a designer."

Nell stilled her knitting needles. "I'm sorry. I know that's the work you wanted."

"The millinery isn't hiring either. I checked at the mercantile too." Vivian picked at a fingernail. She knew Nell's next question: Have you spoken to Ida about a job?

"Well, then I might have some good news for you. I was in the Blue Grocery yesterday the same time as Mabel Hartley. She runs the Cripple Creek branch of the Colorado Telephone Company, over on Third Street."

Not at all what Vivian had expected.

"Mrs. Hartley told the grocer she needed a full-time telephone operator," Nell said.

"Telephone operator?" Connecting callers was a far cry from creating fashions. But Vivian's dream of becoming a famous clothing designer had come to an abrupt end, just as her dream of one day being a wife and mother had.

The toes of Nell's boots tapped the pine boards with each gentle swing. "Not what you'd hoped for, but…"

"It's a job. Thank you." At least the job of telephone operator would be steady work. Unlike costume design or even sewing jobs, which could ebb and flow like the ocean. There was no guarantee that work at the millinery or the mercantile would have been steady either. "I'll go to the telephone company when I leave here. After we've had a chance to visit awhile."

Nell's smile brightened the freckles scattered over her nose. "Good. All our visits so far have been hectic."

"And crowded." A songbird chirped in a nearby sycamore tree, and Nell's needles clicked in a restorative rhythm—the sights and sounds of bliss. Vivian relaxed against the porch swing and watched Nell work. "You're knitting a blanket?"

"A baby blanket."

"For a baby?" Vivian straightened. "Something I should know?"

A shadow darkened Nell's blue eyes. "It's not for us." She laid the blanket on the swing beside her. "I'm starting to wonder if I'll ever bear Judson's children."

"I'm sorry. I didn't mean to—"

"I know." Nell pressed her hand to her chest and sighed.

Vivian fidgeted with the flouncing on her skirt. She wasn't the only one who couldn't have what she wanted. The difference was that Nell deserved a family.

Nell wiped a tear from her cheek. "I'm tired of reminding myself that Judson and I have only been married thirteen months. I'm tired of hearing about women who waited many years before bearing children, and others who never did."

"It must be hard."

"I know I should be content with what God has given me. I want to trust the Lord. I do trust Him, but I'm so weak."

Vivian shuddered. She could write a book on personal weakness, and she was ready to defend Nell's right to question God.

"I'm sorry. You didn't stop by to listen to me complain." Nell pulled the blanket onto her lap. "Having to wait isn't the worst thing that can happen. An explosion in a tunnel killed a miner last month. His widow expects to deliver their first baby in just weeks." The needles resumed their clicking. "The blanket is for her. Eleanor. She's rather sickly. I don't know how she'll ever manage on her own."

Vivian felt her shoulders droop. That was Nell, always tending to the needs of others. Vivian could never measure up to her sisters. Ida ran a business. Kat was not only a writer for a national publication but also a mother. And Nell had charity running through her veins. She made baby blankets for widows when she longed for a baby of her own. As a child, Nell had been the one to gather all their dolls and coax them to eat imaginary food with a real spoon. Her heart ached for a baby, and she'd be a fine mother.

"Come with me to see Eleanor Saturday morning," Nell said. "I'd like you to meet her."

It would probably do Vivian good to meet more people in town, especially those less fortunate. "It would give me more time with you."

Nell nodded. "We can meet at the corner of Fourth and Bennett at ten o'clock."

"I'll be there."

"Wonderful. If I finish the blanket in time, we can deliver it Saturday."

Vivian studied the basket of clothing at Nell's feet. The dressing gown on top had a needle and thread stuck in it. "Mending?"

Nell nodded. "Yes. I wanted to finish a few more rows on the blanket first. The fires last year left many families homeless. That clothing belongs to the widows and orphans the Sisters of Mercy are helping."

"You're amazing, Nell Sincl—Archer."

"Because I mend clothes?"

Vivian nodded. "Among other things."

"Sewing is something I can do to help."

Vivian reached into the basket and pulled the dressing gown onto her lap. "I might as well make myself useful while we visit." She pinched the ripped side seam together and began stitching.

They talked about Miss Hattie, living in a boardinghouse, and the Sisters of Mercy. Then Nell cleared her throat. "Viv-i-an."

Vivian stilled her needle. Her name in that tone from this sister meant Nell had romance on her mind. Only this time, Nell and Ida and Kat were married, and Vivian was not. She met her sister's gaze anyway.

"I know you cared for Gregory and hoped to marry him one day," Nell said.

"That didn't work out, and Gregory went his own way." He wasn't the marrying kind. Vivian jabbed the needle through the seam a bit more forcefully than necessary and stabbed her finger. She stuck it in her mouth to seal the wound. Not so easy to assuage her bleeding heart.

"There are other men, you know."

Vivian tied off the thread and snipped it with her teeth. "The deputy and I are committed to stopping the robberies. I was a witness, and he is quite thorough. That's all."

"I didn't mention any names."

Vivian swallowed hard. She'd just set her own matchmaking trap.

Nell grinned, a calculating gleam in her eyes. "The lawman isn't the only good-hearted, single man in town."

But he was the only one who'd captured her attention.

"Judson works with several eligible fellows. There's Tim Phieffer in shipping and receiving. Melvin Whitman is an inspector at the mine. And there's—"

Vivian raised her hand to stop her sister. "I'm not interested in courtship, Nell." If she could be, Carter Alwyn would be at the top of her list.

They moved on to other topics, and Vivian mended the dressing gown, a skirt, and a shirtwaist, then left Nell to finish the blanket.

A light breeze teased the ringlets dangling at Vivian's collar. From Nell and Judson's home near the base of Mount Pisgah, she headed down B Street toward Bennett Avenue. She dodged a feisty horse pulling a wagon at the corner of Bennett Avenue and stepped up onto the boardwalk. So far, life in Cripple Creek was nothing of what she'd expected. Bank robbers and lawmen. Shop owners who thought her too costly, too young, too weak. Well, she'd show them they were wrong.

"Good day, ma'am."

Vivian looked up into the face of an elderly gentleman doffing a derby.

"Sir." She returned his smile and continued on her way to Third Street.

Although Vivian wasn't fond of the idea, work as a telephone operator would give her a lot of opportunities. And she couldn't sit around doing nothing while waiting for Mrs. Ondersma's business to thrive.

She needed to go where the job opening was. She could do just about anything for a time if she knew it was merely a steppingstone.

The Colorado Telephone Company office sat on the west side, across from the Third Street Café. A blue metal factory-made storefront and gold lettering on the glass door embellished the two-story brick building.

Vivian drew in a deep breath and wrapped her gloved hand around the doorknob. As Father would say, nothing ventured, nothing gained, so she entered.

A woman rose from a small desk and tucked a sprig of gray hair under the circle of braid that clung to the back of her head. "May I help you, miss?"

"I was told there is an opening for an operator."

The woman looked Vivian over and tugged the banana-yellow pinafore straight on her bright orange linen dress. Surely that wasn't a required uniform. If so, Vivian already knew this wasn't the job for her.

"Your name?"

"Vivian Sinclair."

"Have a seat on the bench there." She looked past Vivian at the wooden deacon's bench against the wall. "I'll let Mrs. Hartley know you're here."

When the woman dressed like a fruit basket had disappeared through an open door, Vivian seated herself. A chorus of *pr-ring, pr-ring, pr-ring* overpowered the muffled female voices emanating from the other side of the wall. She looked through a stack of magazines on a side table until footsteps drew her attention back to the door.

"Miss Sinclair?"

Vivian looked up into a smiling face and stood. "Yes."

"I'm Mabel Hartley, the manager here. Someone told you we needed another operator?"

"Yes, my sister, Nell Sinclair... I mean, Mrs. Judson Archer."

Recognition registered in Mrs. Hartley's gray eyes. "She's come here for donations to the benevolence fund. I am short one girl." She glanced toward the open door. "If you'll follow me, we can go to my office and discuss your qualifications."

Mrs. Hartley was about Vivian's height, but fleshy. A cacophony of bells and chatter filled the room they entered. Vivian followed Mrs. Hartley past three young women seated at desks in front of panels covered with holes and flickering lights. Thankfully, they all wore different patterns of dress in various colors. No uniform. She could do this.

The operators pulled cords out of the table in front of them and plugged them into the holes with lights next to them. Vivian was sure she'd heard the words "Who are you calling?" twelve times between the door and the narrow steps in the corner of the room.

Upstairs, the manager's office was modest but neat and clean. Mrs. Hartley pointed to a wooden office chair and then seated herself behind the oak desk. Vivian folded her hands in her lap.

"You saw the operators at the boards?" Mrs. Hartley asked.

"Yes ma'am, I did."

"Then you saw that our work here is rather clear-cut. A telephone operator receives incoming calls and directs the caller to the intended recipient." Mrs. Hartley opened a drawer. "You think you could do that?"

It sounded easy enough. "I would do my best."

"You're young and bright. I say we give it a try." She pulled a form out of a folder and handed it to Vivian. "Fill this out and bring it back with you Monday morning."

"Monday. Yes, thank you."

"You'll begin your training at ten o'clock."

Vivian had walked halfway to the boardinghouse before her new reality sank in—she was a working woman. Helping Aunt Alma unpack boxes of fabric and thread and stock shelves in her dry goods store in Portland didn't count. On Monday she would begin her first real job. She was finally on her way to becoming a self-reliant woman.

TWELVE

⌒⊝⌒

A surge of hope powered Vivian's steps as she strolled down Fourth Street Saturday morning. At the corner, she stepped up onto the boardwalk. Nell walked toward her down Bennett Avenue and waved. In Nell's other hand, a paper-wrapped bundle dangled by the string that bound it.

"You finished the blanket," Vivian said as they walked.

Nell sighed. "Just last night."

"But you finished it. When you set your mind to something—"

"Yes, well, it's a Sinclair trait, which means I'm not the only one." A smile reached Nell's blue eyes. "Any success in your search for employment?"

"I went to the telephone company when I left you Tuesday and spoke to Mrs. Hartley."

Nell's eyebrows arched. "And?"

"And I start work at the telephone company on Monday."

"That's wonderful!"

Vivian wasn't sure how she felt about being a telephone operator, but she was thankful to have a job.

Nell paused at a busy intersection and waited for a donkey cart to pass, barely turning her head to the right. "This is Myers Avenue." She spoke the street name in a whisper. "We have to turn left to get to Poverty Gulch where Eleanor lives, but *good girls* don't frequent Myers."

Blameless girls. Girls who weren't living a lie. Feeling like an impostor, Vivian followed her sister's lead and looked straight ahead as they continued down the hill behind the depot.

They'd just walked under the trestle and down into the Gulch when three little girls ran toward them in flour-sack dresses, all of them shouting her sister's name, their arms open wide. "Miss Nell!" "Mith Nell!"

Nell pulled them into a hug. "Girls, this is my sister, Miss Vivian."

"Pleased to meet you, ma'am," they said in unison.

Nell introduced them. "These are the Zanzucchi sisters, Jocelyn, Jaya, and Julia."

Smiling, Vivian looked at each one in turn, spending more time on the youngest sister. "Girls, it's a pleasure to meet you."

The oldest of the Zanzucchi girls smiled, then focused her dark-eyed gaze on the package in Nell's hand. "Is that for Miss Eleanor's baby?"

"Yes, it's a blanket." Nell looked down at the youngest child, who still clung to her leg. "But now, I have a little something for you."

"For uth?" The big-eyed girl looked about four years old.

"Yes. For you." Nell poked her belly, and she squealed. "For you, and for you." When she reached for the other girls, they jumped back, giggling.

Vivian couldn't help giggling too while inwardly struggling to understand God's reasoning, or at the very least, His timing. Nell was so good with children and longed for one of her own to present to a husband who adored her. And here she was, taking a baby blanket to a woman who'd lost her husband and would have to raise a child on her own. It made no sense to Vivian.

"But it's not our birthday, Miss Nell." This big sister stood just as poised as Ida always did.

"It's not?" Nell asked.

A frown creased the littlest one's chin, and she shook her head, causing ripples of sunlight to flow down her long raven hair.

Nell pulled three candy sticks from the pocket of her calico skirt. "We'll just have to call these an 'I love you' gift."

"Candy!" Jaya rocked side to side while Nell handed out the candy.

"You're welcome. But you have to go straight to your papa for permission." Nell glanced toward one of the canvas tent cabins that dotted the area. "Can I trust you to do that?"

Jocelyn was the first to nod. "Yes ma'am. Thank you." She reached behind her sisters and nudged each of them in the back.

"Yes ma'am," Jaya said.

Vivian felt herself grimace. Jocelyn reminded her of Ida. Always doing the right thing and expecting it of others. Another reminder that not going to Ida for a job had been the right choice. Vivian was destined to be a disappointment, and there was too much at stake to see it in Ida's eyes every day.

"Yeth ma'am." Julia's pigtails danced. "Thank you."

Vivian followed Nell's lead and waved as the girls scrambled toward their shanty like cats after a mouse.

"I need to ask Doc Susie about Julia's speech impediment." Nell turned away from the girls, toward the sound of a running creek. "Having just come from medical school, our woman doctor may know of new treatments or exercises that could help."

Nell stopped outside a mud-chinked log cabin nestled in a clump of oak trees.

"Miss Nell." The voice sounded flat. A woman whose face bore lines far beyond her years peered out from an open flap window. "You brought someone with you?"

"My sister, Vivian."

"Welcome. Please come in."

Nell opened the door and they stepped inside. The one-room cabin was sparse but clean, with only a rocker, a straight-back chair, a crate table, and a rope-bed in the living area. Eleanor stood at the simple table, wringing her hands.

"You don't look well. Should I find Doc Susie?" Nell asked.

The widow shook her head, her lips pressed.

"Perhaps a gift will cheer you up, then." Nell held the package out to her. "I brought you something."

Eleanor stared back with watering eyes.

"For the baby," Nell said.

A tear trickled down the widow's ashen cheek. Vivian understood warring emotions, and it was obvious Eleanor was waging an epic battle.

"Let's sit down." Nell pulled out a chair and waited for Eleanor to ease herself into it. The girl's belly was so round, it was hard to believe she had another month until the baby's birth. When they were all seated, Nell slid the package across the table to Eleanor.

Her fingers trembling, Eleanor dragged the strings off the wrapping and laid it open. She stared at the blanket. "You need to keep it."

Nell looked at Vivian first, her brow furrowed, then at the widow. "I don't understand. You don't like the blanket? I knitted it special for your little one."

"I'm going to wed."

Nell tapped her thumbs. "You're getting married?"

Eleanor nodded and pulled a telegram from the pocket on her apron. "I knew Douglas in Philadelphia. Our families lived in the same neighborhood. He heard about Lars's death and has asked me to marry him."

Nell was the Sinclair family romantic, so why wasn't she offering the woman her well-wishes? Instead, a frown dulled the freckles bridging her nose. "Are you sure this is what you want to do?"

Eleanor tucked a thread of brown hair behind her ear. "This is what's best. Douglas will wire the money for my trip home." She stared at the gift. "The baby won't be going with me."

Nell gasped. "What? You can't mean that. A baby is a gift from God. It's your baby...a part of the husband you loved and lost."

Eleanor sniffled and folded her hands. "I can't stay here alone. I can't work with a baby to care for." She drew in a quick breath. "I need to marry, and—"

"He doesn't want the baby?" Heat burned Vivian's ears.

Eleanor shook her head. "Douglas is a good man. I know he'll treat me well." She drew in a deep breath. "I must do what is right for all of us."

Nell groaned and covered her mouth with a trembling hand. Vivian swallowed against a lump of emotion in her own throat. It wasn't hard to imagine Nell's confusion. Not only had God chosen to give Eleanor and not Nell a baby, but now the widow didn't even want her child.

"I want my baby to have a mother and father who can welcome it with open arms and open hearts," Eleanor said. "Parents and kin who will cover it with love."

"You're giving your baby away?" Nell asked.

Eleanor bit her top lip. "I want you to take my baby." She slid the blanket across the table to Nell and looked her directly in the eye. "Your baby. I want you to keep the baby as your own."

"Raise someone else's child?" Nell leaped to her feet and paced the short length of the room. "I always thought…"

Her sister didn't have to finish the sentence for Vivian to know what Nell wasn't saying. Nell had grown up believing she'd birth her own children.

Eleanor wiped a tear from her cheek. "Nell, you said a baby is a gift from God."

Nell sat back down. "Yes, a heritage from God."

"You don't believe He can use other people to deliver His gifts?"

Tears spilled down Nell's cheeks. She nodded and captured Eleanor's hand.

Vivian pulled a handkerchief from her reticule and blotted her own tears. God hadn't answered her sister's prayer in the way they expected, but Nell would have a baby.

Perhaps Cripple Creek was where Vivian belonged after all. She'd start a new job Monday. Did she dare to believe that God was working things out for her too?

Carter pulled a spatula out of a drawer. Hot cakes sizzled on the griddle. The one-hole potbelly in his second floor apartment wasn't much of a cookstove to speak of. Hot cakes weren't much of a Sunday supper either, leastwise not compared to the spread he was sure the Sinclair sisters had laid out. Three Sundays ago he'd enjoyed a roasted pork loin and candied sweet potatoes at the parsonage.

That was before the fourth Sinclair sister arrived in town. Before Vivian Sinclair stood up to him on the train. Before she decided to ignore him and he'd determined to avoid her.

Just as well.

Spatula in hand, he scooped up his golden-brown hot cakes and slid the stack onto a blue enameled plate. They weren't roasted meat, but the cakes still reminded him of breakfast at his mother's table. He poured maple syrup over the hot cakes until they swam in a pool. Seated at the table against the wall, Carter clasped his hands and bowed his head. *Lord God, thank You for Your provision of this food. My home. My stove.*

While he breathed in the sweet scent of his meal, Carter recalled Tucker's prayer for him.

And Lord, please give me the grace and strength I need to accomplish the task You've set before me. Please keep Your hand upon all those involved in bringing these men to justice. Amen.

He'd just cut into the stack of hot cakes when he bowed his head again.

And Lord, I could also use an extra helping of grace and strength where Miss Vivian Sinclair is concerned. Thank You. Amen.

He filled his fork with hot-cake layers and devoured his first bite.

Maybe it was all in his imagination anyway. Perhaps their unfortunate first encounter on the train would always hinder their chance of a true friendship. Or anything more.

He'd chosen to do the avoiding today, when Tucker invited him to join the family for Sunday supper. Romance could never work for him. Not as long as he was a lawman. He wouldn't put a wife through what he'd watched his mother endure. An officer of the law could be called upon at any moment to walk away from his family and risk never returning to them.

He lifted his mug and breathed in the heavy aroma of coffee before enjoying its rich warmth.

The sharp sound of the buzzer above his door propelled him to his feet, and he banged his thighs on the table. The downstairs office was locked today, but the sheriff had insisted Carter install the buzzer so he could be reached in case of emergency. Usually it was rung by truant kids dared by their friends.

More buzzing. Not kids then.

Carter grabbed his hat off the peg. By the time he reached the bottom step, he could see Edgar Hamilton waving at him through the window. Carter met the saloon owner at the door and motioned for him to come in.

"I know it's Sunday, but Sergeant Grady down at the police department thought I should tell you something."

Carter pointed to two chairs along the far wall. "You want a cup of coffee?"

Edgar raised his hand. "Gotta get back to the bar."

Carter sat beside the balding bartender. "You have a problem over there?"

"A drunk shot up my piano last night."

"Sounds pretty normal for a Saturday night. And well within the jurisdiction of the police department."

"That's what I thought until I reported it to Grady this morning and he asked me if the guy said anything."

Carter sat up straighter. "I'm listening."

"Heard him say his cousin was a fool to go and get himself shot by a greenhorn miner, then he paid for his drinks and the piano with a stack of silver dollars. Grady thought he could be talking about the fellow—"

"Mac shot."

Nodding, Edgar smoothed his thin mustache. "One more thing, deputy. The more I've thought about it, the more I remember him lookin' like the shorter man Miss Sinclair described for the sketch."

Carter popped up out of the chair like a man on fire. He took two long strides across the room to his desk and pulled the folder of posters and drawings from the drawer. Returning to the chairs, he slid out the sketch of the stockier guy and showed it to Edgar.

The saloon keeper nodded. "A bulbous nose. A rounded face. My artwork didn't quite match him, but her description sure did."

Carter's pulse quickened. At least one of the outlaws was still in the area.

All he had to do was figure out why.

THIRTEEN

he moment Vivian stepped through the door of the Colorado Telephone Company on Monday morning and heard the commotion on the other side of the wall, her stomach knotted. What had she been thinking, accepting a job as a telephone operator? What little experience she'd had with a telephone at Aunt Alma's dry goods store involved being connected, not connecting other people.

The woman Vivian had seen Tuesday rose from the desk and met her at the end of the counter. "Miss Sinclair."

"Good morning, Mrs.…"

"Wilkening. Miss Mara Wilkening." Miss Wilkening stuck a pencil in the gray braid that sat at the nape of her neck and glanced up at a wall clock. Five minutes to the hour. "It's good to see you are prompt."

Suddenly, Vivian was thankful Ida had drilled into her the importance of the timely habit.

Miss Wilkening took the completed form from Vivian and glanced at both sides before setting it on the desk. "Follow me." She spun around and marched to the open door in the back corner.

Her steps far less sure than Miss Wilkening's, Vivian watched the older woman's stiff carriage. The clerk's dress wasn't orange today, but her lime green frock didn't do much to flatter her pole-thin shape either.

Vivian would work on that once Miss Wilkening had proven she was capable of producing a smile.

Vivian expected to follow Miss Wilkening to the stairs leading to the manager's office. Instead, they stopped beside an empty chair at the end of the row of switchboards.

"This will be your work station." Miss Wilkening clapped her hands like a crack of thunder, drawing the attention of all three operators seated in front of their respective boards. "Girls, this is Miss Vivian Sinclair." The clerk looked down at Vivian with narrowed eyes that made her feel even smaller than her five feet two inches. "Vivian will work alongside you." Her words were pointed at the others, but her steely gray eyes pinned Vivian. "On a trial basis."

Reminding herself to breathe, Vivian smiled at the other operators. "Good morning."

"Victoria." Miss Wilkening pointed to the girl seated closest to them first. "Alice. Eva."

None of the three girls spoke to her, but each of them nodded, and the dark-haired girl at the far end waved. Not one of them wore a hat, and all were dressed like farm wives. Perhaps during breaks, Vivian would have an opportunity to suggest more becoming costumes.

When Miss Wilkening jerked her hand like an orchestra conductor, the young women all turned back to their boards and began pulling cords to and from lighted plugs. "All right, then," Miss Wilkening said. "Let's you and I get down to business."

"Yes ma'am."

"First off, this is a job, not a summer fashion show at the opera house, Miss Sinclair." Miss Wilkening's gaze settled on Vivian's hat. "You'll need to remove that."

Swallowing her own bite of sarcasm, Vivian set her reticule on the chair and removed the first of several hatpins. While she continued her task, setting the pins on the shallow desk, Miss Wilkening stared at the chair.

"You won't need your reticule either. You're here to work, not to primp."

The book of Ruth came to mind, along with Ruth's bitter mother-in-law. Perhaps, like Naomi, Mara Wilkening had been forced to leave Judah and bury her husband and then her two sons. Had she said to her family, "Call me Mara" because the name for *bitter* suited her best?

"To save us both time, I'll put them in a cupboard for you," Miss Wilkening said.

Vivian handed over her belongings. As her supervisor crossed the room to a bookcase of open cubes, her heels clicked against the wooden floor. When Vivian's hat didn't fit into the box with her reticule, Miss Wilkening set it on the top shelf. Now Vivian would need to ask for help at the end of the day to retrieve her hat. And the shelf probably hadn't been dusted since it had been built.

Miss Wilkening returned and tapped the back of the empty chair. "Sit. We've lost valuable time."

Vivian lowered herself onto the chair, staring at the panel of lights and plugs in front of her, fully aware that, with this sour woman by her side, the day would feel too much like Ruth and Naomi's journey to Judah.

❦

On Friday evening, after her first week as a telephone operator, Vivian carried a box of ribbons from her trunk to her dressing table, where she'd carefully laid out several sheets of paper from her sketch pad.

She was hard pressed to find anything to like about her job. Although she'd seen improvement in her skill at operating the switchboard, she was still having trouble keeping all the cords and plugs straight. And Mara Wilkening's incessant clucking had done nothing to boost Vivian's confidence.

Vivian chose six ribbons from the box—all different colors. She ran the purple one through her fingers. How she missed working with different materials, textures, and colors. Designing and making the outfits for Ida's move to Cripple Creek last autumn was the most fun she'd had in a long time. Vivian lifted the lid off her hatpin box, then studied her makeshift switchboard. The divider boards from her trunk sat on the table and leaned against the mirror. For now, the silky ribbons would serve as the cords connecting her imaginary callers. She pinned one end of a ribbon in each of the penciled circles that indicated cords. After a quick review of her board list, she pretended the head of the pin that held the yellow ribbon in place was flashing.

Swallowing a giggle at the silliness, Vivian imagined she heard a voice in her provisional earpiece. "Who are you calling?"

She practiced connecting six calls and only looked at the list once—for the plug that belonged to the banker, Harry Updike. Why was his plug such a challenge to recall? She had no trouble remembering which plug connected a caller to Deputy Carter Alwyn.

Vivian stared at the purple ribbon and thought of something she should like about her job.

Her work kept her so busy that avoiding the deputy would be easy.

FOURTEEN

ᴐᴥ

*V*ivian had been working as a telephone operator for two weeks and one day. Last week she'd done a much better job of keeping the lights and plugs and cords straight on the switchboard. Her practice had paid off, and she'd received her first payout on Friday, then enjoyed a Fourth of July picnic up on Tenderfoot Hill after the Sunday service. Yesterday she'd made a couple of mistakes on the connections, but the girls all said Mondays were the most difficult. Today, the promise of daily improvement spurred her steps through the door of the telephone company, five minutes before nine o'clock.

"Good morning, Miss Wilkening."

Her taskmaster met her at the end of the counter. "Miss Sinclair, Mrs. Hartley wishes to see you."

"All right." Vivian had yet to receive a cordial greeting from the office manager.

She followed the stiff orange dress through the open door and up the stairs. Apparently the company manager personally informed new employees that they'd passed the test of working on a "trial basis."

Mara Wilkening tapped on the office door, and when Mrs. Hartley responded, she opened it.

The manager stood behind her desk, a weak smile edging her lips. "Miss Sinclair, please come in." She pointed at the chair in front of her desk, and Vivian seated herself. Vivian expected Miss Wilkening to leave, but instead she hefted a second chair and settled into it six feet away from Vivian.

Vivian drew in a deep breath and focused on the company manager. "Mrs. Hartley, I'm thankful for this opportunity to tell you how much I appreciate your patience while I learn my job." She leaned forward. "I've never done anything like this before, but I'm beginning to feel more comfortable in the job."

"That's what we're here to discuss." The whining tone of Mara Wilkening's voice reminded Vivian of the droning stamp mill in Victor.

"Yes. Mara has some concerns," Mrs. Hartley said.

The mother hen jerked her back straight. "We both know they are more than mere concerns."

"Yes." Mrs. Hartley rolled a pencil in her fingers. "Some feel you are a liability to the company."

"A liability?" Vivian tried to swallow her panic. "I was both faster and more efficient at my job last week."

"Mara did mention that, but we still have a bit of a situation."

Why was she talking in riddles? *Liability. Situation.* "I don't understand."

"I'm afraid the only agreeable resolution is to let you go."

Heat raced up Vivian's neck. "You're firing me?"

"I'm afraid so, dear. You made a lot of mistakes."

"Am I the only one who makes mistakes her first week?"

"No." Mara Wilkening looked her straight in the eye. "But you've been the only one who misconnected the same person eight times in two weeks."

Vivian squirmed. The banker. "This is about Mr. Harry Updike?" Both women nodded.

"I know those boards and plugs and cords can be confusing." Mrs. Hartley pulled open her desk drawer. "But Vivian, Mr. Updike is a major stockholder in the company."

"I'm losing my job because of a man who barks like a bulldog on the telephone. Am I the only one he flusters?"

Pressing her lips together, Mrs. Hartley pulled three dollar bills from the drawer and held them out to Vivian. "Here is payment for yesterday and today."

Vivian reached for the money. "I'm willing to personally apologize to Mr. Updike if you'd be willing to give me another chance. I'm sure I could smooth things over for you."

Mara Wilkening raised a leathery hand, her steely gray eyes narrowing. "What's done is done."

Truer words were never spoken. And now Vivian had one more thing she wished she could undo.

As she followed the mother hen out of Mrs. Hartley's office and down the stairs, her legs felt as if they were lifting bricks. The incessant bells on the telephone board echoed off the constricted staircase. The operators' repetitious replies made her left eyelid twitch. When they stepped onto the floor, the chatter ceased. The cords stilled. Three pair of eyes watched Vivian's every move. Even the flickering lights on the panels behind them seemed to mock her. They knew she was a failure.

"Make sure you haven't left anything on the shelf," Miss Wilkening said.

Vivian glanced at the shelves on the far wall. "I left nothing there." And there was nothing here for her, even if Mrs. Hartley had agreed to a second chance.

Lifting her head, Vivian put one stylish leather shoe in front of the other and walked past the counter, through the door, and out into the sunlight. Another mockery.

Relief quickly replaced her disappointment. She was free of that awful job and that awful woman. If only she could figure out how to replace the humiliation of being marched out past the other girls.

Vivian walked up Third Street as if she had somewhere important to go. She'd been in town a full month. She'd been turned down for several jobs and been fired from another. She couldn't even answer the telephone properly.

For lack of a better idea, Vivian turned right at Bennett Avenue and slowed her pace on the boardwalk. Friday's payout allowed her to pay Miss Hattie for the last two weeks' room and board. She still owed rent for this week. And she needed to purchase necessities for her hair and skin at the mercantile.

Any of her sisters would do what they could to help her, but she'd been the baby long enough. It was time she stood on her own two feet.

Walking past the millinery shop, Vivian couldn't help glancing through the window. A gaggle of girls close to her age fussed over hats and looked like they were having fun doing so. Vivian would've fared better working there. She drew in a deep breath and continued down the walk.

When she came upon the vacant bench in front of the post office, it seemed the perfect place to contemplate her next move. Once seated, Vivian pulled a pendant watch from her reticule. Twenty minutes past nine o'clock. More than seven hours to fill before Miss Hattie expected her home.

Vivian set her reticule beside her on the wooden bench. She wasn't like her sisters. Just because they'd come to Cripple Creek and found success didn't mean she would. She was bound to fare better in Denver, if only getting there didn't require train fare and money for lodging.

Three of the girls she'd seen through the window poured out of the millinery, toting packages in each hand. The farm girls at the telephone company could learn a thing or two about how to dress and carry themselves from these three. So could all the other women Vivian had seen out and about this morning. The girls walking toward her were all lovely— tall and shapely. And friendly. The one with dark hair and green eyes smiled at her.

Vivian greeted her, and the young woman stopped and glanced at Vivian's reticule. "I like your costume. Very stylish."

Vivian's spirit lifted. "Thank you."

"Are you a working girl?"

"Not anymore." Vivian sighed. "I left my job this morning." It wasn't a completely honest answer, but she couldn't bring herself to admit she'd been fired.

"Well, we work for Miss Pearl over at the Homestead House. She has an opening for a downstairs hostess—a day job, and I'm sure she'd be partial to someone who wears her clothes with superb chic, as you do. Miss Pearl will be back at the house this afternoon, if you'd like to come by and talk to her."

"Thank you." Vivian watched the girl swish past. Her bags brushed against the flouncing on her skirts.

Vivian had never thought of herself as chic, but she did like the idea of working somewhere she might be appreciated, even welcomed.

Carter disliked only one thing more than he did hanging around sa-loons, looking for the mysterious second train bandit—spying at the Homestead House. Even if it was only three or four times a week. For-tunately, this was Tuesday morning, which meant the *other women* were out and about town, and Pearl had joined them. It wasn't likely the suspect would visit her in the middle of town in broad daylight. Just in case he did, Carter had asked a couple of shopkeepers, grocers, and the postmaster to keep an eye out for any male companions they didn't recognize.

Which left Carter free to think about other things. For starters, a full breakfast—eggs, ham, potatoes, and biscuits drenched in butter and honey. He stepped onto the boardwalk, anxious to let the Third Street Café do the cooking today. As an added bonus, perhaps the ac-tivity in the eatery might keep his mind off Vivian Sinclair. He'd been doing a poor job of it on his own. Except for polite greetings at the back of the church the past two Sundays, he hadn't spoken to Vivian since seeing her in Victor, but her absence did little to hamper her ability to divert his attention.

"Deputy!" The voice came from behind him. "Hey, Alwyn, wait up."

Carter stopped midstep and turned. Bart Gardner from the *Cripple Creek Times* galumphed toward him like a mare about to foal.

Carter didn't have anything against newspapermen, but their hun-ger for a story had them on the hunt, and he was their prey. Reporters from three other newspapers in town had already been in his office this week, and it was only Tuesday.

The portly man closed the gap between them and came to a stop uncomfortably close to Carter.

"Mornin', Bart."

"You find Mac's killers yet?"

"We're closer than we were on Friday when you came by my office, but nothing is resolved yet."

"You said that last week."

"It's still true." Carter felt a sudden cramp and stretched his neck, first to the left, then to the right. "It's also still true that I can't divulge any leads or information that might tip the law's hand and give the outlaws an advantage."

"Of course not, but there must be something you've discovered that you could share with me. Something to show people you're doing the job you were hired to do."

Rage was about to replace the blood that ran through Carter's veins. Apparently his disdain showed, because the newsman took a long step backward, putting a little distance between them.

"Didn't mean to imply that you're not doing your job," Bart said. "I'm sure you are."

"Rest assured you'll know when the men who robbed the train and the men who killed Mac are found." Carter didn't bother sharing that he was convinced they were the same men who had robbed the bank in Victor. "Good day, Bart." He tapped the brim of his hat and turned to leave.

"One more thing, deputy. You know of someone bright looking for a job, send them my way."

"Will do." Carter made his escape up Bennett Avenue.

He'd just crossed Fourth Street when he spotted Miss Sinclair sitting on the bench outside the post office. When she met his gaze, she seemed completely unaware how much trouble her naiveté could cause her.

He removed his hat. "Miss Sinclair."

"Deputy Alwyn."

Carter looked around at all the men hanging out of shop doors and lining the streets. "Miss Sinclair, an unusually high number of men are out and about town this morning. Do you know why?"

She looked up the boardwalk, then out toward the street, and shook her head. "I hadn't noticed, but I really haven't been in town long enough to know usual from unusual."

"How about the women? Did you notice that the women are different this morning from those you're accustomed to seeing about town?"

"Some, perhaps."

"Tuesday mornings from eight o'clock to eleven o'clock are set aside for the *other women* to do their shopping."

"Oh." Blushing, she glanced toward the millinery shop, and he guessed she'd seen the women without realizing who they were.

Carter gripped the brim of his hat with both hands. He needed to get her off the street. "I was following my growling stomach to the café. Would you care to join me for a bite to eat? Or a cup of coffee perhaps?"

She studied him, arching a thin eyebrow. "Tea?"

"I'm sure they have it."

A controlled grin sparked her brown eyes. "I suppose a cup of tea with you would be permissible."

He took the first step, and they walked to the café in silence. When Carter held the door for her, the faint hint of lavender trailed her, and he fought to remember why he'd decided to avoid her in the first place.

A dark-haired matron seated them across from each other at a table against the wall, and then the waitress met his gaze. "Coffee, deputy?"

Carter nodded. "And two eggs over hard. Bacon. Sausage. Hash. Biscuits."

The waitress flipped the brown braid off her shoulder and studied Vivian from the black lace frill on her hat to the ruffled hem on her purple dress. "For you, Miss?"

"I'd like a cup of ginger tea and a piece of peach pie with cream." Vivian pointed to the bell jar on the counter displaying a whole pie.

He hadn't even had breakfast yet, and Vivian was eating dessert? "It can't be any later than ten o'clock, and you're ordering pie?"

"Is that a problem?"

"Not for me." Yes, definitely independent. And the real problem was that he found her attractive on many levels.

The waitress jotted on her notepad and looked up at him. "Will that be all, sir?"

Carter looked across the table at Vivian.

"Yes, thank you," she said.

"Very well, then." The waitress dropped her pad and pencil into her apron pocket. "We'll get those right up for you."

As soon as the waitress walked away, Vivian regarded him, her dainty chin angled slightly. "You have more outlaw business to discuss, I presume."

"Not exactly. Not at all, actually." He pressed his back against the chair for added support. "I know you attributed your attempt to ignore me in Victor to not getting a job you wanted and to family matters, but…do you have something against lawmen?"

"I assure you that I have nothing against lawmen, Deputy Alwyn." She fidgeted with the napkin in front of her before meeting his gaze. "I was simply trying to discourage you."

"Why would you feel a need to do that?"

"Because, I don't want to *encourage* you, Carter."

"You used my given name."

"So I did."

Before he could respond, the waitress arrived with a big mug of steaming coffee and a dainty teacup on a saucer.

"Thank you." They spoke in perfect unison.

"The rest will be up in a minute." The waitress headed toward the diners seated at a corner table.

Carter returned his attention to the puzzling woman sitting across from him. "You used my given name. Does that mean you like me?"

Vivian stirred a spoonful of sugar into her cup. "It means I would like you, if I could."

"Meaning I'm unlikable?"

She moistened her lips. "Meaning I can't trust myself."

"To like me?"

Vivian nodded.

"I see." So it wasn't just his imagination or wishful thinking—she was drawn to him too. They were both attracted to each other, but apparently each of them had personal reasons to avoid romantic entanglements. And he didn't have to know her reasons to respect them. "I can't offer any more than friendship either, Vivian."

She opened her mouth long before the words came out. "Friendship is good." Relaxing against the chair, she tucked her hair, the color of caramel taffy, behind her ear. "Now I have a question for you."

"That's fair." He wasn't sure whether to welcome a query from her or to brace himself.

"Might you know of anyone looking to employ a well-dressed young woman from Maine with a passel of sisters and a knack for bewildering deputies?"

Carter chuckled. "Just so happens that I do."

"Really?" Surprise crinkled her forehead.

"Yeah, Bart Gardner over at the *Cripple Creek Times* told me just minutes ago that he needs someone bright to work in his newspaper office."

"Thank you." Her smile added golden flecks to her brown eyes and threatened to render him speechless.

What were his reasons, again? Oh yeah. He didn't want to bring a wife into his life as a lawman.

Perhaps it was time to rethink what Tucker had referred to as his calling. Right now, being a shopkeeper or a rancher or even a mucker in a mine sounded good if it meant he could pursue more than friendship with Vivian Sinclair.

FIFTEEN

⟡

The newspaper man stood beside a contraption that filled the room with a constant *whirr-clickety-clack.* It was all Vivian could do to resist covering her ears, but she was here to ask for a job.

Feeding sheets of paper into the smelly machine divided the man's attention. "You said you're here about an opening for employment?" he shouted.

"Yes sir."

He studied her and shook his head. "I'm afraid I don't have anything for you, young lady."

She'd had quite enough of people deciding what she could and couldn't do based upon her age or gender or size. And she probably had all three strikes against her here. Vivian blew out a long breath. Never mind that such an action wasn't becoming of a lady.

"Sir." She hadn't intended for it to come out in a huff, but the volume did gain the man's attention. "Just moments ago, I was told that you spoke this very morning of an opening here at the *Cripple Creek Times.*"

"This morning, you say?"

Vivian nodded. She started to cross her arms for emphasis, but thought better of it.

"Deputy Alwyn?"

"Yes sir." She kept her chin held high. "You told him you were looking for someone bright to work in the office."

He looked down at the floor, stained black. "I did."

"Well, sir, that would be me."

"But—"

"Please, sir." Vivian allowed her bottom lip to jut out ever so slightly, a tactic that used to work on her father. "I'm new to town, and I need the job."

Mr. Gardner's face softened, and his shoulders slouched. "You'll need to leave the fancy clothes at home."

"I can do that." Why had her eye chosen this particular moment to start watering and itching?

He glanced down at the filthy apron stretched tight across his middle. "You'll need to wear an apron."

Vivian nodded. That was easy enough.

"You'll start Monday morning. Eight o'clock."

"Yes. Thank you, Mr. Gardner. You won't regret hiring me." Smiling, she walked to the door.

She was now a newspaperwoman.

᠈᠊ᡘ᠊

Carter hadn't intended to go to the parsonage from the Third Street Café, but the more he considered his calling and reflected on Vivian Sinclair, the more he thought about how much he respected Tucker Raines's opinion. He could count on his friend to be honest.

When Carter didn't find the reverend inside the church building, he walked the flower-lined path to the parsonage. He'd rapped the brass knocker only once when the door swung open.

"Deputy?" Ida Raines looked past him. "Is something wrong?"

"No ma'am." Not unless she wanted to count the way her sister had him tied up in knots. "I'm sorry to bother you. I wondered if I might have a word with your husband. I checked at the church." He glanced toward the brick building behind him. "But you're home and—"

"Please, come in." She waved him into the small entryway. "I was on my way to the icehouse for the afternoon. I'll let Tucker know you're here."

As the Sinclair sister moved to the closed parlor door, Carter couldn't help noting the similarities between her and Vivian. Although Ida Raines was three or four inches taller, both possessed narrow noses and high cheekbones.

Mrs. Raines tapped on the parlor door before opening it. "Carter Alwyn is here to see you."

The reverend stepped into the entryway and reached for Carter's hand. "Good to see you."

A slight smile tipped Ida Raines's mouth as she looked Carter in the eye. "Mind if I ask you a question?"

He had no room for a bigger icebox in his apartment, but he'd let her give the sales pitch anyway. "I don't mind."

"Was your *meeting* with my sister this morning planned or by happenstance?"

He gulped. How could she already know about the two of them eating together at the café?

"Tucker mentioned he saw her talking to you in front of the post office," Ida continued.

Carter shot the reverend a look meant to scold him for squealing. Tucker shrugged. "Sisters. Sorry."

"Yes, seeing Vivian was unplanned." Carter shifted to his other leg.

"So she was on her break at the telephone company?"

She worked at the telephone company? He brushed his hand through his hair. Vivian had asked him for a lead on employment. But it wasn't his place to meddle in a family. He needed to choose his words carefully.

"Dear, I doubt Carter came here to play a game of Yes or No with you," Tucker said, saving him. He shooed his wife toward the door. "Off you go. He doesn't need a big sister. Or a matchmaker." The reverend turned to Carter, his eyebrows arched. "Do you?"

Carter shook his head.

"See there." Tucker patted his wife's back. "Your services, though very capable, aren't needed here."

Ida glanced at Carter, a gloved hand in the air. "If you should change your mind... I know my sister very well and could give you some pointers."

Carter couldn't believe he was actually considering taking Ida up on her offer. Fortunately, she squeezed Tucker's hand and stepped outside before he could give in to the temptation.

The reverend watched his wife saunter down the path, then turned back to Carter, a smile on his face. "Got to tell you, deputy, these Sinclair sisters are really something."

"I'm discovering that." What that *something* was, exactly, Carter couldn't yet pinpoint.

"Ida made lemonade. I was about to pour myself a glass. Can I get you some?"

"Sounds good. Thanks."

Tucker pointed to the parlor. "I'll be right in."

A vase of black-eyed Susans topped a round, oak lamp table between two wing-back chairs. A Bible lay on the side table by one chair, and a copy of *The Word and the Spirit* by Charles Spurgeon lay on the floor next to the other. Carter chose to sit at one end of the settee, where he had a clear view of the landscape painting on the wall. Pikes Peak rose out of a bank of gray fog, tipped in pure white.

Right now he felt surrounded by fog, impatient for a breakthrough.

Laying his hat on his lap, Carter let himself imagine a life like this. A home. A favorite place to sit and read. A woman in his life to tease and hold hands with. A wife to come home to. Or in the reverend's case, a wife who came home to him.

Tucker walked in carrying a glass of lemonade in each hand. "My sister painted the picture."

Carter took a glass from him. "Mrs. Peterson, correct?"

"Yes, I forgot you met Willow before she went to Colorado Springs to be with my folks." Tucker sat across from him in one of the wing-back chairs. "She gave me the painting when we went to see them last month. Didn't get it hung until this week."

Carter raised his glass to his mouth. The lemonade was a perfect balance of sweet and sour, just what he needed to quench his thirst.

Tucker leaned back in his chair. "What's on your mind?"

A few things, including his friend's sister-in-law, but where did he begin? His friend showed no signs of filling the silence with more questions or assumptions. Carter liked that about him.

After another gulp of lemonade, Carter set his glass on the sofa table. "How do you know that what you're doing is what you're intended to do?"

"In my work?"

For starters. Carter nodded.

"I didn't know for a long time. Thought it was itinerant preaching until I found out my father was sick and my mother needed me to help with the ice business. My plan was to return to California as soon as possible."

"So how did you know you were supposed to stay here? Return to preaching and marry?"

"That's a big question. A series of them, actually. But for me, they were all related." Tucker paused and scrubbed his clean-shaven face. "I had a change of heart. I knew I was supposed to stay. I suddenly had a strong desire that I believe God placed in my heart, along with an opportunity I eventually recognized as God's provision for His plan."

Was Tucker talking about the church or about Ida Sinclair? Did Carter dare think that Vivian could be part of God's plan and provision for his life?

"In your office a few Sundays back, during your prayer, you asked God to 'protect me in this, my calling.'"

Tucker straightened. "I remember. Had the robberies on my mind."

"So you think I'm called by God to be a lawman?"

"You don't?"

"I don't know. I hadn't thought of my work in that way before. My dad was a lawman."

Tucker nodded, sympathy etching lines into his brow. Carter had told his friend the story.

Carter picked up his half-empty glass. "So, am I 'serving justice' because God called me to it, or am I a lawman because it's what my father did?"

"Seems we have some things in common. Me with the ice business and you with the law." Tucker swirled the ice chunks in his glass. "You think you're a deputy simply because it's what your father did? That you have to carry on his work?"

"Maybe." Carter took another drink. "Or some sort of mission to avenge his death."

"You probably want to save families from suffering the loss you suffered."

Carter looked up at the painting again. "I have the desire and was given the opportunity, but… I'll think about it." He swallowed his resolve to ignore his feelings. "Between you and me?"

"Yes, I learned my lesson." A grin deepened the laugh lines at Tucker's eyes.

"Vivian Sinclair."

The pastor leaned back in his chair again. "Forgive my ignorance, but what's the problem? Vivian isn't interested in a lawman?"

"I'm not interested in bringing a woman into the life of a lawman."

"Not interested, or afraid to do so because of what you and your mother lived through?"

"It's too dangerous."

"And that's why you're questioning your choice of profession?"

"Partly."

Tucker peered up at his sister's painting. "Keep trusting God. Keep your heart open to Him. He'll lead you through the fog."

Nodding, Carter stood. "I best get back to the office. Thanks."

"I'll be praying for you."

"Appreciate it."

Tucker held the door open for him. "Do you think if your mother knew then what she knows now, she would've chosen not to marry your father?"

Carter positioned his hat on his head and looked at his friend. "I don't know."

And he wasn't sure he wanted to.

Sixteen

ᘉᘉᘉ

*V*ivian sneezed again and followed it up with a huff of frustration. That was at least the tenth sneeze in the two hours since she'd arrived at the newspaper office. The worst possible time for a cold. She needed to make a good impression her first day on the job. Not an easy task when she seemed to be waving a blackened and wet handkerchief about. Stuffing the handkerchief back into her apron pocket, she sniffled and resisted the impulse to wipe her watery eyes with her hands.

"Miss Sinclair, are you all right?" Mr. Gardner spoke above the *clickety-click, swish-clunk* of the monstrous press he wrestled. He was already more pleasant to work with than Mara Wilkening.

Vivian nodded and held her breath in an attempt to stifle another sneeze. "Yes sir." Except that her eyes felt like they'd been rubbed with salt and her nose was sure to be as red as a tomato.

When her boss resumed feeding paper into the rotating mass, Vivian returned her attention to the work table. She pulled one letter at a time out of the pan of solvent, patted each creviced piece of metal with a cotton cloth, and then set each letter in a clean pan on the table.

It wasn't the work she'd expected to do here. In her mind, an office job involved typing and filing and answering the telephone. Certainly, she'd rather handle fabrics rinsed in lavender water than letters dipped in a solvent that smelled worse than ammonia, but she much preferred working with a newspaperman than a telephone woman. This paid better, and she found the entire process rather intriguing. Until today, she had no idea what went into creating those huge sheets of paper that had captured her father's attention with every new edition of the *Portland Press Herald*.

The next two sneezes didn't even wait for her to retrieve the handkerchief from her pocket. Hoping that was the last of them, she carried the cleaned and dried letters to the other end of the table, where Mr. Gardner had placed the type tray.

"Remember to mind your p's and q's now." The hard-working man laid a two-foot-by-three-foot sheet of paper over a drying rack. "A place for every letter, and every letter in its proper place." He hadn't scowled at her once. She would like this job.

"I will, sir. I'll be most careful."

Cleaning type was something she could do. This work made much more sense than the willy-nilly lights and plugs and cords on the telephone switchboard. Scooting onto a stool at the table, Vivian began fitting each of the cleaned type letters into their proper place in the distribution box.

By four o'clock, thousands of letters had been swished in solvent, patted dry, and properly tucked into bed in the tray. Unfortunately, she felt like she'd been swished and dried and was now ready for bed too. All she had left to do was wipe down the table. She'd nearly made it through her first day.

Two more sneezes struck. She yanked her soiled handkerchief out of her pocket. The sneezes continued, five in a row. The inside of her nose tingled, and her throat felt scratchy. Two symptoms she hadn't noticed earlier.

Mr. Gardner rose from his desk and walked across the room toward her. She sniffed back another sneeze. "You've been sneezing like a skunked dog all day." He lifted the type tray off the table and studied her. "And, frankly, you look like you've been on a binge."

"Yes, I'm sorry, sir. I seem to have a cold." Vivian blinked hard against the grit in her eyes. "I plan to stop by the pharmacy on my way home and pick up some menthol salve. I'm sure I'll be like new by tomorrow morning."

Shaking his gray head, he carried the tray to the rack at the printing press. Sliding the tray into place, he looked at her and brushed his mustache. "You weren't sneezing last week when you were here."

"No, but I do remember my eyes started watering and itching a bit."

The corners of his mouth sagged into a frown. "While you were here?"

"Yes." She squeezed the word out, trying to resist another sneeze.

"And Tuesday after you left, did your eyes water and itch?"

"Not for long."

"Were you sneezing on your way to work this morning?"

"I don't suppose so."

"Then this isn't a common cold."

"It isn't?" Nothing like this had troubled her at the telephone company. If this wasn't a cold, then what was it?

"It's the solvent or the ink. Could be both." He pulled a fresh handkerchief from his pocket and handed it to her.

"Thank you." She wiped her watering eyes.

"Seems you may not be cut out for newspaper work."

"But I am."

"Some folks just can't take the solvent."

"This can't be." Vivian glanced at the grimy window. "I could open the window to air out the room some."

He smiled. "We work with paper."

"Of course." A warm flush climbed her neck. "That would be a problem."

He nodded and wiped his hands on his apron.

"But I like working here," she said.

"You do?"

"Yes, it's a little dirty and stinky, and loud, but working with the letters is rather fun. I did a good job, didn't I?"

"Yes, but I'm afraid, for the good of your health, you'll need—"

"No."

"Yes. You need a job that's better suited to your status, anyway. This is menial work for a young lady with your breeding." He glanced at the handkerchief in her hand and tapped his bulbous nose. "You have ink on your face."

She wiped the top of her nose, adding a big smudge to his kerchief.

"The top of your right ear is black too."

Ink—and egg—on her face. Her sisters were all successful in their lives, and she was a complete failure. Couldn't keep God's laws. Couldn't keep a job. She hadn't even lasted a full day at this one.

Thirty minutes later, Vivian trudged up the hill on Fourth Street. Two jobs in one week, both of them gone.

Mr. Gardner had paid her two dollars for the day's work. With that and what she had left from the telephone company, she'd have enough to pay this week's rent, but that would leave her nothing for incidentals.

Purchasing postage stamps. Sending telegraphs. A train ride to Victor when Etta Ondersma changed her mind.

When another sneezing fit threatened, Vivian stopped at the corner on Golden Avenue and pulled Mr. Gardner's handkerchief from her pocket. Four sneezes this time that made her chest ache and weakened her knees. Why must she always be so stubborn? If she'd accepted Mr. Gardner's offer to drive her to the boardinghouse in his wagon, she'd be in her room by now.

Ida wouldn't have been fired from her first job...any job. Ink and solvent wouldn't have made her sick. And, feeling this bad, Ida would've accepted the offer of a ride home.

Miss Hattie was right. Sisters did help one another. Vivian and her sisters had always been there for one another. Until Father split them up for his move to Paris.

If she wasn't so stubborn, she would've gone to Ida for a job before she went to the telephone company.

Vivian blew her raw nose and tucked the wadded handkerchief into her pocket. She willed herself down the street to Miss Hattie's. One step after another, slow but sure, all the way to her room.

～✄～

Friday, Vivian sat at her dressing table and pinned a cameo just below her lace stand-up collar. Sealing her lips, she breathed through her nostrils.

Her clear nostrils.

She'd finally quit sneezing halfway through supper on Monday. Her eyes had stopped watering and itching Tuesday. And by the time she'd retired that evening, the redness in her eyes had faded. Mr.

Gardner had been right—it wasn't a cold that had assailed her, but rather an adverse reaction to the newspaper environment.

Which meant she was back where she'd started—jobless.

Vivian lifted the lid off the metal box of pins and noticed her hands. The ink stains remained, especially on her right hand—the one she'd used to retrieve the inky letters from the tray. She was indeed a marked woman, physically and figuratively. Not the kind of woman a man could love and want to wed. And since her transgression had erased marriage from the picture she'd imagined for her life, she needed to persist in finding a suitable job that would allow her to support herself. Sighing, Vivian twisted her hair at the back of her head and stabbed a comb into it. If only it were that easy to tack her past in its place—behind her.

She carefully set the mesh summer hat on her head. She was tempted to telephone Etta's Fashions in Victor to see if anything had changed, but she wasn't going to beg. She'd done that with Mr. Gardner at the newspaper and then had to quit. Humiliation snapped at her heels no matter what she did.

She lifted an envelope from her dressing table. The letter had come to her from Ida just weeks after her eldest sister had left to start a new life in Cripple Creek the previous year. Vivian slipped the onionskin stationery from its matching envelope and reread the message.

1 November, 1896

My Dear Vivian,

I'm faring well and finding success in my work for Mollie O'Bryan.

Oh, how I wish I could have brought you to Cripple Creek with me.

Partly because I already miss you terribly, and partly
because I'm concerned about you. Father is gone to Paris, and all
three of your sisters have moved to Colorado.

Vivian drew in a deep breath. She'd cried for weeks after saying
goodbye to Ida. Aunt Alma had done everything in her power to con-
sole her, but Vivian missed her family—her sisters most of all.

Vivian, your heart is especially vulnerable right now,
with all of us gone.
You've accused me of not liking Gregory. You said I was
jealous of the time he spent with you. There's more to it.
Gregory impressed me as the kind of boy who may
sympathize with you, then possibly try to take advantage of
your emotional weakness.

Another apt description—emotional weakness. And Gregory's attentions had made her feel stronger, in control. A costly delusion.

Why was it so much easier to see behind you than ahead? It wasn't
fair that her sisters were so wise and she so severely lacking in wisdom.

Ida had been right about Gregory, and Vivian so wrong. As it
turned out, she did need to be told what to do and what not to do. If
only she hadn't resented Ida's counsel. If only...

She knew now that it wasn't Ida's fault her little sister was stubborn
and a poor judge of character. Vivian had no one but herself to blame
for her mistakes. And there was a lot about life and business that she
could learn from her sister.

Vivian folded the letter and tucked it back into its envelope, then
returned it to her trunk. She angled her hat slightly and pinned it in

place. Reticule in hand, she descended the stairs and walked out the front door, hopefully into a new relationship with her eldest sister.

The Raines Ice Company was located on four acres just below the depot. Ida had explained the reasoning—easy access to the ice being delivered on the train. Working for Ida, Vivian would learn not only how to be a good sales person, but also how to run a successful business. Information that would come in handy when she'd earned enough to shift her attention to her dream of being a fashion designer and owning her own clothing company.

Heeding Nell's warning about Myers Avenue, Vivian walked down Bennett instead. Just before the depot, she turned right, continuing down the hill and across the railroad tracks. The icebox showroom and Ida's office were housed in a brick building adjacent to a rock-lined icehouse. An OPEN FOR BUSINESS sign hung from the doorknob. A bell jingled when Vivian opened the door, announcing her presence, and Ida and a customer glanced her way.

"Vivian, it's good to see you. You can wait at my desk if you'd like, and I'll be right with you." Ida returned her attention to the balding man in an oversized herringbone suit.

Vivian seated herself in the desk chair along the wall and watched her sister in action.

Wearing a burgundy linsey-woolsey dress, her hair sculpted by tortoise shell combs, Ida swept her hand across the well-stocked showroom, then rested her fingertips on a beautiful appliance with brass hinges and decorative carvings. "This Monarch is the finest icebox available today, Mr. Updike."

"Mr. Harry Updike?" His full name escaped Vivian's lips before she could stop it.

Her sister cocked a thin eyebrow and the man crossed his arms.

"Pardon me." Vivian had come looking for a job, not trouble. And causing her sister to lose a sale would be trouble.

Ida dipped her chin, which meant a question was forthcoming. "You know Mr. Updike?"

"Only the name...from the telephone company."

The banker huffed, a hint of recognition in his beady eyes.

Vivian looked away, studying a pencil on the desk in front of her. She'd told her sisters she'd been fired because of a disgruntled shareholder, but given the circumstances, she should have remained silent.

Ida turned back to her customer, and Vivian held her breath. "Mr. Updike, have you decided which icebox you'd like to have delivered to your home?"

Vivian's eldest sister was full of surprises, and once again, Ida had demonstrated wisdom, or at the very least, discretion.

The banker opened and shut the door of the food compartment. "Your finest looks suitable, Mrs. Raines, but for this defect."

Vivian startled. Ida wouldn't try to sell anything with a defect, certainly not in secret.

Mr. Updike stabbed a thick finger at the top corner of the icebox. "I'm certain you don't expect me to pay full price for damaged goods." Even in person, he sounded like a bulldog.

Vivian resisted the temptation to walk over and see the defect for herself, but she did straighten in her chair for a better view.

Tilting her head, Ida examined the corner of the icebox. She pulled a handkerchief from the seam pocket on her dress and wiped the top of the appliance. "Thankfully, Mr. Updike, it was a mere smudge, not a flaw."

If a thorn in one's flesh took human form, it would have jowls and be this banker.

Ida offered Mr. Updike a smile, one Vivian recognized as second rate. "We can deliver your icebox tomorrow morning, and you'll have the finest appliance on your block. I only need your payment."

Yes, Vivian would learn a lot working for Ida. And the best part was that Mr. Updike would already have the newest icebox, so there would be no reason for him to trouble her.

Ida made quick work of the sales transaction. As soon as the bell jingled behind the banker, Vivian stood and met her sister's gaze. "Nice work."

"Thank you." Ida sighed, hard enough to puff out her cheeks. "It took everything I had in me to resist giving that rodent a tongue-lashing. He's the one who insisted Mrs. Hartley fire you, isn't he?"

"Yes. Thank you for resisting. He would've lost that battle for sure, and I'd just as soon put that all behind me."

Ida nodded. "I'm glad you stopped by." She pulled her reticule from a desk drawer. "It's been too long since my bowl of oatmeal this morning. Can I buy you lunch?"

"I'd like that."

Ten minutes later, Vivian sat across the table from Ida in the Third Street Café. The same table she'd shared with Carter Alwyn the day she told him she couldn't like him. The day he'd said he, too, had only friendship to offer her.

After they'd given the matronly waitress their order for peppermint tea and roast beef sandwiches, Ida rested her hands on the table and met Vivian's gaze. "How are you?"

"I'm well. Getting a little thick around the middle from Miss Hattie's fine cooking, though."

Ida chuckled. "I don't see it, but I know what you mean. She loves to cook. Kind of sad that she doesn't have a family for whom she can cook."

At least Miss Hattie had enjoyed having a husband, even if her George had lived too short a life.

"I heard you had to quit your job at the newspaper." Ida arched her brows. "The work made you sick?"

"Yes. The chemicals and the ink." Vivian moistened her lips. "Actually, that's what I came to the icehouse to discuss with you."

"Oh?"

"You've helped Tucker build ice delivery into a successful business." Vivian watched the waitress set their cups of tea on the table. "Thank you."

"Your food'll be ready shortly." The waitress flipped a long brown braid over her shoulder and spun toward the kitchen.

Ida pulled the saucer toward her. "I can't take all the credit for all the success. Tucker built the icehouse before we married. And Otis Bernard takes care of organizing and supervising the wagon drivers and the deliveries."

"And you take care of the bookkeeping and icebox sales."

"I do." Ida stirred sugar into her cup. "Are you asking me for a job?"

Vivian moistened her lips again. "Yes. I'm sure it must come as a shock. I've not been appreciative of your concern the past year, but—"

"Two years, almost to the day you turned sixteen."

Nodding, Vivian drew in a fortifying breath. "Two years. I've changed a lot since then." More than she could say.

"I can see that you have." Ida's smile brightened her blue eyes.

"I'm sure with all you do here, and being a pastor's wife, you could use some help in the store."

Ida took a sip of tea. "Vivian, I'd love to hire you—really I would, but I can't."

Vivian reached for the sugar bowl, trying to hide her disappointment.

"We've expanded the business a fair amount, hired several more delivery drivers, and I'm afraid money is a little tight right now. Too tight to hire anyone else." Ida's frown reflected Vivian's regret. "Things might change, and if they do… I suppose I should think more positively than that. *When* they do, I'll let you know. But I'm sure you'll be happily working elsewhere by then."

Vivian stirred the sugar into her tea, a bit more briskly than she intended, and the spoon tinked the sides of the cup.

Ida had been her last hope. She couldn't even get a family member to hire her.

SEVENTEEN

ᐁᘐ

Vivian pinched the clothespin and pulled her red gored skirt off the line. She sighed, feeling pinched herself. The end of July already, and she had significantly fewer prospects for a job than she had two months ago.

In the past several weeks, she'd eliminated a long list of options. Etta's Fashions. The millinery. The Colorado Telephone Company. *The Cripple Creek Times.* The Raines Ice House. The mercantile. Glauber's Clothing. The confectionary. Attorney at law. The Butte Opera House. She'd applied for an office job at the Colorado Trading and Transfer Company. She couldn't even get hired as a maid at the National Hotel, the largest in town. And those were just the first dozen places she'd tried. She freed her plaid shirtwaist and added it to the basket at her feet. Saloons and smoke shops were the only options she'd passed up.

After pulling the last two pieces of her laundry from their pins, she carried the full basket to the kitchen door. She had the boardinghouse to herself for most of the day. She didn't expect Miss Hattie back from her Women for the Betterment of Cripple Creek luncheon until late afternoon.

Vivian set up the ironing board in front of the stove and laid a folded sheet over it. She pulled the hot sad iron from the stove and a shirtwaist from the basket at her feet. When she'd moved in with Aunt Alma two years ago and had to start doing her own ironing, she quickly developed a new appreciation for all that Tilly, their household domestic, had done for her family before Father left for Paris. Now, taking in ironing seemed all that was left for Vivian to do.

As she pressed the sleeves on her broadcloth shirtwaist, memories from that Tuesday and her time at the bench on Bennett Avenue washed over her. She thought about the girl who stepped out of the millinery, looking like she'd just walked off the pages of a fashion magazine. She'd spoken to Vivian as if they could be friends. *"Are you a working girl? We work for Miss Pearl over at the Homestead House. Opening. Daytime hostess. Partial to someone as chic as you. Come by and talk to her."*

At the time, Vivian didn't know the Homestead was one of the places on Myers Avenue—the street *good girls* didn't frequent. Then Carter Alwyn had come along and enlightened her.

Tuesday mornings the *other women* do their shopping.

Little did the deputy know how much more she identified with the group on Tuesday mornings than she did with the respectable women every other day of the week. And he couldn't know. Just one more reason she should be grateful she and the deputy had come to an understanding concerning any mutual attraction.

"I can't offer any more than friendship either, Vivian." And she had no doubt he meant to keep his distance from her. She'd overhead her family and Miss Hattie invite him to Sunday supper on several occasions during the past few weeks, and he'd always declined.

The dark-haired girl had said the opening at the Homestead was for a downstairs hostess during the day. Most likely serving food and drinks. A job that sounded innocent enough.

Vivian snickered. But what did it matter what the job was or where? She wasn't blameless, and certainly no better than those girls. Besides, everyone else had turned her down.

The Homestead was her only lead. She'd be stupid not to at least talk with this Miss Pearl.

Two hours later, Vivian walked down Fourth Street toward Bennett Avenue wearing white gloves. The ink stains had faded from her hands, but she felt anything but spotless. Still, it wasn't as if she intended to work as one of the *other women*. It just happened that an available job required her to work in such an establishment.

She'd done worse. The first time she surrendered herself to Gregory's desire and her own lust for love, she vowed it would never happen again. Not until they wed as he'd promised. Then a second time. A third. Who would do that? The answer sent stomach acid into her throat.

The next time they were alone together, they stood in the grand entryway of his parents' home. Gregory took her hand to lead her up the stairs to his bedchamber, but she stood her ground. She couldn't do it anymore. Not like that. She told him no and asked when he planned to marry her. His guttural laughter still echoed in her heart and mind, almost as deafening as the statement that followed.

"Don't be silly. I have no intention of marrying you. Any girl who has sullied herself can't be my bride."

Vivian wiped a tear from her cheek. Shaking his head like a stern schoolmaster, Gregory had opened the palatial door of his home and motioned for her to leave. That was the last time she'd seen him.

At the corner of Fourth and Bennett, Vivian sidled up to a tall brick building and looked around. When she was satisfied no one was watching her, she continued south to Myers as if she were going to Poverty Gulch. Except when she arrived at the corner, she turned right instead of left.

The Homestead House stood on the north side of the road, and the white two-story building looked more like a palace than a brothel. Not that she knew what a house of ill repute looked like. But this one was crisp and clean. Light blue filigree hung from the roof, shading the house like a fancy hat brim. The same light blue framed the two open windows at the second story. Lace curtains fluttered in the breeze. The front door was to the left of a glassed-in alcove that added an elegant charm.

Vivian pressed a hand to her waist. She could do this. After all, she was only here to talk to the woman. There was no harm in that. She'd find out if the job was still available. It wasn't as if she'd committed herself to the work. She'd hear what Miss Pearl had to say and look at the place before making a decision.

And if she did take the job with Miss Pearl, it would only be temporary. It wouldn't take her long to make enough money to go to Denver. There were bound to be several dress designers there with enough business to share.

Vivian drew in a deep breath and reached for the brass latch.

A bell chimed as she opened the door and stepped inside. The carved rosewood ceiling of the foyer captured her attention. Velvet wallpaper lined the entry, and her shoes sank into a plush Persian carpet. She'd never seen so much opulence.

Footsteps sounded on the ornate staircase, and Vivian turned. The dark-haired girl she'd spoken to that Tuesday descended the steps with the flair of a stage actress and a painted face fitting for a matinee.

The girl smiled. "I remember you. It's been three weeks."

Vivian nodded. "You mentioned an opening for a daytime hostess." She leaned forward. "Downstairs."

A smile added sparkle to the girl's coal black eyes. "You decided to apply?"

"Is the hostess job still available?"

"As far as I know."

"Good." It was good, wasn't it? "I would at least like to talk to Miss Pearl about it." Vivian glanced from the crystal chandelier above her head to the Persian carpet. "This place is—"

"Extravagant, I know." Clasping the frilled edges of a fine paisley shawl, the girl floated off the bottom step. "Nothing but the best for Miss Pearl."

"And for her girls." A woman who looked like the palace queen sauntered into the room. Her lace gloves matched her green satin gown. She wore her shiny red hair up in a pompadour.

"This is the young woman I mentioned seeing out on a Tuesday morning when the girls and I were shopping," the black-haired girl said. "Said she was out of work."

"I remember the story." The queen shifted her attention to Vivian, her painted red lips pursed. "You've never been a *working girl,* have you?"

"No ma'am," Vivian said. "Not in that way."

"You probably hadn't even seen a real *working girl* until…what was it, three weeks ago?" the queen asked.

"I don't believe so. No ma'am." Vivian extended her hand. "I'm—"

The woman raised her hand abruptly. "No real names." Her painted eyebrows narrowed. "One's former life…private life is just that—private."

That was an advantage. Vivian wouldn't have to worry about being linked to anyone else in town, anyone whose respectability could be at stake.

"I go by Pearl DeVere—Miss Pearl—in the business." Miss Pearl strolled around Vivian, her emerald green skirts whispering with each move. "You'd need plumping up a bit, and a tighter corset that would give you at least some semblance of a waist and a bust. Shorter than the others too." She stopped in front of Vivian and looked her in the eye. "Violet. You look like a Violet to me."

A color that wasn't quite a true blue. "Yes ma'am. It suits me."

"Very well. Violet, join me in the parlor, and we'll discuss the possibilities." Miss Pearl started across the foyer.

"Ma'am."

With measured ease, Miss Pearl turned to face Vivian, a penciled eyebrow raised.

"I want to discuss the hostess job. During the day. Downstairs." Vivian knotted her hands. "I'm not interested in… the other kind of work."

"I understand." In the manner of a true lady, Miss Pearl pinched the sides of her skirt and lifted it ever so slightly. "Opal, dear, would you ask Mary to bring us some tea? Something with a little zing in it, please."

"Of course." Opal disappeared into the hallway.

Vivian pressed her gloved hand to her middle, hoping to calm the bees buzzing in her stomach, and followed Miss Pearl into an imperial parlor. Her eyes feasted on the large room—a cranberry swirl glass chandelier, green velvet drapes, a large Persian carpet, an electric lamp with a red tasseled shade sitting on a polished black walnut table.

Miss Pearl lowered herself onto a rosewood settee as if this were her throne room. She looked up at Vivian and pointed to a swing rocker. When Vivian sat down, Miss Pearl regarded her with a knowing smile, as if she were amused by Vivian's awe. "So, Violet, what do you wish to do with your life?"

Vivian startled at the sound of the unfamiliar name. She picked a piece of lint from her skirt. "I want to design fashions, ma'am. Mostly gowns."

A sudden, sharp laugh escaped Miss DeVere's perfectly rounded mouth.

Vivian straightened, gripped the arms of the chair, and met the madam's misty-eyed gaze. "Miss DeVere, I'm really quite good at sketching new designs."

"Call me Pearl. I wasn't laughing at you. I'm sure you are." She pulled at her gloves, one finger at a time. "That's what my family in Indiana thinks I'm doing here—designing dresses for the wives of the rich in this area." Laughing again, she gestured toward the lavishness surrounding her. "And now *I'm* the rich in this area."

Vivian squirmed. Her family thought she was a good girl. They'd never suspect her of working here either.

"You'd make a lot more money and much quicker working for me than you would working as a dress designer," Miss Pearl said.

A woman as dark as the soot in a hurricane lamp stood in the doorway. When Miss Pearl nodded, she entered the room, carrying a tray.

"Thank you, Mary," Miss Pearl said.

"Welcome, Miss Pearl. I fixed them both the way you like it." Mary handed a teacup and saucer to the madam and then glanced at Vivian. "Do you like your tea sweet, miss?"

"A spoonful of sugar, please." Vivian watched as Mary stirred in the sugar and delivered her cup. "Thank you."

"You're welcome, miss." Mary shifted her gaze to the woman of the house. "You needin' anything else, Miss Pearl?"

"That'll be all, Mary. Thank you."

Mary had no sooner cleared the doorway, when Miss Pearl turned toward Vivian. "How good are you at acting?"

"I don't understand."

"We're in the entertainment business here, and we take our work quite seriously. Our clients are all men willing to pay well for the *entertainment*." Miss Pearl lifted her teacup to her lips in a manner suited to the most refined of ladies.

"The hostess too?"

Miss Pearl peered at Vivian over her cup. "Yes, even the hostess in the game room and in the music room, which is where you'd work, is considered an entertainer. Nearly every room in the house is our stage."

"I see."

"We each have our own chambers, and there are two bathrooms upstairs."

Vivian gulped. "I have a room elsewhere, and I need to maintain that room and my presence there."

Miss Pearl tapped her chin with a painted fingernail. "Actually, I think that could work out perfectly. We have clients at all times of the day and night, but you'd do your entertaining as hostess during the day." The palace queen played with the curls dangling at her neck. "You can treat your work here like a day job and go home, or wherever it is you go, before the dinner bell sounds."

"Thank you."

"There will, however, be an occasional evening required."

Vivian picked at a fingernail. How would she ever explain being away from the boardinghouse after dark?

"I love to throw parties," Miss Pearl said. "We're having one next month—the last Friday. I'll need you here for that."

Vivian nodded and lifted her cup. She'd raised it no higher than her shoulders before a pungent odor ascended into her nostrils, causing her to gag.

Miss Pearl covered her mouth, but not before Vivian detected a grin. "I like my tea with a shot of brandy in it. You've never had even a sip of alcohol, have you?"

"No ma'am." Vivian set her cup on the table beside her.

"The men will like you. You're fresh, like newly fallen snow."

Vivian kept her secret to herself, yet again. Fresh, she wasn't. Fallen, yes.

"We stock cigars and serve drinks in the game room and in the music room. And some of our guests take meals."

The grandfather clock in the corner chimed three, and Miss Pearl stood. "I have enough time to give you a tour of the house and show you to the room you'll use to get into character. Miss Opal will find you a wig and give you a few pointers on how to conduct yourself. Then be back here tomorrow at ten o'clock sharp."

Nodding, Vivian stood. This wasn't going to be as humiliating as she'd supposed. She could grow accustomed to the smell of alcohol and cigar smoke, but what about Miss Hattie? She looked at her new boss.

"Don't worry," Miss Pearl said. "We have sweet-smelling toilet waters to hide the odors. You'll find an assortment atop the bureau in your room."

Vivian's acting skills obviously needed work. If Miss Pearl could tell what she was thinking, Miss Hattie and her sisters would surely see right through her.

EIGHTEEN

arter glanced up at the mantel clock. Again. Half past five. He and Boney Hughes had stopped by Miss Hattie's Boardinghouse nearly an hour ago to talk with Vivian, and she still wasn't back.

The landlady told them Vivian had gotten the job at the newspaper but had to quit due to problems working with the chemicals and ink. Miss Hattie pulled her teacup from the side table beside her chair. "Vivian's been out looking for a job most every day."

Commendable, and he hoped she found suitable work, but the thought of her returning home so late in the day made his shoulders tight. It wasn't safe for a young woman like her, attractive and naive, having only recently come from the East. "You said Vivian...um, Miss Sinclair usually returns home by four o'clock?"

"Yes. But if she's found work, those arrangements could detain her."

"Of course."

"Don't forget...she does have a passel of sisters." Boney drained his coffee mug. He'd chosen to sit on the brick hearth. "Could've met up with any one of 'em and stopped somewhere to jaw."

Miss Hattie stiffened and narrowed her eyes at the miner.

"Now don't go gettin' your feathers ruffled, Hattie," Boney said. "Didn't mean any disrespect. Just sayin' that those young women could outtalk a gaggle."

Carter snickered, earning a scowl from the widow.

"Don't encourage the old coot," she said.

"Yes ma'am."

"For your information, Boney Hughes, women don't jaw." She stuck out her pinky and raised her cup to her mouth. "We leave that to old miners."

Boney chuckled, revealing gaps between his teeth.

Miss Hattie leaned toward Carter. "Are you ready for a refill?"

"No ma'am. Thank you." Carter lifted the cup to his mouth and breathed deeply of the brew's aroma, hoping to adjourn his nerves. Contrary to his first impression, Vivian wasn't a mere girl. She was a bright young woman, and he needn't worry about her. But he did, anyway. She was his friend, after all.

"Hattie, you might want to give the deputy a nice, calming chamomile next time." Boney grinned, holding out his pinky.

Miss Hattie nodded and walked to the window. "You do seem a little edgy where our youngest Sinclair sister is concerned, deputy."

"Miss Sinclair is new here. A single woman." He probably shouldn't have emphasized that point, given Miss Hattie's reputation as a matchmaker. "She's inexperienced with the West and its ways. I don't like the thought of any young woman being out alone when the sun goes down."

A woman like Vivian shouldn't have to work for her livelihood. She should be courted and wed to a man who...

Who what? Carter argued. With himself.

A man who appreciated the love and affection of a bold and independent woman and provided for her.

Miss Hattie pulled the lace curtain back from the window. "Vivian has a good head on her shoulders. She'll be in before dark. Why, that looks like her now."

"See." Boney looked Carter's way, and then joined Miss Hattie at the window. "All that fuss over nothin'."

Miss Hattie and Boney suddenly looked at one another. Their brows furrowed and their chins dipped.

"Perhaps I spoke too soon." Miss Hattie let the curtain close.

Carter went to see for himself. "You saw her?"

Miss Hattie nodded. "I thought she was headed home, but she's just standing there across the street."

Boney stepped away from the window, and Carter pulled back the lace curtain. Vivian stood at the corner, looking like a princess in her purple dress. A reticule hung on her arm. Her hands were tucked in white gloves and clasped in front of her. After seeing his bay hitched to the rail out front, she'd no doubt stopped in her tracks. And why not? He'd been avoiding any social gatherings that involved her family.

He'd said, and she'd agreed, that their relationship had to stop at friendship. And despite a few hold-out feelings to the contrary, he still believed it.

Then she looked up. Time seemed to stop as they stared at each other, never mind that a window and an entire road stood between them, and he couldn't ignore the fact that he wanted more than friendship.

She looked away and stepped into the street. Carter ran a hand through his hair and followed Miss Hattie to the door. Vivian stood on the porch, staring at them, her eyes wide.

"We saw you at the corner, dear. Did you lose something?" Miss Hattie asked.

"No, thank you, ma'am." Vivian stepped over the threshold and looked up at Carter. "I was thinking."

"About how to avoid me?" He hadn't meant to say it aloud.

Vivian quickly shifted her attention to the old miner.

Boney pressed his hand to his shaggy beard and bowed. "Mr. Boney Hughes, ma'am."

"Vivian Sinclair. It's a pleasure to meet you, Mr. Boney. My sisters speak highly of you."

"The pleasure is mine, Miss Vivian." Boney shook her gloved hand.

She turned to Carter. "Deputy Alwyn."

Feeling more like a schoolboy than a lawman, Carter straightened his shoulders. "Miss Sinclair." So they knew one another's names. Despite his intention to remain detached, Carter wanted to know more. "How are you faring in your search for a job?"

Vivian's head reared slightly. "Fine, thank you." She removed her shawl, her movements deliberate and as smooth as butter. "Were you just leaving?"

Miss Hattie grinned, clearly as amused by Vivian's candor as he was. "Honest mistake, dear, seeing how we were all gathered in the doorway, but the men came to see you."

"Me?" She didn't look him in the eye.

"Yes." His mind returned to the Third Street Café. Neither of them was open to romantic entanglements, but they'd agreed that friendship was good. So why was Vivian so uncomfortable around him today? Had she changed her mind? He cleared this throat, hoping to dislodge those thoughts. "You mentioned having sketched the clothing of the two bandits on the train."

"I did. That's why you're here?" Her shoulders relaxed.

"Yes, we'd like to take a look at them, if you don't mind."

She glanced toward the stairs. "I'll bring them down and meet you in the parlor."

"I'll have a cup of tea for you when you come down, dear." Miss Hattie spun toward the kitchen while Vivian climbed the stairs, her head held high.

Carter felt a tug on his arm and looked down into the leathery face of the old miner. "Shall we do as the lady says, deputy?"

Ignoring the gleam in Boney's eye, Carter nodded and led the way back into the parlor.

They'd just walked to a round table in the corner when Vivian sauntered into the room, carrying a sketch pad. She'd removed her stylish hat and gloves. "I don't know how helpful these will be."

He didn't either, but it was good to see her again. On business. "You heard about the miner who was killed in his cabin the day I saw you in Victor?"

"Yes, Miss Hattie told me the awful news."

"Boney saw two men leaving Mac's cabin the afternoon the young miner was killed."

"You think they're the same men who robbed the train?" She set the sketch pad on the table and seated herself.

"We have reason to, yes." Carter sat on one side of her, Boney on the other.

She began flipping past page after page of sketches of children's clothing. "Uh, I was playing with costume ideas for my niece." The pink coloring returned to her cheeks.

She wanted children. That was nothing that should cause a young woman embarrassment. At one time, he'd fancied himself a family man...a father.

Carter nodded, unable to get any words past the lump in his throat. He needed to put any and all thoughts of a future with this woman to rest. Regardless of what his mother would or wouldn't have done had she known his father wouldn't survive, he couldn't ask a woman to step into that kind of uncertainty.

"Here they are." Vivian opened the pad to a page full of sketches of men's outerwear.

She pointed to a single-breasted overcoat with a wide collar and big buttons. "This is the coat the tall one wore." She moved her finger. "And his hat. I only had a quick look at his boots, but I think these are close."

Boney peered over his coffee mug. "Didn't get a look at the boots, but same kind of coat and hat I saw that day at Mac's."

Carter guessed that if he ever saw that coat or hat, even those boots, he'd recognize every crease and smudge. Vivian's talents would be wasted anywhere here in town. Tomorrow morning, he'd call Etta Ondersma himself and put in a good word for her. "Your attention to detail is amazing, Vivian."

Her brown eyes seemed to reflect his own mixed feelings. "Thank you." Quickly shifting her attention back to the sketches, she flipped to the next set of drawings. "This is what the shorter man wore."

Most of the items didn't come as a surprise to him. She and Boney had described them pretty clearly, but neither had mentioned seeing a belt buckle. She'd sketched one in the bottom right corner.

"You saw his belt buckle?" he asked.

She nodded, focused on the drawing. "When he tripped and spun around to glare at me, his coat caught on the seat in front of me."

"A racehorse with the word *Derby* below it?" As in Kentucky Derby, perhaps?

"Yes. The buckle was silver. This is a crude likeness, to be sure."

"A lot better than crude, miss." Boney smoothed his beard. "Why, those fancy cameras they have nowadays wouldn't capture as much detail as you did."

"Thank you, Mr. Boney. I enjoy drawing clothes. But I usually sketch fashion designs for women, not the fashion faux pas of scoundrels."

The miner laughed, and so did Carter. Miss Sinclair was anything but predictable.

"Deputy, this one's talented, humorous, *and* an eye-catcher." A sly grin parted the whiskers on Boney's face. "If I was you, I'd snatch her up right quick."

Vivian gasped, her coloring deepening to a rosy red.

Heat rushed up Carter's neck and burned his ears. Shifting in the chair, he looked down at the sketch. But the old rascal was right; if he knew what was good for him, he'd take Vivian's hand and not let go.

Nineteen

⟋⟍

uit squirming like you're sitting in a bed of mad ants." Opal hooked her fingers under Vivian's chin. "If you don't hold still, you'll end up with stripes up into your hair."

Vivian sat in a well-appointed bedroom, wearing a silk chemise. A velvet black ribbon adorned her neck and two silk violets sat atop the dark wig on her head like a table decoration. She gripped the sides of the chair to still herself and looked up into Opal's painted face. "I'm sorry. I'm sure you're doing a wonderful job, but wearing this stuff...being here is normal for you."

Opal raised a thick eyebrow. "I wasn't born doing what I do."

"My face feels like I got sloppy with the maple syrup." Vivian folded her hands in her lap. "I'm sorry. I don't mean to be difficult. I know there's a lot here that I'll have to get used to."

Opal held a fluffy brush over the can of face powder the way an artist would hold a brush to a palette of paints. "You have nothing to worry about. Miss Pearl treats us all real good, and so do her clients." A satisfied smile graced her light brown face. "The way I have you looking, you're sure to be a favorite hostess in no time." Leaning forward, Opal brushed ochre on Vivian's cheeks, then set the brush on Vivian's table and stood. "I wish I had your high cheekbones."

"And I wish I had your height."

Being here with Opal was almost like sisters playing grownup. But that was Vivian's private life, and this was to be her other life for a time. As long as she kept the two separate, everything would be fine.

Vivian peeked in the mirror. Her face was at least a shade lighter, almost white, and her lips several shades darker, a blood red. Long brown curls draped her bare shoulders. No one would recognize her like this. Looking at herself now, *she* couldn't even say who she was for sure.

Two bedrooms. Two dressing tables. Two mirrors. Two lives.

Violet.

"It won't take you long to get used to things around here. Pretty much the same day to day."

Opal pulled a sapphire blue Sunday dress from the wardrobe and helped Vivian into it. Buttoned and cinched, Vivian wrapped a silky cream-colored shawl below her shoulders, and then chose an embroidered lace fan from the shelf.

"You ready to go downstairs?" Opal asked.

As ready as she'd ever be. Vivian nodded and followed her new friend to the door. At this point in her life, all she knew was one foot in front of the other, so down the stairs she went.

Opal had given her a tour of the Homestead yesterday. The game room, the music room, and even the modern kitchen, complete with a full staff. Vivian paused at the doorway into the game room and drew a fortifying breath. Cigar smoke hovered over one of the green leather-topped tables where three men sat playing cards. One of the many things she'd have to grow accustomed to at the Homestead House.

Opal sashayed into the room, right up to the table. She made it look so easy. The men paused their game, and the tall beauty conversed with them as if they were lifelong friends. Opal was acting, that was all…playing a character.

Vivian squared her shoulders. She could do that.

Miss Pearl stood in front of the liquor cabinet, her arm draped on the herringbone-patterned shoulder of a man much shorter than she. She turned and met Vivian's gaze.

After whispering a few words to her companion, Miss Pearl swept her pink brocade skirt forward with a gloved hand and glided to the center of the room. "Gentlemen." She held her other hand out to Vivian.

Vivian's cue to make her entrance. Another deep breath. Miss Pearl gave her a gentle nod, and lifting her shoulders, Vivian entered the room. Smiling, she kept her steps measured and slow, her head held high, and the fan poised near her neck—just as Opal had taught her.

Then she saw that the man at the liquor cabinet had turned around. His balding head was fringed with gray hair. He'd bought an icebox from her sister, and according to Mrs. Hartley, he was a major stockholder in the telephone company. Despite her many undergarments, a shiver shot up Vivian's spine. This man knew her family.

Just play your character, Vivian. Violet doesn't have a history with Harry Updike. Suddenly she was thankful for the gooey mess on her face and the tight wig on her head.

Miss Pearl glanced from Vivian to Mr. Updike, then to the three men seated at the table. "I'd like to introduce the newest addition to our family here." She smiled at Vivian with the pride of a mother introducing her newborn child. "Gentlemen, this is Miss Violet."

All three of the men at the table greeted her with a nod, but the youngest stood. "Miss Violet."

"Gentlemen." Vivian tilted her head slightly and smiled. "I hope you're enjoying yourselves."

"Yes ma'am." The curly-headed blonde didn't look much older than Ida, in his early twenties perhaps. "And I'm enjoying the view."

Vivian's neck and face warmed, and she fluttered her fan. "Thank you kindly." She quickly shifted her attention to the other men. Acting, that was all. "It's a pleasure to meet you all." She waved her gloved hand toward the cards. "I won't keep you from your game."

When they returned their attention to the cards, she looked up at Miss Pearl. Her newest boss winked at her with a look of pure satisfaction.

Vivian was doing her job and doing it well. Fanning herself, smiling, and being friendly seemed easy enough. And since that was primarily all she had to do as hostess, that was all she'd think about.

"Gentlemen, Violet and Opal will serve your lunch this afternoon. Enjoy." Miss Pearl laid her hand on the arm of the banker in the oversized suit and sashayed out of the room.

Vivian joined Opal at the ornately carved walnut bar against the far wall, where her friend poured drinks from a cut-glass decanter, and whispered. "How did I do?"

"Fine. No, much better than fine." Smiling like a teacher proud of her student, Opal poured another drink. "I tripped on my own toes my first day here and landed in a man's lap."

Giggling to hide her mortification at the mere thought, Vivian pulled a tray out of the buffet and reached for a glass.

"Unfortunately, he wasn't my client." Opal added a drink to the tray. "Took me weeks to convince his girl that I wasn't trying to take her business. Just clumsy."

"That's terrible. I'd say things are going well for me then."

"So far, so good."

Then why did she feel so bad?

TWENTY

〜◎〜

*H*er head bowed, Vivian stared at a knot in the pine flooring between her feet. Tucker Raines seemed like a good man—a perfect match for her sister Ida. Vivian didn't have any legitimate complaints about his preaching, but when it came to the closing prayer, Tucker was as long-winded as a winter gale down the Eastern Seaboard. She pressed the toe of her shoe to the scar on the floor and closed her eyes.

It wasn't that she was anxious to return to the boardinghouse, not with Deputy Alwyn joining them for Miss Hattie's birthday celebration, but she was ready to leave the church. Except for keeping secrets, she wasn't really doing anything wrong, but it didn't feel right to sit in church as if she were *as Christian* as the rest of them.

Vivian laced her fingers. The last time she'd seen Carter Alwyn, he was concentrating on her drawings of the robbers' attire. When he saw the belt buckle she'd sketched, he seemed quite pleased with her. But Carter Alwyn was set on seeing justice served. Without a doubt, he would find fault with her workplace and postulate about her activities there. Her ability to keep her job might very well depend upon her performance that afternoon.

A tap on Vivian's knee alerted her that she'd missed her brother-in-law's "Amen." Nell stood beside her, even her smile reverent, and probably assumed the distraction was due to praying rather than plotting. The weight of Vivian's workplace suddenly wrenched her heart. Nodding, she rose from the pew.

While her sisters and Miss Hattie mingled in the aisles, Vivian made her way through the crowd. She was out in the foyer, nearly to the door, when she noticed the balding man shaking Tucker's hand. He was only a couple of inches taller than she was and wearing an oversized herringbone suit.

She gasped. The worst thing she could have done. The man who had waited impatiently for Miss Pearl at the game room door on Friday now stared at her. And so did the sour woman standing over him. She bore a staggering resemblance to Vivian's old boss, Mara Wilkening.

"Are you all right?" Tucker looked positively pleased to see her. He held out his hand.

Time to perform. Vivian brushed a blond curl from her face and accepted his steadying grip. "I'm fine, thank you." She glanced at the floor to steady her nerves. "I must have tripped on something."

"Have you met Mr. Updike?" Tucker asked.

You mean the man who got me fired from the telephone company? The same Mr. Updike who frequents at least one brothel? "We saw each other informally at the icehouse last month." Vivian watched the banker's face for any sign of recognition and extended her hand to him. "Mr. Updike."

"Yes, I remember." His smile was anemic, at best, but that didn't mean he recognized her from the brothel.

"Mr. Updike, this is my sister-in-law, Miss Vivian Sinclair." Tucker sounded far too proud.

"Miss Sinclair." Mr. Updike, on the other hand, sounded un-interested.

The mother hen look-alike glared at him. "Miss Sinclair, I'm Mrs. Updike." She shook Vivian's hand. "It's a pleasure to officially meet you."

"Thank you." Fighting a compulsion to gag, Vivian looked around and caught a glimpse of Ida talking to someone on the other side of the foyer. She didn't want to give herself away by behaving rashly in front of the banker, but she could only take so much of him. Meeting his wife had pushed her to the limit. "Gentlemen, Mrs. Updike, if you'll kindly excuse me, I need to speak with my sister."

Before lightning strikes us all.

The good news was that Mr. Updike didn't seem to recognize her, and if he did, he was sure to keep quiet about it. The bad news—she wasn't the only person in the church living two contradictory lives.

Carter couldn't remember when he'd laughed so hard. Otis Bernard's ten-year-old son Abraham was a natural entertainer. Everyone at Miss Hattie's dining table sat squarely in the palm of the boy's hand. It wasn't so much the depth of his jokes as the enthusiasm with which he deliv-ered them.

Carter wiped his eyes and looked around the room. Morgan and Kat, Tucker and Ida, Judson and Nell, and Otis and Naomi and their four boys filled the room as one family. And the Sinclair sisters and their husbands treated Carter like one of the bunch. All but one, who had busied herself in the kitchen most of the afternoon.

Vivian strolled into the room. A flower-decorated cake rested on the palms of her hands like a bouquet. "Happy birthday, Miss Hattie!"

Everyone chimed in, and the four Bernard boys gathered around the beloved widow at the head of the table.

"Thank you, dears." Miss Hattie hugged the boys and then looked around the table at each of her guests. "My thanks to all of you for making this birthday blessed. From the breakfast Vivian served this morning to the great preaching and even to the jokes." She patted Abraham's dark cheek.

"You're welcome, Miss Hattie." Abraham beamed. "You just let me know when you're ready for another joke. Still got a lot you haven't heard."

"Thank you, but we best find someone to cut this cake before I'm forced to put all I've learned about being a lady behind me and dig into my dessert fingers first."

Vivian looked across the table at Ida. "I remember you being more of a cutup than I am. Would you do the honors?"

Smiling, Ida shifted her attention to her husband. "Reverend, perhaps the job should be yours. You seemed to do a mighty good job of cutting into your conversation with Mr. Updike this morning to introduce him to my little sister."

"You saw that, did you?" Tucker asked.

Ida nodded, quirking an eyebrow.

"It was effective. As soon as he saw her, he clammed up, and so did his wife."

Tucker stood and accepted the knife from Vivian, who wore a thin smile on her colorless face. No doubt Harry Updike had put on a show for his wife like he'd done in Carter's office. Had that insensible man said something in front of the youngest Sinclair sister? If so, Carter had a new topic for his next conversation with the banker—a lesson on propriety.

Ida stirred sugar into her teacup. "I'd hardly consider Mr. Updike's rants a proper conversation to pull Vivian into."

Tucker sliced into the cake. "Ida's right. I shouldn't have used you as a buffer, Vivian. I apologize."

Vivian offered Tucker a rigid nod and rubbed her arms as if she'd experienced a sudden chill.

The reverend looked at the children at the center of the table. "Truth is…" He leaned toward Vivian, his voice low. "Harry Updike is someone you probably want to avoid."

"For certain." Abraham didn't whisper. "That man's real prickly."

Carter laughed. He couldn't have said it any better.

Naomi Bernard glared at Abraham, but her thinly disguised grin quickly gave way to a giggle. Everyone in the room joined her.

Except for one. Vivian, her brow puckered, pulled the teapot off the table and left the room.

Something had upset her today. Even before the church service, she'd seemed preoccupied. Carter laid his napkin on the table and rose from his chair. He didn't bother to excuse himself before following her into the kitchen.

Vivian wasn't filling the teapot, nor was she anywhere near the stove. The teapot sat on the cupboard where she stood with tears running down her face.

The sight of her crying wrenched Carter's gut. He wanted to take her into his arms. Comfort her. Tell her they could be more than friends. Fortunately, his feet felt planted at a safe distance, just inside the kitchen door.

Sniffling, Vivian turned and looked up at him. "I'm fine."

More tears, powerful enough to free his feet, and he took a step toward her. "Did Updike say something to upset you?"

"No." She wiped her face. "Ida just likes to be the big sister."

Another step. "Are you having trouble at your new job?"

She startled, then moistened her lips. "My job is fine. Thank you." A tear clung to her lower eyelash.

"Miss Hattie mentioned that you'd found employment. I felt somewhat responsible for your trouble at the newspaper and hoped you'd found a more suitable job."

Nodding, she stared at the teapot.

"Something, or someone, has you upset." He reached for her hands and felt both relief and remorse when she didn't pull away. Her hands felt so small in his. The warmth of their connection sent a chill up his spine, and looking into her glistening brown eyes did nothing to steady him. He didn't want to encourage her down a path neither of them felt able to walk, but he did care about her.

Vivian looked down at their clasped hands but didn't pull away. "I'm pleased for my sisters and for Naomi Bernard. They all seem happy." She sniffled, and her lips quivered. "Married and settled."

Carter felt gut-punched. Vivian was new to town and single. All of her sisters were married and starting families. It made perfect sense that Vivian would want that too. And so she should. She was a beautiful, bright, and enterprising young woman. Was she having second thoughts about keeping their relationship confined to friendship?

He lifted her hands to his chest. "Perhaps we should reconsider—"

Footsteps sounded behind him, and Vivian pulled away. His hands feeling stung by the loss of her touch, Carter turned and faced Miss Hattie.

"Doesn't seem there's much for me to do here." The widow snickered and spun toward the door. As soon as she left the room, Vivian grabbed the teapot and marched to the stove.

He reached the cast-iron kettle before she did. He looked into her misty brown eyes. "Vivian."

"We can't." She pressed the teapot into his hand and stepped away. "You can't."

Before he could ask why, she walked out of the kitchen, leaving him with questions and a pot of tepid water.

TWENTY-ONE

❧

*M*onday morning ribbons of golden sunlight striped Vivian's bed. Birdsong followed as she dressed for the day. She'd completed three full weeks working as a hostess at the Homestead. She'd settled into it rather quickly, once she'd recovered from seeing Carter waiting for her at Miss Hattie's that first day, then watching Mr. Updike lead a dual life. Setting aside her emotions to become another person had proven an easier task than she'd first thought possible. To say she enjoyed working at the parlor would be an overstatement, but the job was more pleasant than she'd expected. Miss Pearl was easy to work for, and Vivian had shared plenty of chatter and giggles with Opal and Colleen, her chambermaid.

The best part was that Miss Pearl paid her each Saturday. Vivian had already received three payouts, generous ones. Far more money than she'd made working for the telephone company. More than she would have ever made at the newspaper or any of the other places where she'd inquired. Her rent was paid through next week, and she still had money to pay Miss Hattie for the first two weeks of September.

In addition, she'd had enough left for her necessities and even a few fun items. Strolling down Fourth, Vivian glanced at her feet. Today she wore the new calfskin shoes she'd bought last week. With this Saturday's pay, she'd complete the outfit with the matching reticule.

Her steps light, Vivian walked alongside the new brick building that stretched to the corner, humming a song from one of Miss Hattie's phonograph cylinders. Her landlady did enjoy her music, no matter how many times she'd heard a song in one day. But the widow was just the right blend of warm and caring with plenty of charitable involvements to keep her busy. Vivian liked her.

Vivian finished humming the tune with gusto. In just a matter of weeks, her humiliating search for work had ended, and she was happier than she'd been in a long while.

All she had to do was avoid thinking about that Sunday in Miss Hattie's kitchen. Avoid thinking about how Carter Alwyn had held her hands, infusing her with strength by his simple touch. Avoid recalling the sentence he'd started.

"Perhaps we should reconsider..."

Had he changed his mind and decided he could offer her more than friendship?

Thankfully, her landlady had interrupted them. Even if Carter had changed his mind, nothing had changed for Vivian. And there was nothing she could say or do to erase her past, which would always stand between them.

She shook her head. No more thinking about the what ifs and if onlys. She couldn't afford that luxury. She needed to keep her eyes on a more realistic future.

"Vivian."

Vivian was stepping up onto the boardwalk at the corner when the sound of her name challenged her resolve. Ida hurried toward her down

Bennett. What was her sister doing here? This wasn't a good time. Vivian stilled her steps anyway and waved as Ida approached.

"I thought that was you," Ida said. "I'm glad I caught you before you went in to work."

Think, Vivian, think. Vivian offered her sister what she hoped came across as a sweet smile. "I'm surprised to see you out and about this time of morning." *Mortified* would've been more precise. "Aren't you usually hard at work in the showroom by now?"

"Normally, I am. But I had banking to tend to and letters to mail. I'm on my way to the icehouse now." Ida glanced up at the National Hotel housed in the brick building beside them. "What about you? Are you headed in to work?"

"Yes." Vivian laughed nervously. "I was on my way to work." She shifted to the right, toward the hotel's main door on Bennett. This was where Miss Hattie and her family thought she worked. She'd told them she was a hostess...at the hotel. She'd *tried* to get a job there. She'd hoped to be a server in the main dining room, but she was the wrong gender and the wrong color.

"I should let you go." Ida smiled. "Good to see you."

"Yes, and I'll see you again on Saturday morning at Miss Hattie's."

"Bright and early."

Nodding, Vivian walked across the front of the building and ascended the steps. At the door to the National Hotel, she looked back at the boardwalk, where her sister still stood, watching her. Vivian waved and reached for the door of the four-story building.

A side door off the right side of the lobby caught her attention. Squaring her shoulders, she entered an expansive buffet room, perfectly situated on the corner of Bennett and Fourth. A smattering of folks dotted the dining area. Vivian smiled at them as if she belonged there and strolled toward the window.

She looked out at the boardwalk and sighed. Ida was still out there, and now she had company, a stylish, red-headed woman Vivian didn't recognize. Whatever could they be discussing that was more important than Ida getting to work? Vivian hadn't left the boardinghouse early enough for detours and lallygagging. She glanced up at the clock on the diagonal wall. It showed the time as two minutes before ten o'clock.

Ten o'clock sharp, Miss Pearl had said. Vivian would be late today. How late apparently depended upon her sister. Ida didn't seem to share Vivian's sense of urgency today.

"May I help you, miss?"

Vivian looked up into the oval face of a Negro man. "No, thank you, sir. I just wanted to enjoy a little sunlight without having to go out in it." Smiling, she pointed to the window. "Do you mind?"

"Not at all. Enjoy the sunlight, ma'am, and you let me know if there's anything I can do to serve you."

"I will, and thank you." Vivian turned back toward the window. Ida no longer stood on that stretch of the boardwalk. Vivian walked back to the door, ignoring the folks staring at her. Thankfully, she only had to cross Bennett, walk down one block and over one lot to get to work.

But first, she had to be sure she didn't have an audience.

By the time Vivian reached her dressing room at the Homestead House, Colleen had Vivian's undergarments laid out on the bed and her pink dress hanging on a hook from the open wardrobe door. Vivian closed the door behind her and fumbled with the buttons at the side of her skirt. Two sharp taps followed by two light taps on the door told her Colleen had seen her come up the stairs.

"Come in, Colleen."

Her chambermaid stepped inside, her black and white uniform spotless. "Morning, Miss Violet, I was beginning to worry about you." Colleen reached for the troublesome buttons. "You have some troubles getting here, did you?"

"Only unexpected delays." And tedious detours.

"Well, don't worry. I'll have you ready in plenty of time." Colleen loosened the skirt and began on the buttons on the back of Vivian's shirtwaist. "At least it's Monday. If it were Wednesday, you would've been late for your appointment."

"My appointment?"

"With the doctor. No one told you?"

Vivian couldn't push words past the knot in her throat, so she shook her head.

Colleen helped her step out of her private-life clothes. "The doctor will be here to examine you before you dress for work on Wednesday."

Vivian swallowed hard. "I don't want a doctor. Why would I need a doctor? There must be some mistake." She crossed her arms, suddenly feeling naked despite her undergarments. "Miss Pearl didn't say anything about having to see a doctor."

"She may have thought Miss Opal mentioned it to you, but no need to worry. It's not until Wednesday."

"I don't want a doctor."

"You all have to have a doctor sign off on you before you can get the work permits from the city."

"Work permit? I don't understand any of this."

"It helps ensure your health while keeping everything legal for Miss Pearl. The doctor won't take long. It'll be over before you know it."

A doctor. Did Morgan do this kind of work? Would Kat even allow it? Vivian fanned herself. Her life had turned into a stage play, and she the lead actress. But how would she keep her roles straight if her private life refused to remain private?

∽◉∽

Carter stirred the dried beef chunks that sizzled on the stove in a white gravy. He topped two slices of honey-wheat toast with the creamy beef mixture and sprinkled the results with a liberal amount of black pepper. With a mug full of steaming coffee in his other hand, he carried his meal to the wood-plank table near the window.

He didn't much care for the stark light of the bare bulb hanging from the ceiling, so he turned up the wick on the kerosene lamp on the table and pulled the cord on the electric light.

Finally, he was ready to eat.

Carter bowed his head, enjoying the silence and the savory scent of his meal. It wouldn't taste as good as his mother's version, but it wasn't bad for a bachelor's cooking.

Lord God, I thank You for this food. And I ask for Your strength, Your grace, and Your protection as I and so many others pursue Pickett and his gang. In Jesus' name, I pray, Amen.

His first bite took him back to Leadville, to his mother's kitchen. It'd been too long since he'd seen his mother, but he couldn't make the trip to Leadville anytime soon. Not with outlaws active in his territory. And even if she did finally agree to come see him, it wasn't safe. Not yet.

Boney Hughes had come into town this morning, and they'd

frittered away most of the day. Carter had spent so much time studying maps of the fifty square miles north of town that his eyes wanted to cross. Boney pointed out more nooks and crannies in the hillsides than there were combs in a beehive. He knew of played-out mines and deserted shacks that might attract vagrants and desperados. The deputies in Divide were taking care of their fifty square miles, but that still left Carter with a lot of ground to cover.

So far Pickett and his friends had managed to dodge him and a passel of other lawmen, but the shorter bandit had shot up a piano in Cripple Creek after Mac's death. Two weeks ago, Edgar heard talk in his saloon of three men seen in the Pass who fit the descriptions of the bank robbers. They were fools to still be in the valley, and getting careless. At least one of them would soon make a mistake.

That was what Carter was waiting for. That was why he'd go out in the wind and hide in the shadows on a Monday night. His hunch told him Pearl DeVere was the reason the outlaws were still here. And if the man who bought the horse from her was feeling lonely tonight and showed up at the Homestead House, Carter could put an end to the robberies.

A hunch wasn't much to go on in most circles, but he had one, and his hunch told him the man who bought the dapple-gray horse would make a mistake that involved a certain house on Myers Avenue.

Carter chewed his last bite of beef and drained his coffee cup. He set his dishes in the wash bucket and looked out the window. Twilight, and not all the shops had closed yet. Still too early to make his move. He had some time to kill.

He went to his chest of drawers and pulled out the writing box his mother had given him when he left Leadville. He carried the wooden box to the table and pulled out a piece of stationery and a fountain pen.

He planted his elbows on the table and tapped his chin with the tip of the pen.

Dearest Mother,

It had been at least six months since his last letter. He reread her last missive before putting pen to paper again.

I am well. I hope you are too, Mother, and that you are enjoying your summer. We haven't experienced any real heat here yet. In fact, it's the end of August, and still moderate.

As far as the temperature was concerned, that was true. Where Vivian Sinclair was concerned, *moderate* was not an adjective he'd use. She could be hot, then cold, with the mere mention of a name. Or a day of the week. The young woman's sensibilities were definitely a puzzle he had yet to piece together. An undertaking he wanted to pursue.

Vivian was younger than he was by eight or nine years, and naive. He needed to be patient—let her become more established in the community. Perhaps by then, he would have figured out what to do about his job.

Thirty minutes later, Carter had finished the letter to his mother and another to Mac's family. He put away the writing box and, on his way to the door, pulled his hat off the hook.

Carter didn't walk all the way to Myers Avenue. Tonight he'd watch the house of ill repute from a different angle—diagonally from the alley. At least for a while. He wanted to make sure he didn't miss anyone trying to sneak in through the kitchen door.

Crouched in the dark, he watched one man after another—all shapes and sizes—head to the front steps of the brothel. Most didn't seem the least bit concerned with discretion. Others appeared nervous, scanning their surroundings like a church mouse on Sunday mornings. Electric lights glowed in upstairs windows that did little to hold in the sordid laughter and the phonograph music.

Carter had been watching the place for nearly an hour when he spied a man walking up the street in the shadows. The light spilling out of the sporting-house windows was just enough for him to see that the man wore a derby and an overcoat. Granted, those were plentiful and popular items of clothing, but on such a temperate summer night, the coat seemed out of place. And the man was thick in the middle, like the shorter of the bandits—the man who bought the horse from Pearl.

Carter waited to make his move until the man passed the front corner of the house. Quietly, he made his way to the front of the house, catching the man on the first step. "Sir, I'm Deputy Alwyn, and I'd like to have a word with you."

The man stilled but showed no sign of turning around.

His hand on his gun, Carter stepped around him and looked into his face. His features didn't share any similarities with those Vivian had described for the sketches, but they were indeed familiar.

"Deputy." He seemed to be studying the ground.

Carter drew in a deep breath, disappointed on many levels. "I believe this means I will no longer have the displeasure of your company in my office on Tuesday mornings. Isn't that right, Mr. Updike?"

The banker nodded before continuing up the steps.

TWENTY-TWO

❧

'm only a daytime hostess in the game room." Vivian stood in front of the wardrobe in her room at the Homestead House, tying her pantaloons with trembling hands. This humiliation was second only to the day Gregory said he could never marry a girl who had sullied herself.

Doc Susie looked up at Vivian from where she sat at the dressing table. Her hand rested on the form she'd been filling in since the exam began. "Are you sure you want to do this, Miss…*Violet*?" She glanced around the room. "Work in this kind of place, I mean."

It wasn't the work so much as it was the lie she was living. Vivian nodded and swallowed her regrets. "I'm sure."

Another lie. She'd lost count. But none weighed as heavy on her heart as her omission in Miss Hattie's kitchen two and a half weeks ago. Carter Alwyn wasn't supposed to follow her out of the dining room. He wasn't supposed to ask about her job. His tender concern shouldn't have surprised her. Nor the way his touch affected her, giving her tingles that seemed to have more to do with his thoughtful, protective nature than with a physical connection.

No, she wasn't sure she wanted to work in this kind of place. She knew she didn't, but she wasn't like Kat or Ida or Nell—free to follow her heart if it led her to romance. She didn't have a future with Carter or with any respectable man.

Doc Susie stood. "Here it is then." She pointed to the paper she'd left lying on the desk. "Be sure you give it to Miss Pearl."

"I will."

Doc Susie pulled her black bag off the foot of the bed. "I'll see you again in a month."

Vivian nodded. She had to be realistic. It would most likely take her two or three months to earn the money she needed to go to Denver and start a career in fashion design.

"At least you're in a clean and safe place. So many of the girls I see aren't." The doctor tucked a stray lock of brown hair into the bun at the back of her head. "If you have any problems, come see me."

Vivian took a tentative step toward her. "I will."

"Is there something else?" The doctor's eyes were nearly as blue as Ida's.

"I, uh, wondered...do you keep your work private?"

Doc Susie held the black bag against her stomach. "Are you asking if I keep the names and particulars of my patients confidential?"

"Yes ma'am."

"Your secret is safe with me."

"Thank you." As a sigh of relief escaped Vivian's lips, the doctor left the room and then closed the door behind her.

After Colleen helped her dress for the afternoon, Vivian pulled the medical form off the table. Miss Pearl's bedchamber was at the opposite end of the carpeted hallway. Before Vivian reached the closed door, the proprietor's raised voice singed the hair on the back of her neck. The other girls had all gone downstairs to prepare for the day guests. Vivian didn't want to intrude if Miss Pearl had company or was in a discussion with one of the staff. Nor did she wish to leave Miss Pearl alone up here if there was trouble.

More shouting straightened Vivian's spine. She raised her hand to knock, but thought better of it. What if she was wrong? What if Miss Pearl was only playing a role as part of the entertainment? If that was the case, overreacting could cause them all grief.

"Be reasonable, Pearl." A man's voice dripped the words like honey on a biscuit. Not prickly Mr. Updike's voice. Deeper than the banker's, a baritone with an accent.

"You be reasonable. He found the horse I gave you." Miss Pearl sounded angrier than Vivian had ever heard her.

"Keep your voice down." A southerner?

"He found it dead. The same day Mac died."

The miner Miss Hattie told her about. The man in Pearl's room had her horse? It died the same day as Mac? Had he been involved? Vivian's head began to throb, and she stepped back from the door.

"You did all of it, didn't you?" Miss Pearl asked.

"For us. You can't blame me for wanting to give you the best. I did whatever I did for our future."

Could the man in the room with Pearl be the bandit? The one who killed Mac?

Miss Pearl groaned. "He came here asking questions. I don't need the law breathing down my neck."

The police? Or Carter?

"And what a pretty neck it is."

"Oh no you don't!" Miss Pearl's heels tapped the floor as if she were stepping away from the man. "For all I know, he could be watching my place right now."

Vivian covered her mouth. Could Carter really be out there, watching the Homestead? Had he seen her?

"You have nothing to worry about." Was that the voice of the man she'd tripped on the train? "He won't see me."

"Don't touch me, you fool."

Vivian tensed. "Miss Pearl?"

Silence.

A few seconds later, the door whooshed open. The madam stood before Vivian, not a hair out of place, looking calm and collected. Whoever the man was, he didn't want to be seen. He'd disappeared. Was that licorice Vivian smelled, or was it just her imagination?

Leaning forward, Miss Pearl glanced out into the hallway. "Violet. What are you doing here?"

Vivian needed to keep her voice steady. "I'm sorry to bother you, I just—"

"Were you listening at my door?"

"The doctor told me to give you this form." Vivian handed her the medical form.

"Yes, of course. Thank you." Miss Pearl's smile didn't reach her eyes. "The phonograph isn't just for music anymore. I have a couple of cylinders with outstanding dramatic readings. I'll have to let you listen to them."

Vivian nodded. Miss Pearl had an answer for everything, but Vivian didn't know what to say.

"Some other time. Right now, we need to get downstairs." Miss Pearl stepped into the hallway and slammed the door shut behind her.

"Yes ma'am." Vivian started down the staircase, her chest and face hotter than a busy stove. Was Miss Pearl breathing down her neck, or was it just the secrets and lies?

She should tell Carter what she'd overheard. But then she'd have to tell him how she'd been in the position to hear it.

∽◦∽

Carter climbed the stairs to his apartment. Time for another cup of chamomile tea, his mother's favorite remedy for just about anything and everything. He'd been nursing a headache all morning.

He should've been thankful Harry Updike hadn't come around yesterday morning. He'd had suspicions, but now he knew for certain why the banker's wife was so bent on cleaning up Myers. When Updike wasn't posturing in a show of disdain for the seedier side of Cripple Creek, he was sneaking off to at least one sporting house. Mrs. Updike wanted her husband back in their home.

In the meantime, the men who robbed the banks and the train and killed Mac for his sock of gold were still loose and free to add to their list of criminal charges. Friday was the big party at the Homestead House—and his next stakeout outside the white gingerbread palace of ill repute. He hoped and prayed the leader of the gang wouldn't be able to resist the gathering.

Carter finished his tea and had just set his cup in the sink when the bell on the door downstairs jingled. "Be right down," he called.

The postmaster's son, Archie, stood just inside the door, holding a slip of paper. The kid was as gangly as a fresh colt—all legs and arms—and just as busy. When Archie wasn't working for Jesse over at the livery or sorting mail for his father, he was delivering mail or telegrams.

Archie spotted Carter in the upstairs doorway. "Good day, Deputy Alwyn."

"Hey, Archie." Carter took the stairs two at a time. "You ever get to go fishing anymore?"

"Not till Sunday, sir." Before Christmas, the lad would have a deeper voice. "A telegram came for you."

Carter pulled a coin out of his trouser pocket and exchanged it for the telegram.

"Thank you, deputy."

"You're welcome. Happy fishin', Archie."

The bell jingled on the boy's way out, and Carter settled into his desk chair. Sheriff Otto Caldwell in Louisville, Kentucky, had sent the message.

> Leon Kelso. Stop. Son, Elton. Stop. Cousin, Timothy Kelso,
> Pickett. Stop. From here. Stop. Wanted in seven states between
> us. Stop.

Carter added the telegram to his case folder.

Leon Kelso, Elton Kelso, and Timothy Kelso.

He had names.

And by the end of the party Friday night, he hoped to have at least one of them in shackles.

TWENTY-THREE

*M*iss Pearl had asked to see her before she went down to the party. Vivian stood in front of the full mirror on her wardrobe door, willing herself to breathe through her fears. She'd seen to all the details. She'd checked her reticule three times to make sure she had the key to the back door of the boardinghouse. After she spoke to Miss Pearl, she'd telephone Miss Hattie to let her know she'd be late, not to wait up for her.

"You look real pretty, Miss Violet." Colleen stood beside her. "You'll for sure be one of the most handsome girls at the party."

Vivian smiled at the girl who had become a friend. "Thanks to your help."

"My pleasure, miss." Colleen swept a strand of red hair off her face.

The cranberry taffeta gown Miss Pearl had picked out for Vivian to wear was exquisite. A narrowed waist, a black velvet insert in the center of the bodice, and puff sleeves made of ecru lace that matched the trim at the scooped neckline. The only things Vivian would change in the design were the black velvet bow and broach over her bust, and she would have chosen a higher neckline.

Vivian tucked an ostrich feather into the wig of ringlets on her head and looked over at her chambermaid, who hung Vivian's private-life clothes on a silk-wrapped hanger.

"If that'll be all, Miss Violet, I'll just finish straightening up your room before I go home for the night."

"Yes, thank you." Vivian moistened her lips. "I'll leave you to it and go see Miss Pearl."

"Oh, just one moment, miss."

Vivian turned back toward the bed, where her chambermaid held the matching lace gloves Vivian was to wear to the party.

"Miss Pearl would've fainted away had I shown up gloveless on a party night. You're the best, Colleen." Vivian slipped her fingers into the gloves.

"I heard the gown Miss Pearl is wearing to the party tonight cost—" Colleen's green eyes widened, and she slapped her hand over her mouth. "Dear me. I've spoken out of turn."

Vivian raised a gloved hand, palm out. "I won't tell anyone. The secret is safe with me." What was one more secret floating on a sea of them?

"Thank you, Miss Violet. I wouldn't want to get anyone in trouble for talking about it. She didn't mean any harm." Colleen bent toward Vivian, her hand cupped at her mouth. "The gown is just so beautiful that she…it came all the way from Paris, you know."

Paris, where her father lived. If only he had let her join him in France. "I didn't know."

Colleen turned her attention to the everyday unmentionables still lying on the bed. "Enjoy the party, miss."

Vivian would settle for surviving the party—her first evening on the premises.

She walked to Miss Pearl's room at the far end of the hallway, drew in a deep breath, and knocked. "Miss Pearl?"

The bedroom door swept open and Vivian felt her jaw drop. Miss Pearl stood before her, looking like an angel. The rumored ball gown was made of shell-pink chiffon adorned with sequins and seed pearls.

"You look... well, there aren't words for how beautiful you look," Vivian said. "Like an angel."

Miss Pearl chuckled. "An angel, you say?"

"Yes ma'am." A fallen one, perhaps. But according to the preacher in Portland, fallen angels were also quite comely.

"It was a gift." Miss Pearl did a slow turn. Her auburn pompadour shone under the chandelier overhead. "Eight hundred dollars' worth."

Suddenly aware that her mouth gaped open, Vivian pressed her lips together.

"You look quiet lovely yourself. The cranberry color definitely favors you." Miss Pearl glanced down at Vivian's felt lace shoes. "Those brown eyes of yours will have men falling at your fancy feet."

"Thank you."

"You've done very well here. The men really like you."

Vivian accepted the compliment, trying to ignore the war her feelings waged within her.

Miss Pearl snapped her lace fan open and fanned herself. "Miss Violet, it's time you started earning your keep."

"Earning my keep?"

"Yes. I had a gentleman request you for his private entertainment tonight."

Vivian's stomach knotted. "Private entertainment?"

"Don't look so surprised." Miss Pearl pursed her ruby-red lips. "You're an entertainer in a sporting house."

Vivian drew in a deep breath, raising her shoulders and her head. "I agreed to the job of hostess, not to…that kind of entertaining."

The last word came out on a whisper but seemed to echo off the wallpapered ceiling. Pouring drinks, delivering cigars, and serving fruit compote and sandwiches was one thing. Vivian hadn't allowed herself to think about the other.

"You can't have really expected to remain a mere hostess." Miss Pearl pulled a toilet water decanter from her dressing table and gave her mostly bare chest a spritz. "The other three girls work the downstairs and the upstairs, and I expect you to do the same."

Vivian pressed a hand to her roiling stomach.

"If you want to keep your job," Miss Pearl said, "you will entertain upstairs."

Vivian had tried to find work elsewhere…everywhere. Unless she was willing to throw herself on the mercy of her sisters, she had to keep this job. She swallowed hard. "I do want to keep my job, ma'am."

"That's more like it." Miss Pearl returned the spritzer to her dressing table.

Vivian had a pretty good idea who the special request had come from, and he seemed nice enough. He'd been showering her with attention since she'd started. "The young man from the card game?"

"No, although he may be next in line."

"A line?"

Miss Pearl let out a laugh that defied her queenly attire and shooed Vivian toward the door. "I'll be down in a few minutes and introduce you to him at the party."

Nodding, Vivian shut the door behind her, the click rattling her to the core. She forced her quaking knees to carry her down the stairs.

Being here and working upstairs wasn't what made her a soiled dove, she reminded herself. This was merely a paying job. The damage had been done long before she'd stepped foot in this town.

The man who'd requested her tonight was no different than Gregory.

At the parlor door, Vivian glanced at the ornate grandfather clock in the corner. Half past five. She still had time before the guests arrived. Time to at least try to settle her stomach.

A smorgasbord of smells assaulted her as she entered the kitchen, a beehive of activity. Roasted pork, fresh-baked breads, peach desserts—most likely with too fancy a name for her to pronounce. She'd never seen so much food in her life. And she didn't feel like eating even a bite of it. The colorful display took her back to the family house in Portland and Tilly's Sunday spreads—the way it was before her family separated.

Mary looked up from the center counter, where she prepared a tray of raspberry puffs. "Why, Miss Violet, you look mighty pretty, you do."

"Thank you. I thought if it wasn't too much trouble I'd have a cup of tea before the party."

"No trouble at all. Betts has some steeping."

Betts wiped her hands on her apron and pulled a cup from the cupboard. "I'll have your tea for you in two shakes."

Vivian took a small step toward the stove. "I prefer my tea without brandy, Betts."

Mary's laugh was easy and infectious.

"Yes miss." Betts grinned. "I prefer mine with a little whiskey, myself."

A knock sounded on the kitchen door, and Mary looked down at her gooey hands. "Would you get that for me?"

Nodding, Vivian pinched her skirt on one side and swished across the room. She opened the door. A mountainous man the color of cast iron stood in front of her, holding a big block of ice.

"Much obliged, ma'am."

Vivian couldn't move words past the lump in her throat. Thankful for her painted face and the pesky wig, she dipped her chin and turned her face away from Otis Bernard, the man whose son had told jokes at Miss Hattie's birthday party.

Was there no one in this town who didn't frequent this place for one reason or another?

∽⊘∾

Carter had taken refuge from the coolness of the night—and from sight of the passersby—behind a wagon, where he had Liberty tied to a post just in case he needed his horse. Every few minutes, he walked across the street and made another lap around the Homestead House. Was this how Moses felt at Mount Sinai, like he was going in circles with no end in sight?

Carter had watched while one dapper-looking man after another darkened the door of the sporting parlor. The bowler hats and dandy suits all blended together.

While he expected the bandits to make a stupid mistake, he didn't expect to see Leon Kelso, the fellow who bought the horse from Pearl, stroll up to the front door. Nor did he expect Pickett to walk up, show Carter his scarred face, and turn himself in. Carter couldn't say what the mistake might be, but he had to be ready. And if Miss Pearl was important to Kelso, it was more likely he'd be here for the big party than in a saloon tonight. Carter had seen many a man fall for the promise of a prostitute's love.

For the past hour, he'd seen no one come or go. The house glowed with electric lighting, and the windows offered silhouettes of those wining and dining inside. Pearl DeVere knew how to endear herself to the influential. Donations to the widows and orphans. Baseball uniforms for the boys in town. Extravagant parties with enough food to impress the pharaohs.

Stringed instruments began to play a gentle waltz, and the sound of voices softened. The madam was known for many things, including her love of live music. And as the shadows began to spin in time with the music, Carter couldn't help noting that he hadn't been to a dance since his father died. He couldn't think of anything he'd done socially the past several years, in fact, outside of an occasional meal at the Raines's home. Witnessing Vivian Sinclair's tears in the kitchen that Sunday nearly three weeks ago and holding her hands for mere seconds hardly counted for courtship.

He tugged the collar on his jacket tight and buttoned it. August in Colorado was as unpredictable as the women. Once the sun dropped below the Sangre de Cristos, a damp coldness swept through the night air. Carter breathed into his hands to warm his face. The scent of impending rain filled his nostrils. An hour ago, he'd thought about going home and getting the gloves he'd forgotten, but that would likely be the time Pearl DeVere walked out on the arm of a man he didn't recognize. Perhaps a man wearing a belt buckle with a racehorse on it.

Nothing had ever been that easy for Carter, but he had to hope for a break, and he'd rather it happened in town than out on a wild chase in the mountains.

∽⌒

Vivian hadn't been able to turn off her emotions tonight. In an attempt to settle herself, she patted the back of her neck with cool water and paced the small necessary on the second floor. How could she have thought working in a sporting house was a good idea?

The answer came quick and easy. Money. She'd desperately needed a job, and Miss Pearl was hiring.

The young man she knew from the game table had asked for her first dance of the night, but according to Pearl, he wasn't the mystery man who had requested her entertainment. Her knees quaked and her hands trembled. At least one of the men who frequented this place was an outlaw. And she'd withheld important information from the deputy she cared about. How could she have done that? Any of it? The old Vivian never would have stooped to working in a brothel. Not the Vivian who valued her good name.

She dried her hands on a towel. What if the unidentified client was the man from Miss Pearl's bedchamber on Wednesday? The man she'd overheard fighting with her boss? If he knew she'd heard him confessing to the robberies and killing for their future—his and Pearl's...

Nothing mattered more to Carter Alwyn than catching the men responsible for the train robberies and killing the miner named Mac. How could Vivian not tell him what she'd heard?

Vivian flipped the dark hair off her shoulder. The wig. The face paint. The fancy ball gown. No matter how hard she tried to pretend, she wasn't Violet. She'd thought her transgressions with Gregory had ruined her, that what happened to her didn't matter. That she didn't deserve better. Maybe she didn't, but Carter deserved to know the truth.

What she'd done with Gregory, what the women did here, what Miss Pearl expected of her tonight—all of it was wrong. And now it was time she did the right thing.

She'd seen Miss Pearl walk up the staircase alone less than an hour ago. Perhaps she was still in her room. Vivian had to end this charade tonight. Right now.

Vivian walked quickly along the hall and then stopped to listen outside the door at the far end of the hallway, in case Miss Pearl had a guest. Nothing. After two minutes, when she still heard no sound from the room, Vivian knocked. "Miss Pearl?"

Silence. The hostess might be resting, but what Vivian had to say couldn't wait. Swallowing her anxiety, Vivian opened the door.

Miss Pearl lay on top of her Irish point spread. She still wore her stunning pink gown, but her party shoes lay beside the bed.

Vivian took slow steps toward her. "I'm sorry to wake you, Miss Pearl…"

The madam's eyes were open, but her chest wasn't moving. Her lips were blue, her skin ashen.

"Miss Pearl!" Vivian gagged and forced herself to breathe past the knot in her throat. She laid her hand on Pearl's bare arm. Clammy. She put her fingers to the woman's neck to feel for a pulse the way she'd seen her father do with Mother. Nothing.

Miss Pearl was dead.

Vivian closed Pearl DeVere's eyelids and had just turned to go find Opal when a man wearing tails and a top hat rushed toward the bed, trapping Vivian against the wall.

"What's wrong with her?" he demanded.

"She's dead."

"No." His fleshy face twisted, and he patted Miss Pearl's hand. "Wake up, darling. I'm here just as I promised, to see you in your gown." When she didn't rouse, he stiffened and scowled at Vivian. "What did you do to her?"

She recognized the pungent odor of licorice-root first, then the belt buckle. The shorter bandit from the train grabbed her arm. Her knees quaked. "Nothing. I-I came up to—"

"You killed her!"

Shaking, Vivian stomped his foot and jerked out of his grip. Her shin slammed into the bed frame, and a sharp pain shot up her leg. Swallowing hard, she jumped back, dodging his grasp.

"You'll pay for this!" he shouted.

While he struggled to regain his balance, Vivian ignored the cry stuck in her throat and raced out the door. She didn't look back as she dashed down the stairs, her skirts rustling and her sore shin screaming at her. She wanted to scream too, but she didn't want anyone stopping her. She had to reach Carter's office. He'd know what to do.

If there were people in the foyer or in the hallways as she ran past, she didn't see them. Her vision blurred by fear, Vivian rushed to the kitchen as fast as her heavy gown would allow and pushed through the swinging door. "Telephone the police!" she yelled. "Miss Pearl is dead!"

Amidst a flurry of gasps and objections, Vivian ran past the kitchen help and out the back door. A sheet of cold rain blasted her, and she swiped at her face and ran up the alleyway behind the Homestead House. Muted light from windows and the glow of the street lamps on Bennett provided just enough light to direct her wild steps.

Only three blocks to go. To remain concealed for as long as possible, she'd take Second up to Bennett. When she reached the sheriff's office, she'd tell Carter the truth. All of it.

Vivian was nearly to the corner when she heard footsteps slapping the muddy road behind her. Her back and arms ached under the weight of her skirts as she forced a faster pace from her tired legs. Rain stung her eyes. A furious pulse pounded in her ears. Still she ran. How could she have been so stupid? So blinded?

God, please help me.

At Third Street, Vivian changed her plan and veered right onto Bennett, hoping to slow her pursuer, and praying Carter might be out on the street or looking out his upstairs window. Or anyone who could help her. She couldn't keep this up. Her sides ached and her throat burned.

Footsteps splashed the mud behind her. He'd caught up to her.

Thick arms coiled around her middle and lifted her off the ground. She kicked and flailed, but he was too strong and she too tired.

"You killed my Pearl," he growled in her ear. "Now you belong to me."

Vivian stopped fighting. She wasn't surprised God hadn't answered her prayer. Wasn't surprised He hadn't saved her from this treacherous man. She didn't deserve saving. Her change of heart was too little, too late.

TWENTY-FOUR

◇

*C*arter stepped out of the shadows for another lap around the Homestead House. He adjusted the collar on his coat again. Huffing, he tugged his hat forward to keep the chilling rain off his face. If he wasn't so stubborn, he'd call it a night and go home. Change out of these wet clothes. Enjoy a hot cup of coffee and climb into bed.

Shouts from inside the house erupted like sudden bursts of thunder. A shiver coursed up Carter's spine as people poured down the front steps, murmuring and wailing. He dashed into the crowd.

"I can't believe she's dead," one woman cried.

He tensed. "Who's dead?"

"Poor Miss DeVere."

Carter charged forward, showing his badge. "I'm the Sheriff's deputy. Let me through."

The crowd parted like the Red Sea, and he rushed into the house.

"Up there." A heavyset woman, her dark cheeks awash with tears, pointed to the staircase.

He took the stairs two at a time. At the landing, he followed the sobs and somber voices to the bedchamber at the end of the hallway. Three working girls stood huddled in the corner. Pearl DeVere lay atop her bed, a sheet covering her face.

Carter approached the body and pulled off the sheet, letting it fall to his feet. No blood, and no sign of a struggle. But the madam of the house was clearly dead.

Pulling his notepad and pencil from his shirt pocket, Carter looked at the girls. "I'm Deputy Alwyn. Please tell me what you know."

A dark-haired girl wiped tears from her paint-streaked cheeks and joined him beside the bed. "I'm Opal. Our cook, Mary, pulled me out of the ballroom. Said one of the girls told her Miss Pearl was dead. We came up here. When we found Pearl like this, I laid the sheet over her."

Carter looked at the other two girls. "Which one of you found her?"

The redhead and the blonde he'd seen the day he came to talk to Miss Pearl about the horse shook their heads.

"It wasn't any of us, deputy." Opal sniffled. "It was Violet."

Miss Pearl had told him she had three girls. "Violet?"

"New girl, been here about a month."

He hadn't seen a fourth girl coming and going during his watch or in town on Tuesdays.

"Until tonight, Violet only worked afternoons," Opal said.

"Where is she now?"

"Mary said Violet ran through the kitchen and right out the back door like a fire lit her tail."

Carter had chosen the wrong shadows to hide in, and in the noisiest of neighborhoods. He made notes, and then looked at the other two girls. "Did either of you see or hear anything?"

The blonde stepped forward. "I saw a man go into Miss Pearl's room just minutes after Violet came up."

"Did you recognize him?"

"It was Leon. Don't know his surname."

Opal nodded. "He's Pearl's special friend. They were always ex-changing gifts. She gave him a horse a few weeks ago."

Leon Kelso from Louisville, Kentucky.

"She told us he bought her this gown." The redhead glanced at the pink pearl-studded dress Miss Pearl wore.

"Did you see this Leon after you were summoned to the room?"

"No, and he wasn't in the room when I came up. I haven't seen Violet again either."

There was a good chance a prostitute and a robber were on the loose together. Was one or both of them responsible for Pearl DeVere's death, or did the sporting girl have other reasons to hide from the law?

❧

Vivian sat in the mud with her hands tied to a saddle behind her, her feet strapped together. Her captor lay just five feet away, wrapped in a bedroll while she shivered under a smelly, wet horse blanket.

He'd taken her below the depot, where he retrieved a chestnut, and she'd ridden with him up a dark path, whipped by overhanging branches. Her wig hung from a tree somewhere in the dark. Now the horse stood tethered to a sycamore a few feet away. If she could get to the mare, she could escape, but she'd lost count of how many times she'd tried to stand under the weight of the saddle. It was impossible.

Vivian pulled her knees to her chest and buried her face in her ripped skirt.

She'd blamed her father because he left her in Maine and wouldn't let her go to Paris. She'd blamed her sisters for making her feel like she could never measure up to their level of morality and achievement. Tears pooled at her chin. The truth was that her plight was no one's fault but her own. She'd chosen Gregory's word over God's. She'd chosen to work at the Homestead House instead of swallowing her pride and asking her other sisters for help. Miss Hattie was in no hurry for her rent. She would have waited a few weeks longer.

Vivian blew a knot of unruly hair out of her face. She'd been out to prove she could stand on her own two feet, and look where it had gotten her—tethered to a saddle in the middle of the night with a killer as her captor. She'd lied to everyone who cared for her, and soon they'd all know it. Miss Hattie, her sisters, and Carter.

Lord, I have sinned. With Gregory. Pride. Deceit. Lies. Hiding. Sneaking. And I blamed everyone but myself, even You.

Tears poured down Vivian's face onto the soiled gown. She'd been so selfish. So naive. So foolish.

Please forgive me, Lord. I don't deserve Your help, but I do need You. Please help me.

Within minutes, her tears subsided, and although she couldn't explain it, she felt better. Peaceful and watched over. Perhaps she wasn't alone with this man.

Lord, please be with my sisters and my father. And with Carter.

Vivian leaned against the saddle that weighed her down and closed her eyes.

Moments later, an explosion broke the silence. Vivian jerked her head up to see her captor coming toward her with a rifle in his hands. Beads of sweat streamed down her spine. She tried to jump to her feet, but the saddle pulled her back down, and she flopped onto her side in the mud.

The bandit walked past her, and she twisted enough to see the silhouette of a dead animal that lay just beyond her.

"Good thing you stopped sniffling when you did," the bandit said, "or I'd never have heard that mountain lion growl."

A mountain lion? Vivian's breath caught. "Thank you."

It felt strange to thank him after all the bad things he'd done, but he had just saved her from an animal attack, and she was truly grateful.

Her captor spit and wiped his mouth with the back of his hand. "I should've let the animal kill you and saved myself the trouble."

"I didn't kill Pearl." Turning away from him, Vivian pulled herself back into a sitting position, bumping her hip on a rock as she did. "I went upstairs to tell her I couldn't do that kind of work."

He huffed and stomped back to his bedroll. "Got news for you, missy." His laugh tensed her stomach. "There's men waiting where I'm taking you, and you'll entertain them without pay."

Acid burned Vivian's throat. "Were you the man who requested my company tonight?"

"I planned to teach you not to snoop outside Pearl's door." He spit again. "When I found you with her, your lesson took a turn for the worse."

"She was already dead when I found her." Her voice sounded as shattered as she felt, falling apart with no one to pick up the pieces.

"Doesn't matter if you killed her or not. My Pearl is dead, and you're going to pay."

Curling into a fetal position, Vivian fell onto her side, against the saddle. If she survived this night, she'd find a way to get away from him.

God, help me.

At first light, Carter walked Liberty out of the corral and looked at his bleary-eyed friend. "Thanks for saddling him, Jesse."

"No trouble." Jesse hooked his thumb in his overalls and followed Carter out of the gate. "You sure you don't need me to join the search party?"

Carter palmed a carrot and held it out to his bay, then swung up into the saddle. He wasn't like his father. He wasn't going after the suspects alone. "I'll have two officers from the police department with me. Any more than three of us would be too conspicuous."

Jesse nodded. "Be real careful, you hear?"

Carter tapped the brim of his hat. "I intend to."

Had his father said the same thing to his mother when he left home that day to keep the peace in the red light district? It didn't matter. Carter was setting out to bring in a prostitute, not rescue one.

He returned Jesse's wave and urged Liberty down the muddy road toward the depot, where the two officers were to meet him. He was riding past the train station when he heard a shout.

"Deputy Alwyn!"

He pulled up on the reins and twisted toward the depot steps. Baxter, one of the town drunks, shuffled toward him, waving his worn hat. Carter didn't have time for town gossip or questions surrounding last night's events.

"Wait up, Deputy! I heard about our poor Miss Pearl." Baxter shook his unkempt head. "You heard about that guy who shot up Edgar's piano a couple of months ago?"

Carter swallowed his impatience and nodded.

"I seen him again last night."

Carter perked up. "You did? Where?"

"Twice."

"When? Where?"

"He came into Ollie's all spiffed up, bragging about bein' on his way to the big wingding over at the Homestead House."

Carter nudged Liberty closer to the man. "You saw him again, later?"

"I was going to the Central Dance Hall. Saw him and a little lady walkin' all cozy-like toward this here depot."

If Leon and Violet boarded a train, they could be anywhere by now. "Did you see them go inside?"

Baxter shook his shaggy head. "Nope. They had a horse tied out back and rode off up the hill."

Carter followed the man's gaze. "Toward Ute Pass."

"Yes sir. Thought it might help you to know."

"It does, Baxter, thanks."

Two uniformed policemen rode toward him on sorrels. Clucking his tongue, Carter signaled Liberty to close the distance between them. Both men wore blue double-breasted uniforms with bottle-cap hats. Ten men would've been less conspicuous than these two.

"Deputy." They spoke in unison.

"Morning, gentlemen." Carter pinched the crown of his hat. "We've got a couple of people who fled the scene—a man and a woman. The man is tied to the train and bank robberies. And Mac's death. Baxter said he saw them headed north last night, and I have reason to believe they have a hideout at Ute Pass."

"Yes sir," said the rail-thin officer with a wisp of a chin. "Sergeant Grady told us they were the last people seen at Miss DeVere's room before her death."

Carter drew in a deep breath. "You two up to a chase?"

The heavier one tugged his uniform shirt over his belly. "We're ready, sir."

Carter turned Liberty north and hoped he was ready. No telling what he'd find, but given their brash behavior the past several months, he didn't expect any of the bandits to give up without a fight.

TWENTY-FIVE

~⚬~

*M*emories from Ida's first months in Cripple Creek washed over her as she reached for the new doorbell at Miss Hattie's Boardinghouse. Like Vivian, she'd come to town with high hopes of fulfilling a dream. Unlike Vivian, she'd achieved her goal of becoming a businesswoman within a few weeks. Granted, she'd run into trouble working for the unyielding Mollie O'Bryan, but things worked out all right.

Hopefully, it wouldn't be long before Vivian gained recognition as a costume designer. Her work at the hotel may not afford her much opportunity to mingle with those who would appreciate her fashion sense, but perhaps she'd accept a little help from her big sister. Mollie O'Bryan had commented more than once on Ida's serge suit, one of Vivian's designs. And Mollie had lots of contacts in Colorado Springs and even in Denver. Perhaps she'd be willing to put in a good word for Vivian—one businesswoman helping another.

True to Miss Hattie's hospitable nature, she whisked open the door and reached for Ida's hand. "Ida, dear." She squinted against the bright sunlight, motioning Ida inside. "Come in. Probably muddier than a bog after that downpour we had last night."

"Yes ma'am. I'm not wearing my best shoes for a couple days, for certain." Ida closed the door behind her. She expected to see Vivian strolling down the staircase, overdressed for their Saturday baking project at Kat's. "How are you faring, Miss Hattie?"

She wanted to ask how the landlady was faring with Vivian, but didn't want to ripple the waters with nosy inquiries. Vivian had grown up considerably since Ida had last seen her—probably as a result of her newfound independence.

"Finer than peach fuzz." Miss Hattie tittered. "And I love having your sister here. Of course, I've been busier than a bee in a flower garden, and Vivian and I haven't gotten to spend as much time together as I'd like. But we're getting along just fine." She smiled. "That is what you wanted to know, isn't it?"

"Yes." Ida giggled. "You do know me well, Miss Hattie." She glanced toward the parlor, then toward the kitchen. The house was uncharacteristically quiet. "Where is your newest Sinclair boarder? Kat and Nell are waiting for us, and I was ready for breakfast an hour ago."

"Now that you've mentioned it, I haven't seen her yet this morning." Miss Hattie pressed a finger to her chin. "Why, I've been so busy getting ready for my day that I don't even know that I've heard Vivian stirring."

"She better be. We have big plans." Ida took a step toward the stairs. "More precisely, Nell has plans for us."

"Making banners for the harvest festival, isn't it? Vivian mentioned something about it at breakfast yesterday morning."

Ida nodded, taking several more steps. She pressed her hand to her growling stomach. Knowing Kat, Ida expected her sister to have the scones and sausage patties ready when they arrived.

"You know after last night," Miss Hattie said, "Vivian may have been so tired that she overslept."

Ida straightened and looked over her shoulder at the widow. "Last night?"

"Oh, you don't know...Vivian telephoned me last evening." Hattie tucked a gray tendril of hair behind her ear. "She said she had to work late. Not to wait up for her. Must've been about five o'clock, maybe half past."

"The hotel requires her to work at night?"

Miss Hattie leaned on the oak railing at the bottom of the steps. "Only last night. She's usually home just after five o'clock. But they needed her to help serve during the dinner hour."

"It seems everyone was busy in town last night. Did you hear the news?"

"I had a headache and went to bed with the chickens last night. What news?"

Ida set her reticule on the entry table. "Otis came by the parsonage this morning and told us Pearl DeVere died last night."

"The young woman from the Home—"

"That's the one."

Miss Hattie clucked her tongue. "She wasn't more than thirty-five years old. Did she fall ill?"

"She was found in her bed." Ida lowered her voice. "I heard one of the girls who works there made the discovery." She glanced at the landing, half expecting her little sister to be standing there with her mouth wide open. "Apparently, it was a suspicious death. The girl who found her may have even had a part in it."

"They think someone killed her?"

"I don't know. The city's doctor will examine her body today to figure out why she died."

"Poor woman. That's terrible."

Ida wanted to agree. She should agree; she was a pastor's wife. But was it so bad to have one less of those women around to lead other women astray? Why, many of them were girls younger than Vivian.

"Since Vivian's not coming to me, I better go up and see if she's about ready." Ida started up the stairs.

Miss Hattie huffed and puffed up the steps behind her. "It happened during the party? Several of the Women for the Betterment of Cripple Creek were going. Said they felt obligated to attend the festivities since the woman is…was such a philanthropist. I'm sure it'll be the talk at our luncheon today."

Ida sighed. Since when was one's charitable nature enough to excuse her immorality?

Ida stopped in front of Vivian's door. She didn't hear any activity inside. Her little sister had obviously overslept. Clearing her throat, Ida reached for the doorknob. "Rise and shine, little—"

The room was quiet and the bed empty. Ida glanced from the dressing table to the wardrobe to the open space in front of her sister's trunk. Vivian wasn't there. And everything from the dressing table to the pillow on the rocker was as neat as a butler's suit, including the bed covers.

Miss Hattie joined Ida in the room. "She's not here?"

"No, and I didn't hear her downstairs."

"If she's anything like me, she may have stopped at the necessary on her way down. I'll check." Miss Hattie took quick strides to the end of the hallway and tapped on the door. "Vivian, dear, are you in there?"

No answer. The room was empty.

Ida's stomach knotted. This wasn't like Vivian. She paused on the staircase and looked back at Miss Hattie. "Do you mind if I telephone Kat?"

"Please do." The quiver in Miss Hattie's voice reflected the tension Ida felt in her neck.

Ida walked to the telephone on the kitchen wall, lifted the earpiece off the hook, and looked at their family friend. "I'm sure she's already there, claiming my scone and eating the last of Nell's berries."

When the connection was made, Kat asked the first question. "We thought you and Vivian would be here by now. Where are you?"

Ida moistened her lips. "Vivian's not there with you?"

The answer weakened her knees. Her little sister had expected Ida at the boardinghouse that morning and knew Kat and Nell expected them early. Vivian had told Miss Hattie so just yesterday, and the land-lady's creased brow did nothing to pacify the question pounding in Ida's heart.

Where was she?

∽✿∽

Vivian sat behind her captor as the horse picked its way up a rocky path on the side of a mountain. She should be watching where they were going, but she didn't dare look down. Neither did she wish to stare at the back of the outlaw's head. Instead, she turned away from the edge and closed her eyes.

Letting happier times fill her mind, Vivian recalled running across a summer lawn with her sisters. Climbing onto her father's lap for a story. Standing on a kitchen stool, making jelly rolls with her mother.

By now her sisters would know she was missing, and her heart ached for them. They believed she was a good girl. They trusted her, and she'd traded their trust for lies. Not only had she deceived them, but now she may never have the chance to tell them the truth, express her regret, and apologize.

And what about Carter? He cared for her too. She'd seen it in his eyes and felt it in the touch of his hand. A part of her wanted to believe that if he knew she was gone, he'd come looking for her, but she wasn't sure she could bear the humiliation if he found her.

The horse stopped. Vivian's ear slammed against her captor's shoulder. Her eyes snapped open. They still clung to the mountainside, about halfway to the top. She let her gaze settle on a patch of columbines blooming in the rocky soil.

"That's your new home." The outlaw pointed at a slanted shack to the right, about fifty feet below them.

A new stream of tears slipped down her cheek. Home was Miss Hattie's Boardinghouse. Home was eating breakfast with her sisters. Home was a checkerboard surrounded by her family.

"Too bad you won't be here long enough to pretty up the place." He snickered.

He was planning to let her go? Or kill her after... The shiver up her spine had little to do with her damp clothes.

"You best not waste your time dreaming of freedom, though," he said. "You're coming with us."

Her breath caught. She'd strayed far enough from the people she loved. She couldn't leave the area with this wretched man. "I'll just slow you down. Why not let me go now?"

He shook his head. "You've been nothing but trouble since I first laid eyes on you." Reaching back, he set his filthy hand on her knee and squeezed it. "You've come a long way from the prim and proper girl on the train."

Her hands still restrained behind her back, Vivian dug her teeth into his shoulder. Growling, he jabbed her in the side with his elbow, knocking her off balance. She slid off the saddle and tumbled onto the muddy ground. Her hip struck a rock, and she moaned.

Her captor stood over her, his stare blistering. "You think I'm stupid enough to leave you behind to play the hero?" He grabbed her upper arms and pulled her to her feet. He huffed in her face. "You're our insurance, missy. And our entertainment." He lifted her onto the saddle and swung up behind her. "You try anything like that again, and I won't wait to kill you."

He spurred the horse toward her prison, where two men stared at them from the stoop. The tallest wore a straw hat like the one she'd seen on the second train bandit, only it wasn't as ragged then. Without a bandanna covering his face, she could see the scar on his cheek that scaled up his ear. The younger man, who didn't look any older than she was, had yet to look away. Vivian took a deep breath and let it out slowly, trying to exhale her fears.

"What do we have here, Pops?" the young man asked. Her captor was a father?

"Since when are we allowed to bring them home, Leon?" the taller man said.

"You're not," Leon growled behind her.

The outlaw Carter had referred to as Pickett joined the son in gawking at her. "When did you start foolin' around with anyone but Miss Pearl?"

"She's dead." Her captor spit, then wiped the back of his hand over his mouth. "She's dead, and I'm in no mood for storytelling." He glared at Vivian. "This here's Violet. Leastwise that's her entertaining name." He finally loosened his grip on her hands. "Get her out of my sight."

"My pleasure." The son grabbed her waist and dragged her off the saddle.

Once her feet hit the ground, Vivian jerked away from him. "Keep your hands off me."

"Good job, Pops. You know I like 'em feisty." The young man snatched her hand and pulled her toward the shanty. "Come on, Violet, I'll show you around the place." His lecherous laugh soured her stomach.

Lord, are You here?

TWENTY-SIX

*W*hat kind of establishment would ask a young woman to work late into the night and not see her safely home?

Tucker at her side, Ida walked into the vast reception area of the hotel that employed Vivian.

The clerk behind the mahogany counter smiled and removed his hat. "Reverend. Mrs. Raines."

"Good day, Mr. Beverly." Ida took a deep breath to settle her nerves so as not to embarrass her husband. Vivian's boss may have given her a room for the night.

Tucker shook the clerk's hand.

"I'm sorry I missed the Sunday service," Mr. Beverly said. "Our twins had sour stomachs and my missus asked me to stay home with her."

"We hope they're back in good health," Tucker said.

"Yes, thank you."

Ida cleared her throat. "I wouldn't normally disturb a family member during work hours, but I need to speak to my sister."

"Which of your sisters would that be?" The clerk glanced toward the buffet room. "Mrs. Archer or Mrs. Cutshaw?"

"I do have a lot of sisters." Too many to keep track of, apparently. "I'm looking for Miss Vivian Sinclair, the one who recently joined us here in Cripple Creek."

Mr. Beverly arched a bushy eyebrow. "Oh, yes. I remember meeting her one Sunday."

Ida nodded. "Like I said, I wouldn't normally disturb her during work hours, even though this was to be her day off, but I need a quick word with her."

"Work hours, you say?"

"Yes, Vivian is employed here at the National Hotel."

"I see. In which department does she work?"

Ida looked at Tucker, who shrugged. "I'm not certain. She said she was a hostess."

Mr. Beverly's eyebrows arched even higher. "Let me buzz the manager for you. He'll know where we can find her." He pressed one of several buttons on the wall behind his desk.

"Thank you." The words had no sooner left Ida's mouth than a dapper-looking fellow stepped out from a hallway.

"Did you require assistance, Mr. Beverly?" The manager smoothed his thin mustache and smiled at Ida and Tucker.

"Mr. Wilson, this is Reverend and Mrs. Raines."

Waiting through the formalities of greetings, Ida thought she might burst. She just wanted to scold her sister for not telephoning Hattie when she learned she wouldn't be home at all last night.

"They're here looking for a Miss Vivian Sinclair, who is in our employment," Mr. Beverly said.

Ida jumped in. "My sister is a hostess here. I apologize for disturbing her at work, but I only require a quick word with her."

"I see." Mr. Wilson shifted his attention to Tucker. "Mr. Raines,

I'm afraid there's been a mistake. I have no Miss Vivian Sinclair in my employ."

Ida raised her hand, leveling it just above her chin. "Vivian is shorter and thinner than I am. With blond hair."

Mr. Wilson shook his head. "I'm sorry, ma'am. She doesn't work here."

"Thank you, gentlemen." Tucker cupped Ida's elbow. He led her to the door and down the front steps in a foreboding silence.

Ida stopped in the middle of the boardwalk. "How can that be? On Monday, Vivian stood right there on that corner and told me she was on her way to work." She pointed toward the front door of the hotel. "I watched her walk up the steps and into the National Hotel."

Tucker looked her in the eye, compassion and concern stamped on his face. "I'm sorry, but I don't understand this any more than you do."

"For several minutes, I stood here talking to Mollie. I would've seen Vivian leave the building."

"Not if she didn't want you to."

Tears stung Ida's eyes. Why would her sister lie about where she worked?

Tucker enfolded her hand in his. "We'll go to the police department and let them know she's missing."

Ida nodded and matched his hurried pace, struggling to carry the brick he'd tossed her—Vivian was missing.

An hour and a half later, the Sinclair sisters and their husbands had all returned to Miss Hattie's Boardinghouse. Ida trailed a finger down her niece's smooth cheek. The baby's coos and sweet breaths were comforting, and the family had passed her around.

Not all that long ago Ida had held Vivian like this—changed her little sister's diapers and dressed her up like a doll. Mother was sickly, and Ida had found herself filling the role when she herself was still a child.

She looked across the parlor at Tucker, who stood at the front window, gulping coffee from a mug. "Where could she be?" Blinking back a fresh onslaught of tears, Ida drank in baby Hope's smile. "I should have looked out for her. I thought she had a good job."

"She told you she did." Tucker set his mug on the teacart.

How long had Vivian been a liar? Ida sniffled. "We can't just sit here doing nothing. There has to be something we can do."

"Like what?" The lines under her husband's eyes reflected the frustration and helplessness the whole family felt. He looked at Kat and Morgan, Nell and Judson. "We've scoured the town—every diner and hotel that might serve dinner, the telephone company, the newspaper office, the millinery. We telephoned Etta's Fashions. We've talked to everyone we could think of who may have seen Vivian, or at least heard from her."

Nell leaned into her husband's shoulder. "Judson and I checked the depot and the passenger wagons." Tears glistened in her blue eyes. "Tucker is right, we've done all we can."

Ida sighed, her lips pressed together. She hated waiting, feeling helpless. She stood and shifted Hope into Kat's arms, then joined Tucker at the window. "This is my fault."

Judson blew out a long breath. "How do you figure that?"

Instead of looking at her brother-in-law, Ida stared out the window. "Vivian came to me for a job last month."

"She did?" Kat's raised voice did nothing to ease Ida's remorse.

Nodding, Ida faced her family. "I told her after all the expanding we'd done, we didn't have the funds to hire her."

"You told her the truth." Tucker brushed a curl from Ida's forehead, soothing her with his touch. "You're not to blame for Vivian's choices."

"I know, but if I'd given her a job, I could've made sure she was all right. Had everything she needed."

Nell tapped her boot on the braided carpet under her feet. "This isn't your fault. Vivian is a big girl now. Besides, I'm sure we could all find reasons to blame ourselves." Her bottom lip quivered. "I've been so busy with Eleanor...thinking about myself and the baby...I should've asked Vivian how she was doing."

Miss Hattie shifted in the Queen Anne chair and set her teacup on the side table. "Vivian left the house every weekday, midmorning, and returned home by half-past five." She worried the skirt on her apron. "If she wasn't working at the hotel, where was she going every day?"

Morgan sat on the settee beside Kat, holding baby Hope's hand in his. "She obviously didn't want us to know."

"We're sisters." Nell dabbed her wet face with a limp handkerchief. "We don't keep secrets from one another."

Ida knew better. When she worked for Mollie O'Bryan, she'd quickly figured out that the businesswoman's methods for obtaining stock information weren't ethical, and yet Ida had adopted them as her own and denied the truth when Kat and Nell challenged her practices.

Ida pulled the curtain back from the window and watched an ice wagon roll to a stop at the hitching rail. She looked over her shoulder at Miss Hattie. "Are you expecting Otis?"

Miss Hattie stood, shaking her head. "I don't think so. I didn't expect to even be home."

Ida watched the bear-sized man trudge up the walk, her stomach knotting with his every step. "I saw Otis in town this morning and told

him about Vivian. Asked him to keep an eye out for her." Her pulse
quickening, she followed her husband and Miss Hattie to the front
door.

Otis's shoulders slumped. "Ma'am, I have something to tell you."
He looked down at his hat.

"About Vivian?"

She detected a slight nod as he looked past her. Her sisters and
brothers-in-law huddled around them.

Ida stepped forward, her heart pounding. "We're all family here,
Otis. You can tell us what you know."

"Let's go into the parlor and sit down." Tucker motioned for Otis
to lead the way. Ida sat on the sofa across from him.

"I deliver ice to the Homestead House," Otis said.

"Yes." Ida knew the delivery routes by heart.

"I was there…at the House yesterday afternoon."

Ida nodded. "Delivering extra ice for the party."

"Well, ma'am, a young woman opened the kitchen door for me—
all painted up. Had dark hair." Otis's gaze darted to Hattie, then from
one family member to the next, settling on Ida. "She was short…with
big brown eyes." He paused. "She disappeared last night."

Tucker squeezed Ida's hand. "You're talking about the girl they suspect of being involved in Pearl DeVere's death?"

Otis nodded like a man drained of energy.

Nell gasped. "It couldn't be Vivian."

"She turned away as soon as she saw me, but not before I got a good
look at her." Otis drew in a deep breath. "A girl about eighteen started
working at the Homestead at the end of July. Miss Pearl called her Violet. Same eyes and size as your Vivian. Wore a dark wig. Only worked
during the day…until last night."

Miss Hattie gasped. "The end of July? That's when Vivian told me she'd gotten a job at the hotel."

Tucker tightened his grip on Ida's hand, his gaze on Otis. "You believe this girl is Vivian."

"Yes, sir, and I'm surely sorry." Otis wadded his hat in his hands.

Ida opened her mouth to speak, but the words wouldn't come.

"How did you learn all this?" Tucker's voice sounded much too calm.

"My sister, Mary, does the cookin' at the House. Said Violet was the girl who found Miss Pearl. Mary watched her run in a panic out the kitchen door, and nobody's seen her since."

⟋⟋⟋

Vivian sat in a wooden chair across the room from a small potbelly stove, her hands tied behind her. Wind whistled through a knothole in the rough-hewn plank wall, chilling her back. After being forced to camp out in the wild last night, she should have been thankful for the roof over her head, but the two men watching her appeared feral. She'd rather take her chances with a mountain lion.

Pickett looked at her from a crude table against the far wall, where he was chopping up a rabbit he'd shot earlier. He stilled the knife. "My cousin ever pay for your services?"

Acid rose in Vivian's throat, and she wanted to spit it at him. Instead, she weighed her response. Leon was gone for the day. She needed to position herself to catch these two off guard. "I only worked as a hostess in the game room."

Both men laughed, but the younger one slithered toward her, his face close enough for her to see his pores. "So that's what they call it nowadays?" He had an Ozark accent like Pickett. He ran a rough finger down her cheek. "Well, Miss Violet, I'm in desperate need of a hostess, and you're probably more than ready to get out of those dirty clothes." His filthy fingers reached for the scooped neckline of her gown.

"Elton!" Pickett pointed the butcher knife at the young man. "You heard your father. We have to let her alone till he gets back. Wouldn't go against him, if I were you."

Elton slowly stepped away from her. "S'pose I could wait another day for your hostessing." He lowered his gaze to her bodice before returning his interest to a mug of coffee he'd left on a stool.

Thank You, God.

Vivian needed a plan. Leon had obviously remained in the area because of Miss Pearl. Now that she was dead, nothing would hold him here. For all Vivian knew, he intended to leave the area as soon as he returned from town. He'd cleaned up and changed his clothes before going, and she had no idea when he'd be back. If she expected to get away from this place before Leon returned, she needed to overpower her fear and play the role she'd learned at the Homestead.

Straightening in the chair, Vivian met Pickett's gaze. "You probably don't get to go into town like Leon does. And I bet you get real tired of having to cook for yourself."

"Women's work," Pickett mumbled.

"I feel the same way." Vivian smiled. "Why don't you let me do the cooking?" She glanced at Elton, who slouched in a wooden chair near the table, his thumb hooked in a belt loop. "If I take care of fixing the meal, you can relax for a while too."

Elton patted his knee, a lecherous grin on his face. "I'd rather you do the relaxing and let him do the cooking."

She focused on Pickett. "I think you'd like my cooking, and rabbit stew happens to be my specialty." *As of this moment.*

"You're right. I wouldn't mind sittin' around doing nothing." Pickett glared at Elton.

Elton cackled. "Suit yourself, but I wouldn't want her anywhere near me with that knife. She could probably gut you before you had a chance to hand her the salt and pepper."

"I'm not stupid," Pickett spit. "I'm just tired of having to do everything around here. Figure as long as we've got a gal here, I should let her do the work." He didn't bother cleaning the knife before dropping it into a barrel in the corner.

Vivian pressed her lips together. The knife would be too hard to get to now, but there had to be something else she could use to get away from them. Besides, a knife was no match for a rifle.

Pickett knelt behind her and untied the ropes on her hands. "No funny business, you hear?"

Vivian nodded.

Pickett narrowed his eyes. "Leon said we couldn't mess with you, but he didn't say nothin' about we couldn't shoot you if you tried to get away."

Vivian massaged the ache in her wrists, then took unsteady steps toward the remains of the dead animal. She studied the pile of potatoes and onions in the sink and looked at Pickett, who'd seated himself in the chair she'd occupied. "I'll need some whiskey."

Elton snorted. "Yeah, well, wouldn't mind having some myself, but Pops said to stay out of it."

Think, Vivian. "He's probably in town, eating a steak and thinking little about those of us stuck here. Hardly seems fair to me." Dipping her chin, she looked at Pickett. "I wouldn't need much, but the whiskey brings out the flavor of my stew." She paused. "And that's what makes it my specialty."

Pickett lumbered over to a crate and removed a soiled towel from its top.

"I hope you know what you're doin'," Elton said. "You know how he gets when he's mad, and he's already pretty sore about Miss Pearl being dead."

Pickett pulled an amber bottle out of the crate. "She just needs enough to bring out the flavor." He popped the cork out of the flask and handed it to Vivian, then looked over his shoulder at Elton. "You have any idea how long it's been since I've had a steak?" He rubbed the scars on his face. "Too easy to recognize now. I deserve some good rabbit stew."

Nodding, Vivian set the whiskey bottle on her cooking table and held up an onion. "Do you want to cut up the vegetables, or you want me to do it while you relax?"

Pickett studied her, then retrieved the knife from the barrel. "Remember, we've got guns and we're both watching you."

She was counting on it. While the rabbit stewed in a kettle on the potbelly stove, she chopped up five potatoes and the onion. She added the vegetables to the pot, along with a few pinches of salt and ground pepper. Now it just needed a few drops of whiskey and time to simmer.

She poured some liquor into the kettle, then tipped the bottle to her lips, feigning a swig. How could Miss Betts at the Homestead House stand this stuff in her tea? Licking her lips as if the whiskey tasted better than it did, Vivian set the bottle on the table, close to Elton and Pickett, leaving the cork on the cutting board.

She couldn't guarantee how tasty the stew would be, but if her plan worked, they wouldn't care what it tasted like.

Two hours later, their plates and the whiskey bottle empty, Elton and Pickett sagged in their chairs, looking plenty relaxed.

"I'm glad you fellows enjoyed my stew," Vivian said. "I like having a few more spices on hand, like rosemary or thyme, but—"

Elton muttered a faint, "Uh-huh."

"You liked it too, Mr. Pickett?"

His only answer was a slight grunt as he folded himself over the table and rested his head on his arms. Elton laid his head against the back of the chair and closed his eyes.

Vivian silently counted to fifteen, then lifted the knife from the wash sink and tiptoed out the door.

As soon as her shoes hit the muddy soil, she took off running, careful to hold the knife out away from her. She needed to put some distance between her and the shanty in what little was left of daylight. If Leon returned early and all three of the men came after her on horseback, the knife wouldn't do her any good.

Scrambling down the side of the mountain, Vivian wove through trees, trying to remain hidden. Difficult to do in a red gown. Even dirty, the dress was bright enough to make her stand out like a cardinal in flight.

She'd just stopped to catch her breath when she heard hooves against the rocks behind her. Why hadn't she taken one of the horses?

A gunshot shattered a rock just ahead of her, and she darted down the path.

TWENTY-SEVEN

﹏◡﹏

*C*arter gripped a slab of beef jerky in his teeth so he could tie the saddlebag shut. Liberty pulled against the reins and ripped a clump of summer grass from the ground. They'd been riding for several hours, and they were all ready for a break. Unfortunately, they had precious few hours left to get up that mountain before daylight gave way to darkness.

Stanley tightened the belt on his loose trousers and looked up at Ute Mountain. "They could be anywhere up there."

Carter bit off a chunk of jerky and pulled his canteen from the saddle. "Boney Hughes told me about several abandoned mines and shacks." He gulped water, his last drink for a few hours. "A perfect place to hide out."

"If you're not in a hurry and don't mind crawling over rocks all day." Walt sat on a rock, eating a meatloaf sandwich his wife had made.

Carter swallowed what was fast becoming a familiar longing. Not that he needed a woman to fix him a sandwich, although he'd probably eat better if she did. Of late, he craved the companionship his folks had enjoyed. The comfort of having someone to share the joys and sorrows of life.

While Carter and the two officers stored their canteens in their saddles and untied their mounts, he briefed them on the details of the robberies—banks, train, and Mac, and what he'd learned last night.

He'd just clucked his tongue at Liberty when a distant shot echoed off the rocks ahead of them.

Carter urged Liberty up the trail behind the other two lawmen, the three of them riding in silence. The gunfire had come from this direction, and Carter had a hunch they were getting close to the gang's hideout. That was probably one of them shooting meat for the night's meal.

Carter pushed his hat tighter on his head and nudged his horse. They'd fallen behind the other two. If they didn't come across Leon and the girl soon, he and Liberty would find themselves stumbling around in the dark. The blue skies were giving way to a blanket of clouds rolling in from the northwest.

While the three horses wound their way north, Carter sorted through a barrage of questions. Where did this Violet person fit in? What did Leon and the girl have to gain from Pearl DeVere's death? Maybe there was some sort of a love triangle; the girl got jealous and killed her rival. But what if they didn't have anything to gain from her death? It made sense that Leon would run; he was a wanted outlaw. But if the girl wasn't involved with the outlaw or her boss's death, why would she run?

Several yards ahead, Walt came to an abrupt halt and raised his right hand. Stanley and Carter stopped. Walt held up two fingers and mouthed the word *men*.

Two men. Not a man and woman?

For a second, it was quiet enough that Carter could have heard an Indian scout's steps, then hooves suddenly pounded the ground and headed up the trail.

Liberty lunged ahead of the officers' sorrels. The chase was on, and Carter prayed their pursuit would end the reign of the gang that had terrorized Cripple Creek and the surrounding areas for the past several months.

Up around a curve, Carter caught a glimpse of the two men. One tall, the other of average build. Most likely Pickett and Elton Kelso. The shorter man twisted and fired two shots at Carter. No more than three bullets left in that revolver before the shooter had to reload. Unless he carried a second gun.

Carter folded himself over the saddle horn and whipped the reins, guiding Liberty toward a steep upward path to the right and signaling Walt and Stanley to follow him. According to the map he'd studied with Boney, they'd intersect with the other two men without having to ride directly behind them. Carter couldn't say for sure whether God had called him to this work, but it felt good to be chasing outlaws, to feel like he was getting closer to making Colorado a safer place to live.

He was about fifty feet from where the paths reconnected, ready to make the turn to intercept the two suspects, when he spotted a flash of red cloth clambering down the embankment. The cook at the Homestead had told him Violet wore a red gown last night.

He eased up and pointed that direction. When the police officers indicated they'd seen her, he stopped. "I'll bring her in. You two apprehend the men and take them back to town."

Pulling the reins to the right, Carter clucked his tongue. Liberty turned off the trail and step-slid down the shale bank.

The petite, red blur scrambled down the mountainside, flailing her bare arms. She had to be the prostitute he was looking for, and Leon probably wasn't far away. Carter urged Liberty through the brush to head her off.

He'd just come out on the other side of a stand of juniper when she began tumbling, toes over tangles, and disappeared over a ridge too steep to follow on a horse.

Carter dismounted and retrieved his Sharps rifle from its scabbard. Pearl DeVere hadn't been shot, but he couldn't say who was armed and who wasn't. For his mother's sake, he couldn't take any chances.

He paused at the top of the ridge. The prostitute had landed at the bottom of a wash about twenty feet down. He picked his way toward her. With her dress in rags, the girl lying face down in the mud didn't look like much of a threat. She didn't even look alive.

After setting his rifle on a rock, Carter knelt and rolled her over onto his arm. Her face was a smear of mud and white paint, with a bad scrape on her cheek. He pulled a handkerchief from his shirt pocket and wiped the layers of crud away from her eyes and off the unscathed side of her face.

Narrow nose. High cheekbones. And a mussed braid of hair the color of maple syrup.

His chest clenched.

"Vivian?"

◦◦◦

Vivian's eyelids resisted her attempts to open them. Mud, fatigue, fear—any of those could account for their heaviness.

Suddenly, she floated on a cloud, or was she on a man's arm? Puffs of warm breath bathed her. A covering lighted on her chest, and a strong hand swaddled her. Something or someone brushed her face, including her eyes. An angel's wings?

"Vivian?"

Her real name. A man's voice. No growl, and no heavy accent, but shock punctuated each syllable.

Carter. Her head rested in the crook of Carter Alwyn's elbow, and she longed to find comfort in his warm, brown-eyed gaze. But he wasn't an actor. He didn't turn his feelings off and on to play a role...to entertain.

Teetering between relief and dread, Vivian forced her eyes open and stared into a look of hurt and shame. Carter's jacket lay over her bare skin. Tears stung her weary eyes. "I'm sorry I ran. I thought you were one of them."

"Where's Leon?"

"He went back to town. Left me with his son and cousin, Elton and Pickett."

"You're Violet?" Shame dripped off every letter, stinging her insides.

She wanted to believe she was someone else, that the Vivian she'd perceived herself to be wasn't capable of doing what she'd done with Gregory or of choosing to work where she did. But it was time she faced the truth—she had indeed been capable of living a lie, at least long enough to ruin any chance she had at love or even a normal life. She was a flawed Vivian, not a flirty Violet.

She met Carter's stormy gaze. "I'm Vivian Sinclair—the girl you know."

He shook his head, and she looked away. She deserved his distrust, even his wrath. She'd expected it. But there had been no way to prepare for the betrayal she saw in his dark eyes.

Pressing the coat to her chest, Vivian sat up. Everything from her stubbed toes to her scraped face hurt, but not nearly as deeply as the self-inflicted wounds to her heart. Carter was right—she wasn't the girl he thought he knew, and she could never be that girl.

Without looking at her, Carter shifted the jacket so she could slip her arm into it. The weight of it fell on her shoulders, and she knew the indecency of her dress had prompted his action, not chivalry.

"I'm sorry. I'm sorry for everything." The truth in her apology seared her soul.

Lord, I'm so sorry.

"Did you kill Pearl DeVere?" he asked.

Vivian felt the blood drain from her face. He suspected her of murder? Of working with Leon and his family?

His lower eyelid twitched. "You told Mary in the kitchen that Pearl was dead, and then you disappeared."

"Those men out there are after me." She glanced toward the ravine's edge. And now they'd kill Carter too. "Pearl was dead when I found her. Leon came in and accused me of killing her. As soon as I could, I ran from him." Vivian looked him in the eye. "I was running to your office when he grabbed me and brought me up here. I know I don't deserve your trust, but you have to believe me. I'm no angel, but neither am I a killer. I was Leon's prisoner, not his partner in crime."

"Can you stand?" His voice held the same intensity she saw in his eyes.

She pressed her lips together to help combat the tears and nodded.

"I need to get you back to town." Carter offered his hands to help her up. When she wobbled, he bent down and lifted her over his shoulder like a sack of grain. "This'll be easier for both of us."

Vivian stared at the muddy ground. Undignified, and definitely not the feeling of floating on a cloud, but Carter was right—being carried in this position would be much easier than seeing her transgressions reflected in his eyes.

TWENTY-EIGHT

*da scrubbed a plate clean and handed it to Nell for drying. Thankfully, the men had dominated the table and parlor conversations. They'd talked about everything from the unseasonably cool summer to last week's sermon, from the current value of ore to the patient count at the hospital. Ida and her sisters had quietly picked at their food. Even Miss Hattie only interjected an occasional comment. Baby Hope had been the most vocal, fussing until Kat lulled her to sleep in the rocking cradle next to the kitchen table.

Their silence had carried over into the cleanup. Ida reached for another dirty plate. All she could do was pray and try to keep busy.

She'd just handed Nell the plate when the telephone's raspy bell sounded and stilled their activity. Ida met Miss Hattie's wide-eyed gaze.

"It could be news of Vivian, dear," Miss Hattie said. "I'll let you get it."

Her heart racing, Ida dried her hands and picked up the cone. "Hello?"

"I have the police department on the line for Reverend Tucker Raines."

"This is his wife, Ida Raines."

A man's voice cut in. "Mrs. Raines, this is Lieutenant Thayer."

"Yes. Have you found my sister?" Nell, Kat, and Miss Hattie gathered around her. Ida did her best to maintain her composure as she listened to the latest information. "Yes, thank you."

Ida set the cone in the hook and faced the others.

Kat furrowed her brow. "They haven't found her?"

"She may be on Ute Mountain. That's where Carter and the police officers spotted two of the three men wanted for the robberies. The officers went after the men and just returned to town with them." Ida drew in a deep breath and blinked back tears. "Carter pursued a girl running away from them. She was wearing a red dress."

"It can't be Vivian out there." Nell set the plate on the cupboard. "She wouldn't run from Deputy Alwyn."

Kat crossed her arms. "We don't really know what Viv would or wouldn't do. She lied to all of us about working at the hotel. She left Ida on the boardwalk and strolled through the hotel door just like she belonged there." Her face flushed. "If Viv could work at a sporting house, she could run from the law."

And get tangled up with outlaws.

Any way Ida looked at it, she'd failed as a big sister.

❧

As darkness hovered, Carter added more sticks to the stack on his arm. The same arm that had cradled Vivian Sinclair's matted head an hour ago on the mountainside.

He was fairly certain Walt and Stanley had captured the other two outlaws, but Leon was probably still on the loose. No telling what he'd do if he knew Vivian had escaped and his cousin and son were locked up in the city jail.

Carter looked over his shoulder at the entrance to the abandoned mine where he'd left Vivian. The young woman he'd bought pie for at the Third Street Café. The one he'd nearly kissed in Miss Hattie's kitchen.

The one who'd worked in a sporting house for an infamous madam, who was now dead.

He added another handful of kindling to his bundle. To think he'd hesitated to move past friendship with Vivian because he didn't want to subject her to his job. He'd even considered giving up his life as a lawman for her. He'd told himself he needed to be patient, that she was young and naive.

He'd been the naive one, her fool.

Groaning, Carter started back to their shelter for the night and to the girl who had broken his heart. How could he have been so blind? So wrong? He knew her family. He'd seen her laughing with her sisters and heard her cooing at baby Hope. Miss Hattie adored Vivian. She'd blushed that day on the bench when he told her Tuesday mornings were reserved for the *other women* to shop in town.

Vivian wasn't the kind of girl he'd expect to find in a brothel or entangled with outlaws. Wasn't the kind of girl he'd always blamed for his father's death.

A grayness had settled on the trees and the mouth of the abandoned mine. Temperatures dropped below a waning crescent moon. Carter needed to build a fire before they both froze to death.

The two candles he'd lit inside the mine flickered but offered enough light for him to see that the rocks he'd piled in the center of the

room had been stacked into a fire ring. He set down the armful of kindling and looked at Vivian. She sat on the ground, looking small in his
large jacket. Her tattered skirt formed a tent over her raised knees.

"Thank you." He wanted to say her name but couldn't.

She didn't look at him. "It's the least I can do after all you're doing
for me."

"Making camp in a dirty, abandoned mineshaft?"

She sniffled and swiped at the tears spilling down her soiled cheeks.
"This is much better than last night. I was camped in the open, tied to
a saddle with a rifle pointed at me. At least in here I don't have to worry
about mountain lions." Her eyes widened, and she glanced at the tunnel. "Do I?"

"I checked. There's nothing in there." The image of the rope burns
on her wrists resurfaced and twisted his insides. Questions buzzed him
like pesky flies as he pulled a match from his saddlebags. "Did he, uh,
bother you?" He wanted to scold himself for caring. Tried to make
himself believe she was a prostitute and it didn't matter, that she may
have offered herself freely.

She pressed the collar of his jacket to her neck. "No. None of them
did. The Lord protected me, even though I didn't deserve it."

He lit a match and touched it to the moss under the kindling. "Do
you think Leon killed Pearl?"

"No." She shook her head. "When he saw me in Pearl's room, he
blamed me for her death. Said he loved her. He bought her the gown
she wore to the party."

That answered the question about where money from the robberies
was going—to impress Pearl DeVere. "Why did you go to Pearl's room
when you did last night?"

"To tell her I'd made a mistake." Her voice quivered, and so did his insides.

"What kind of mistake?"

"Taking the job there." She met his gaze. "I couldn't do that kind of work."

"Prostitute yourself?"

Vivian jerked as if he'd slapped her. But he was the one who'd been slapped, and he felt the sting to his core.

∽⎰∼

The fire crackled a few feet from Vivian. She felt safe here with Carter. He'd pulled several clean handkerchiefs from his saddlebags and given her a damp cloth to wash her face. She didn't expect to feel clean ever again, but at least she'd been able to remove one layer of grime and clean the scrapes on her cheek and elbow.

Now she sat wrapped in Carter's bedroll, nibbling on a biscuit. He crouched on the other side of the fire with nothing more than his jacket to keep him warm. With his back against a rock wall, he met her gaze. She didn't look away this time, and neither did he. She had so much she wanted to say to him. But where could she begin?

Carter broke the silence. "I'm sorry I flung you over my shoulder. That I was so blunt. I shouldn't have treated you like that."

He was apologizing? He'd given up his jacket for her, his bedroll. Even given up searching for the others, leaving it to the police officers he'd brought along.

He filled a tin mug with boiled coffee and handed it to her.

"Thank you." She wrapped her hands around the warm cup.

"Seeing you—well, it took me by surprise."

Another wave of shame rolled over her. "You saved me from those men. I never would've made it back up that ravine on my own. Thank you."

He ate the last of his biscuit and gulped coffee, then poked at a burning log with a stick.

"I can't excuse my recent behavior, but..." How could she explain something that mystified her?

He lifted the stick from the fire. They both watched as a tendril of smoke floated up from its glowing tip.

Vivian cared for this man. Probably had since her first night in town when he'd stood at the Raines's hearth, soaking wet, sympathizing with her. He cared for her too. She'd seen it in his eyes between bites of pie at the Third Street Café and in Hattie's kitchen when she'd told him she was fine. He'd seen through the lie and taken her hands in his.

But that was just one lie of many. She'd be a fool to believe his affection for her hadn't completely burned out or drifted out of reach.

"I never meant to hurt anyone." She laced her fingers over the blanket just below her neck. Her eyes began to pool with tears, the shame leaking out onto her cheeks. "I never wanted to hurt *you*."

He pinched the bridge of his nose the way she'd seen him do on the train. "How could this happen? You are an intelligent, beautiful young lady. Loved by many." He added the last log to the fire. "Why would you even consider working at a place like that?"

"I'm not the innocent you and my sisters think I am."

He opened his mouth as if to say something, but didn't.

"I never liked being the baby in the family. My mother died when I was just a girl. My father moved to Paris, leaving me in Aunt Alma's care. My sisters all moved across the country. My aunt had a business to run. I was suddenly relatively independent." Ignoring the irony of her statement, Vivian lifted the candle Carter had given her off the ground and held the wick to the fire until it began to glow. "I made mistakes in Maine."

"We all make mistakes, but they don't drive us to—"

"Prostitute ourselves?" Even if he couldn't forgive her, she wanted Carter to know the truth. "I had a beau, and I thought we would wed when I finished my schooling." She drew in a deep breath. "We shouldn't have been in his house alone that day, but we were. And in a moment of passion, I let him go too far."

Carter's shoulders sagged. She wanted to believe he was disappointed for her, but how could he be anything but disappointed by her?

"You were right." Tears again brimmed her lids. "I'm not the girl you know. Or thought you knew."

Looking past her, he brushed his hair back from his face. What was he thinking? Perhaps it was best that she didn't know. Otherwise, she may not be able to continue, and she needed to tell him the whole story. Regardless of the outcome.

"It happened more than once, and I didn't tell anyone." She couldn't look at him. "I didn't want to come to Cripple Creek, didn't want to face my sisters, but I couldn't stay in Portland either. I wanted to go to Paris with my father and throw myself into designing clothes, but he vehemently opposed that idea."

"But you seemed to like Cripple Creek. I've seen you with your sisters."

"I thought I could make a fresh start here."

"Until the morning I saw you on the bench in town."

"I'd just been fired from the telephone company. Three girls who worked for Pearl came out of the millinery, and I met Opal. I told her I wasn't working, and she told me about an opening for a daytime hostess at the Homestead House."

"Since you were out on a Tuesday morning, she assumed you were a *working girl* without a job."

"Yes. Then you came along and told me about the job at the newspaper. You know what happened there, that I had to quit."

He nodded.

"I owed Miss Hattie for my room. I needed a job. I asked all over town."

"Your sisters wouldn't help?"

"My father paid my train fare. Aunt Alma paid for her own tickets to escort me out here. My sisters had paid my first three weeks rent." Vivian paused for a sip of coffee, letting it warm her insides before continuing. "I was desperate to find my own way, but I'd been turned down by more than a dozen places, including Ida and the ice company."

"She turned you down?" He sounded as surprised as she'd been.

"She felt bad, but their recent expansion was costly."

"That's when you remembered what Opal said." His words came out in a whisper, just loud enough for her to hear over the sizzling wood.

"I know it was wrong, but I felt so ashamed of what I'd done with Gregory...what I'd given up." A wave of humiliation raced up her neck and burned her ears.

"That's why you couldn't let yourself like me?"

Nodding, she pressed her lips together to stave off the tears. "I no longer saw myself as the kind of girl who was above working in such a place."

"It's not the same thing."

From the sincerity in his voice, she drew the courage to keep going.

"Pearl hired me to work as a hostess. I worked during the day serving drinks and lunch in the game room. That's it."

Silence hung like musty smoke between them.

Carter scrubbed his whiskered jaw. "The day Boney and I waited for you at Miss Hattie's and you were standing on the corner?"

"Pearl had just hired me." She met his sad gaze. "I recognized Liberty at the hitching rail and didn't want to face you."

"You knew what you were doing was wrong."

"I did it anyway."

"You said you went to Pearl's room to tell her you couldn't do that kind of work."

"A man…" Tears stung her eyes. "A man had requested private time with me."

Carter's jaw hardened.

"I hadn't worked upstairs, and I didn't want to. I went up to tell her that I quit."

He drew in a deep breath. "Miss Hattie believed you had a legitimate job."

"I told her I was a hostess at the National Hotel. I lied to her. I lied to everyone."

He grabbed another stick and poked at the fire.

"This past Wednesday," Vivian continued, "I overheard Pearl and a man arguing. I now know that man was Leon. They were talking about the dead horse, about him being involved in the robberies and the death of that miner."

"I've been working night and day to find those responsible," Carter said, "to stop them. I've been watching the Homestead, looking for the ringleader. You knew he was there, and you didn't tell me?"

"I should've. Right away." Tears trickled down her face, their salti-ness stinging her cut lip. "When I slipped into the alley last night, I went to find you. I planned to tell you everything...where I worked and what I'd overheard." She swiped at her tears. "I'm sorry."

"I am too." His eyes steely, he tossed the stick in the pit. "We'd bet-ter try to sleep. We have a long ride tomorrow."

Vivian stared at the charred ashes between them and then blew out her candle.

TWENTY-NINE

A t the hint of first light, Carter sat on a rock outside the abandoned mine. Vivian had finally fallen asleep about three hours ago. She trusted him. He'd seen it in her eyes and heard it in her steady breathing. He hadn't slept. Determined to protect her, he'd sat with his back to the wall, watching the doorway and flinching at every owl hoot and coyote yowl.

One bad decision on Vivian's part had led to another, then another. But she didn't kill Pearl DeVere. Neither had she been an accomplice as he'd feared.

Too many things pelted his mind. A selfish man in Maine who had broken Vivian's heart. A devious woman who had hired Vivian under the guise of "hostess." A man who claimed to love Pearl DeVere, while stealing and killing innocent people to buy her gifts. The same man who chased Vivian down an alley and hauled her off to his lair.

Still, how could the well-bred Vivian, raised in a God-fearing home, become Violet—a young woman with a painted face, dressed to tease? She'd lied to everyone who cared for her. For what? Money provided by lusting men?

The Lord protected me, even though I didn't deserve it.

Under the Sunday morning dawn, Carter pulled a worn slip of paper from the billfold in his coat pocket and unfolded it. When he left Leadville for Cripple Creek, his mother had penned a verse from the book of Romans and given it to him.

Therefore being justified by faith, we have peace with God through our Lord Jesus Christ: By whom also we have access by faith into this grace wherein we stand, and rejoice in hope of the glory of God.

He'd assumed the worst of Vivian based upon her employment and speculation about her association with Leon. She'd been honest about her shortcomings when he hadn't even recognized his own. Carter's father had taught him that labels didn't determine a person's character or their worth. He'd demonstrated this truth with his very life. A truth Carter had resented until last night in the smoky cavern, when he saw Vivian instead of who he believed Violet to be.

His father had been fond of saying, "Sitting in the front pew doesn't make you closer to God." Assigning labels to people. Spouting religious dogma, as if grace wasn't enough. Pointing fingers, as if self-righteousness *was* enough. Engaging in gossip, and he'd heard plenty the night Pearl DeVere died. All were equal offenses in God's eyes.

Carter squirmed on the rock. Vivian had fallen into the trap of comparing herself to others, measuring her failures against her sisters' successes. Gilbert's words from that day in Victor rose to the surface of Carter's memory.

"You're out to prove something. I might do the same if I was trying to get out from under my dead father's shadow."

He'd brushed away his friend's observation at the time, but now it held his attention. Vivian had been truthful with him last night. It was his turn to do the same.

Carter took long strides toward the woman he would've died to protect. Two steps into the mine, he stopped in his tracks. He couldn't help staring at her. She knelt over his bedding, rolling it. A smaller blanket flowed off her back onto her muddy, tattered skirt. She'd managed to finger-comb her hair. A few curly locks flowed from the pins in streamers.

Vivian looked up, startled. She stood and faced him. "I didn't hear you come in."

"Vivian, when I saw you yesterday, I assumed the worst. I should've known better." He took slow steps toward her. "I did know better. I'm sorry."

"I don't blame you. I know what decent folks call girls like me."

"Then shame on them." He met her teary gaze. "Shame on me. Because that's not who you are." He was close enough now to see her brown eyes glistening like mist on an autumn leaf. "I see a caring woman with determination and grit."

He gently wiped a tear from her bruised cheek, and she flinched.

Carter looked at the broach that served as a clasp to hold the blanket together at her neck and make up for the low neckline of her dress.

"A resourceful woman."

"More like a desperate woman." A shadow clouded her eyes. "Pickett and Elton had guns. You could've been shot rescuing me."

"I wasn't."

"But we don't know where Leon is. He could still come after us."

"All the more reason to get you back to town. An early start and a steady ride should get us there by noon." Carter took the bedroll from her. "Are you ready to go?"

She nodded. "My sisters and Miss Hattie must be worried sick."

"Had I known you were missing and that those ruffians were holding you captive, I certainly would've been."

She bent to gather the candles from the ground. "Do you think they know?"

"Where you worked?" He nodded. "They would know by now. It's a small town when it comes to gossip."

She wasn't the innocent girl he'd thought her to be. She was a woman who had made mistakes and confessed them. A woman who, in the end, had helped the law find at least two of the bandits.

The woman he loved.

There, he'd admitted it, at least to himself. She'd hooked him the moment she squared her shoulders on the train and glared at him with those fiery brown eyes, a mix of sass and sensitivity.

He hung the saddlebags over his shoulder. It was a short walk to the clump of juniper trees where he'd tethered Liberty. He braced Vivian's elbow to steady her. At least that was what he told himself.

"My father was a sheriff's deputy in Leadville when I was a boy," he told her as they walked. "I worked in his office. Paperwork and cleanup mostly."

She peered up at him. "I heard he was killed on the job. I'm sorry."

"A girl was kidnapped by a raucous drunk."

"He was shot rescuing her?"

"Despite the town council's objections, my father went after them."

"The town council didn't want him to do his job?" Her voice shook with the disbelief at their apathy he should have felt all these years.

He swallowed hard. "She worked at a brothel. They believed it was a risk of her trade."

A frown darkened Vivian's eyes. "They didn't think she was worth saving." The tired tone of her voice reflected the weight of the words.

"They weren't the only ones who were misguided. For the past ten years, I've blamed that girl and her profession for my father's death…for my loss. I made sanctimonious assumptions about the women who chose that kind of work." He paused. "And assumptions about you. Can you forgive me?"

"After all the things you've learned about me—terrible things— you're asking for my forgiveness?"

"God doesn't list sins from the worst down to the slightest and judge a person accordingly. Only people do that."

A smile formed a dimple in her right cheek, and she laid her hand on his arm, sending shivers up his spine. "You're forgiven, deputy." Compassion shone in her brown eyes. And something else he hoped was love.

They shared a lot in common—grace. And that was where he longed to live.

With Vivian.

ᢒᡅᢧ

Vivian and Carter stood side by side atop the last grand hill, looking down at Cripple Creek. Cabins and mines dotted the vast valley below them.

He tipped his face toward the heavens. "God gave us blue skies today. My favorite color—sky blue."

Hers too. She'd ridden behind Carter all morning, her arms wrapped around him. He was a man of convictions and integrity. A man raised by a father who believed everyone and anyone was worth saving, and then lost his life because of that conviction. A man of compassion.

Carter had been shocked to discover she was the runaway girl from Pearl's parlor, to learn of her secret life, but he'd taken care of her. And once the shock wore off, he'd listened to her explanation and shared his own story.

When faith should have sustained her and sent her into God's arms, she'd wallowed in self-pity and turned to Gregory. Now she knew the difference between a superficial man and a man of deep faith and integrity. Her transgressions and the wrenching heartache that followed had readied her heart to receive God's grace. She didn't know what lay ahead for her and the deputy, but she believed God had brought them together.

She was thankful the pretense and lying were over. But she knew honesty carried risks along with the freedoms it offered. Miss Pearl's death and her own disappearance were bound to be fodder for the gossip mills. People would judge her. It was human nature, and she'd certainly judged others before becoming so intimately acquainted with her own shortcomings. Many consequences awaited her at the bottom of the hill, but those that might separate her from her family were the ones she feared the most.

God, help me to trust You, no matter what.

She drew in a deep breath and looked up at Carter. "Are you taking me to the police department?"

"That won't be necessary. You didn't contribute to Miss Pearl's death. You ran from the scene of the crime because you feared for your life. I'll take you to the boardinghouse—that's probably where your family is."

She nodded.

"Once I see the doctor's report on the cause of Miss DeVere's death, I'll know more about the department's investigation." He raked his hand through his hair and returned his hat to his head. "You'll be easy for the police department to find for questioning. I doubt your sisters will let you out of their sight."

She hoped he was right. What if her sisters couldn't even bear to look at her? She'd know soon. Whether she was ready or not for what lay ahead, it was time she stepped out of the secrets and lies and faced her family.

"Are you ready, Deputy Alwyn?"

"I'm ready."

It wasn't pity or even compassion she saw in his eyes. Was it love? Her heart said yes while her mind argued that he couldn't love her. Not after what she'd done.

He held his hand out to her and helped her into the saddle, then swung up behind her. His arms encircling her, he snapped the reins and clucked his tongue. Liberty lunged forward. They rode in silence, no doubt both lost in their thoughts and prayers.

As they drew closer to town, the sound of a band overpowered the *clip-clop* of the horse's hooves. Vivian twisted and spoke over her shoulder. "What do you think is going on?"

"Sounds like it may be the funeral."

"Pearl DeVere's." She faced forward, her heart aching because of all that had transpired in the past. Yes, Miss Pearl had been engaged in a sordid business, but she had a kind and generous heart. And now she was dead.

Carter leaned around her, his right arm bracing her side. His closeness felt right. "From the looks of the crowd forming on Bennett

Avenue, a burial procession is about to begin. That probably explains why Leon turned around and left the hideout so quickly. He couldn't seem to stay away from her."

Vivian didn't want to think about what Leon's presence in town could mean. Carter couldn't let him go. She understood that, but—

"Thankfully, the activity is taking place in the center of town." Carter turned right onto Golden, three streets above the event.

Miss Hattie's Boardinghouse had never looked so good. The yellow siding and white trim looked brighter than Vivian remembered. Liberty hadn't even reached the hitching rail when her sisters gushed out the front door and ran down the steps toward her, their arms open wide.

She was home.

Before Liberty came to a full stop at the hitching rail, Ida stood beside them, her arms raised. Carter helped Vivian slide off the horse, and Ida's arms encircled her, snug like a down comforter on a frigid night.

Vivian drank in her sisters' welcoming hugs and smiles. The dark circles under their eyes attested they hadn't slept much more than she had last night.

Redness rimmed Nell's blue eyes. "I feared you were dead."

"I had moments like that too." Vivian glanced at the broad-shouldered man flipping his horse's reins over the rail. "We have God and Deputy Alwyn to thank that I'm not."

On the train nearly three months ago, she hadn't considered the deputy a gift from God, but yesterday all that changed. She returned Carter's broad smile, thanking God again for helping him find her.

Ida squeezed Vivian's hand and looked up at Carter. "We'll never be able to thank you enough for bringing her home."

"One of those pork roast suppers of yours ought to do it," Carter said.

"Consider it arranged." Ida studied Vivian from her mud-encrusted shoes to the broach-clasped blanket hiding her low-cut neckline, then up to her bruised cheek. "Are you sure you're all right?"

"Morgan went to the parsonage with Judson and Tucker," Kat said. "Should we call a doctor?"

Vivian shook her head. "I promise you—I feel much better than I look."

"It's a good thing," Kat said, "because you look like you were dragged through a knothole and back out again."

"That makes me feel much better." Vivian grinned.

Miss Hattie seemed to glide down the porch steps. "Our girl is home. Thank God!"

Vivian melted into her landlady's matronly embrace, and another fountain of tears flowed over her sore cheek. There was so much to say, but...

"Let's get you inside." Carter cradled her arm and led her up the porch steps behind Miss Hattie.

Sunrays lit Vivian's path across the pine flooring in the entryway. She took a few steps, then paused to take it all in. A vase of yellow roses on the oak table against the wall. The framed painting of the banks of the Missouri River.

A whiff of something hearty filled her senses, and she sniffed the fragrant air. She looked at Miss Hattie, who stood at her side. "Roast beef and a pie?"

"A New England pot roast and peach cobbler."

"Mmm. My favorites." Vivian glanced up Carter. "Not that I didn't appreciate the biscuits and jerky."

His laugh was like music. "No offense taken. I don't know that the grass is any greener in Miss Hattie's kitchen, but it's always tastier." He held her gaze, his brown eyes a mix of tenderness and intensity. "I have to go. Still work to be done."

She admired his strong work ethic and his dedication to justice, but she couldn't help but hope the police department had already captured Leon. If they hadn't… "Please don't go after him alone." Even as she said it, she knew Carter Alwyn would do whatever it took to see the outlaw brought to justice. "Be careful."

"Yes ma'am." He pressed his hat onto his head.

Miss Hattie cradled Vivian's shoulders but spoke to Carter. "Just because we had some prayers answered doesn't mean the prayer meeting's over."

"I'm grateful, Miss Hattie." He kissed the widow on the cheek and looked at Vivian. "I'll come by and check on you tomorrow."

"Tomorrow." Vivian's whisper sounded dreamy, but she didn't care. Nobody could be matchmaking as heartily as she was right now.

Thirty

ॐ

Carter stepped out of the Cripple Creek Police Department onto the crowded boardwalk. He'd talked to Pickett and Elton Kelso in the jail, but he learned more from reading the medical report. The doctor concluded that Pearl DeVere died of an accidental overdose of morphine.

Stanley and Walt had captured two of the three bank robbers, but it was their leader who troubled Carter. Leon Kelso had instigated several robberies and at least one murder in this county and imprisoned Vivian. And he still roamed free.

Carter glanced toward the gathering crowds on Bennett Avenue. If what Leon told Vivian about loving Pearl DeVere was true, the bandit could be among the mourners.

Duty called, but Carter hesitated, and it was Miss Vivian Sinclair's fault. The way she'd thanked him for bringing her home and told him to be careful. The silk in her voice when she whispered *tomorrow* made him feel like he had someone to come home to.

The "Death March" drumbeats echoed off the brick buildings on either side of the street. The Elks Band led the funeral procession, wearing red fezzes and gold-braided scabbards. Four mounted policemen pushed the crowd to the edges of the road. A heavily draped, glass-sided hearse with shiny red wheels ambled past, pulled by sleek black horses. Red and white roses blanketed the casket, and a cross of pink carnations lay on the seat. Buggy after buggy filled with veiled women followed the hearse, many of them wailing. People from all walks of life lined the streets.

As Carter made his way up the street toward the graveyard, he remained close to the buildings for as long as possible, tucked behind clusters of spectators. If Leon came anywhere near this rolling pageant, it'd be the mistake that snared him.

At the edge of town, Bennett narrowed to the cemetery entrance. Very few cabins dotted that windswept part of the mining camp. A man chopped wood in front of a tarpapered shack. A boy struggled to hitch a burro to a cart. A dog howled, harmonizing with the note of the cornets.

The ache in Carter's temples thumped with the beat of the snare drums. Funerals brought back the past. His mother dressed in black. His aunt shepherding him through the day. People like Harry Updike standing under the oak tree, debating the futility of his father's sacrifice for that kind of girl.

Carter hadn't yet reached the gate of the cemetery when a spirited stallion galloped up the hill toward him, the rider waving feverishly. Jesse from the livery. Carter strode toward him.

"The guy you described from the saloon just left the livery. Traded an old mare for a gelding. Headed toward the pass." Jesse swung to the ground and handed Carter the reins of his horse. "This is Reno. You take him. I'll stop by Jon's and let him know you're in pursuit. Watch your back."

Carter swung up into the saddle and swatted Reno's flank.

After Carter left the boardinghouse, Vivian sank into a hot bath. A good scrubbing and a change of clothes made her feel refreshed, but it would take her insides longer to feel clean again.

She and her sisters gathered in her bedchamber at Miss Hattie's. Ida, Kat, and Nell had all welcomed her home, but she knew they had questions and deserved an explanation. Vivian sat in front of the dressing table while Ida pulled a brush through Vivian's clean hair. Kat nursed baby Hope in the rocker. Nell sat on the edge of the bed, eyelid twitching in the silence.

"You never worked at the hotel." A frown creased Ida's chin.

Vivian swallowed hard. "I tried to get a job there. But, no, I never worked at the National Hotel."

The rocker stilled, and Kat looked Vivian squarely in the eyes. "Otis told us he saw you at that house Friday evening. He said you were wearing a wig and dressed like one of them."

Ida stopped brushing. "You left me on the boardwalk and strolled through the hotel door like you belonged there."

"Unbelievable that you could do that." Kat raised Hope to her shoulder. "If you could work at a place like that, and lie about it, what else are you capable of?"

"Stop it!" Nell jumped to her feet, her lips quivering and tears streaming down her cheeks. "We should just be thankful she's safe."

Her sisters had trusted Vivian, and she'd let them down. She'd caused them all so much pain. Heartbroken, Vivian looked at each of her sisters and breathed a prayer for the right words. "I know you're all hurt and angry, and I'm so sorry."

Nell mopped her face with her sleeve. "What did you do there? Did you…" Nell swallowed.

Vivian blinked back her own tears. "I only worked as a hostess downstairs during the day, serving drinks and food. Friday night, Miss Pearl asked me to do the other kind of work." She glanced at Nell, who was looking everywhere but at her. "I couldn't do what she asked. I'd gone up to her room to tell her I quit when I found her dead." She looked up at Ida.

Her oldest sister looked like she had a lemon stuck in her throat. "I just don't understand how you could agree to spend time with those kinds of men."

Vivian pressed her lips together in an attempt to stave off the tears that stung her eyes. She had to keep going. "I know you all are morti-fied that I'd worked in such a place."

"Mostly, we were worried sick about you," Nell said.

"And dumbfounded." Kat laid baby Hope on the bed. "Oh, all right, a little mortified too. How could you be that desperate and not say anything to us?"

Ida's sigh shifted the curls on Vivian's forehead. "Vivian did come to me. Asked me for a job and I—"

"This isn't anyone's fault but my own." Squirming, Vivian breathed another prayer. "I know it won't erase what I've done or the pain I've caused, but I want to tell you what happened. All of it."

Kat seated herself on the bed beside Nell, and Ida set the brush on the table and sat in the rocker. Vivian started with her experiences with Gregory and shared her story. From the letter she'd written to Father begging him to let her come to Paris to meeting Pearl's girls on the boardwalk to Carter finding her near Leon's hideout and bringing her home.

After nearly an hour of talk and tears, Vivian folded her hands in her lap and looked at each of her sisters. Would they be able to forgive her? Now that they knew about all her offenses, would they still love her?

Kat was the first to stand and pull Vivian into a warm embrace. "Welcome home, sis."

Tears flowing, Vivian stepped into Nell's and Ida's hugs. She was right where she belonged.

A smile lit Nell's face, accentuating the banner of freckles across her nose. "Seems to me you've left the best part of the story until last—Deputy Carter Alwyn."

Vivian twirled a curl dangling at her temple. "Well, let's see now. He wears a black hat, but he's one of the good guys."

"We all saw how he had to rip himself from your side." Kat tapped the toe of her shoe on the wooden floor. "There's more to that story, and you did say you wanted to tell us all of it."

"Well, like my sisters, Carter Alwyn understands grace."

Nell raised a thin eyebrow. "And?"

"And…I love him. Not just because he rescued me, either." She paused. "But because he believes I'm worth rescuing. Something I didn't even believe of myself."

Nell clasped her hands. "I love a happy ending…or should I say beginning?"

"I hope so." *Oh, Lord, may it be so.*

"Hello, my dear Sinclair sisters." Miss Hattie's singsong voice wafted into the room. "The fatted calf is ready."

Vivian felt a big smile overtaking her face and led the way to the staircase. She was nearly to the bottom step when the doorbell rang. Her heartbeat stuttered. "It could be the police. Carter said they may come to ask me questions."

"Oh, I hope not. We need to get some food into you." Miss Hattie rushed past her and opened the door.

The oldest Zanzucchi sister stood on the porch, holding a lantern and panting as if she'd just run a race.

"Jocelyn?" Nell rushed toward the girl.

"Eleanor said to come fetch you. To tell you it's her time."

"Oh my. Oh my. The baby's coming." Nell looked at Vivian.

"I'm fine." Vivian squeezed Nell's arm. "Go."

"Miss Naomi's with her now." Jocelyn's breathing had evened.

Nell smoothed the ruffles on her pinafore and pulled her shawl from the hall tree. "This could be the day I meet my son or daughter."

Vivian gave her sister a quick hug and watched her float down the steps toward motherhood.

The Lord's day.

Perfect day for a birth.

Perfect day for a rebirth.

❧

Vivian had asked him not to go after Leon by himself. Carter preferred to honor that request. In fact, company on such a mission was personal policy, one that might have saved his father's life. Carter had been out twice with a posse, but today there wasn't time to gather one. If he had any hope of catching up to the outlaw and capturing him, he had to act quickly.

Did Leon know Vivian had escaped, that his cousin and son had been captured? Carter doubted the police department would have been able to keep the capture under their hats. It also seemed unlikely that Leon could have managed to spend time in town and not hear the gossip.

Jesse had seen the bandit ride north, out of town. He had to be headed back to the hideout. Would he return to the cabin if he knew? Why?

As daylight bowed to shadows, Carter urged the stallion up the rocky path toward Ute Pass. Vivian had shown him the place where she and Leon had camped Friday night. With any luck, Carter would find the outlaw camped in the midst of the same boulders.

Every scuff of Reno's horseshoes on the rocky path reminded Carter of the growing list of Leon's injustices, strengthening his resolve to pursue the outlaw and hold him accountable no matter the cost. Carter now knew how his father had felt that August night when he rode out after a drunken miner and the saloon girl he'd taken at gunpoint. He knew what drove his father to buck the city council and strike out on his own. No one was above the law, and no one was below its protection.

Once Carter reached his target area, he nudged the stallion through the scrub brush at a quieter pace. He didn't see any smoke from a campfire, but that didn't mean the outlaw wasn't here. Carter tied Reno about a hundred yards from the rock formations, which weren't easy to approach without being spotted.

As he made his way toward the boulders, he heard faint whistling and recognized the tune, "Goodbye, Little Girl, Goodbye." It had to be Leon.

The whistling stopped before the end of the song. An owl hooted. A chorus of coyotes howled in the distance. Then a twig snapped twenty feet away.

Carter's stomach clenched. Leon knew he wasn't alone, and he was on the move.

Carter crouched against a wall of granite behind the scrub brush, knowing that if he was spotted, he had no protection. Heart pounding, he lifted his revolver, his finger poised on the trigger as he listened. All he heard was the rising rhythm of his own heartbeat pounding in his ears. Shades of gray shrouded the earth and sky. Squinting, he strained to make out any shadows on the rocks. Where was Leon?

"Show yourself." The Ozark accent came from above him, off to the left. "We've got you covered."

A bluff. Three men had been involved in their gang, and Leon was down two. Carter guessed Leon already knew where he was and just needed a clear shot. But Carter needed to see his opponent as well.

"We?" he called back.

The sound of boots scraping rocks and snapping twigs tightened Carter's throat. He scrambled on hands and knees to the shelter of a stand of rocks and squeezed between them.

"Guess you haven't heard the news," Carter said.

Silence.

"Bound to be real quiet at your place tonight," he continued. "Your son and cousin are doing their talking in jail."

Leon's laugh sounded more like a growl. "You're dreaming, deputy. One's got a pistol aimed at you, the other a rifle."

"The girl who heard you arguing with Pearl, the girl you dragged up to the cabin is gone too."

"She killed Pearl."

"Self-administered laudanum killed Pearl." More crunching and snapping. Leon was below him. "Fancy belt buckle—that racehorse. You get that back home in Kentucky?"

"I'll soon be tending a ranch full of racehorses while you're fertilizing wildflowers."

A stone bounded off the boulders to Carter's right, causing him to jerk toward it. A crack rang out, and a sharp shove on his left shoulder spun him toward the rocks. Fresh, dark blood streaked the boulder. His chest was sticky with the stuff, but there was no pain. All he felt was warmth.

Was it like this for his father? Carter took comfort in that.

The sound of calculated footsteps drew closer, and Carter slumped to the ground. Leon was coming to finish him off.

Carter lay still, the hand that gripped his revolver hidden under a branch. While the steps drew closer, he asked God for the chance to stop this man. If it was his time to die, he aimed to make his death worthwhile.

"You never should've come looking for me alone," Leon said. A sinister laugh sent a shiver up Carter's spine. The man who had been terrorizing his state and county stood within a few feet of him. A dark silhouette against the setting sun, Leon held his revolver at arm's length, pointed squarely at Carter.

Carter heaved his shoulder in an attempt to raise his weapon. The arm responded but couldn't muster any speed.

Before he could pull back the hammer, a powerless click echoed off the rocks. His adversary's gun had misfired. Leon hadn't counted on God's intervention.

Carter summoned all his remaining strength, and some he didn't possess, to raise his gun. The report filled the space between the rocks and echoed across the canyon.

Leon took a step back and dropped his weapon in the dirt. He looked down at the black spot spreading across the bib of his shirt, then at Carter. His eyes closed, and he slumped to the ground.

When Leon didn't move again, Carter gave in to the blackness.

THIRTY-ONE

∽৩৩∿

ivian pulled a large sketch pad from her trunk. After savoring the plate of pot roast together, Kat and Ida had left to join their husbands at the parsonage. From there, Kat and Morgan took Judson down to Poverty Gulch to check on Nell. Less than thirty minutes ago, they'd called Auntie Vivian to let her know she had a noisy nephew.

Seated in her rocker, Vivian glanced from the hobnail lamp on the side table up to the corniced ceiling above her, then to the quilt on her feather bed. Nearly as steady as her breaths, the prayers of thanksgiving just kept coming. Now that she had time alone this evening, time to reflect on the happenings of the past several days, she could see that God's hand was there guiding her, protecting her, providing for her. One man had been her downfall. Another, her salvation.

Breathing a prayer for Carter, Vivian leaned back in the cushioned chair. She flipped open the book of what she called her dream drawings, sketches of women's costumes for all seasons. She knew exactly where her favorite page lay in her portfolio of fashion designs, but saving the best for last, she trailed her finger over the lines of the ball gown on the first page. She revisited her sketches of skirts, capes, shirtwaists, even women's riding trousers before turning to the dog-eared page.

The wedding gown displayed there was the dress she'd designed while Gregory was courting her. But it wasn't Gregory she saw waiting for her at the end of the aisle now. Instead, a brown-eyed deputy with a smile that could melt midwinter icicles dwelt in her daydreams. He possessed a caring touch that comforted her and a heart so full of grace that it spilled out onto those around him.

She'd thought her gown would be accented with a dandelion yellow sash—Gregory's favorite color. But not Carter Alwyn's favorite.

Vivian gripped both sides of the pad and lifted it off her lap. Standing, she clutched the sketch to her breast and twirled across the room, lost in a silent dance.

Wagon wheels churned the street below, then suddenly stopped. Anxious voices drew Vivian to the window. In the darkness, all she could see was the silhouette of a wagon and the glow from the lantern a woman carried up the walk.

Tucker and Ida.

Vivian set the sketch pad on the bed and grabbed her dressing gown from the wardrobe. It was ten o'clock. Miss Hattie had retired for the night.

Fear knotted Vivian's stomach while she secured the tie at her waist. Her sister's presence this time of night could mean only one thing—trouble. She quickly lit her lantern and hurried down the stairs to open the door. Ida and Tucker's solemn faces only served to tighten the knots in Vivian's stomach.

Tucker ushered Ida inside and removed his hat. "Vivian, Morgan called us."

"Kat? Is something wrong with her? The baby?"

"It's Carter."

Vivian's breath caught in her throat.

Ida grasped Vivian's hands. "Jesse and Boney found him. He's been shot."

Vivian's heart pounded in her chest. "Is he alive?"

Lips pressed together, Ida nodded.

"He's at the hospital," Tucker said. "He's asking for you."

⁓⦥⁓

Carter watched Morgan Cutshaw walk toward his hospital bed. He struggled to draw in the breath to speak. "Is she coming?"

"Tucker and Ida went to get her, but we can't wait."

Carter couldn't say for sure that his mother would marry his father all over again, knowing he'd be killed, but he did know her greatest regret. They'd taken her husband to surgery before she could see him, and he'd died on the operating table.

His breathing shallow and labored, Carter gasped in a lungful of air. "I have to wait."

Morgan sighed. "Five minutes, and that's more than I should give you."

Carter closed his eyes. Hopefully God would give him longer. Vivian was the woman he'd been waiting for, even if he hadn't been looking.

"Carter?"

He opened his eyes to a glorious vision. His girl peered down at him, apprehension and tears brimming in her eyes.

"Vivian."

She swept tears from her chin. "Carter Alwyn, I'll have you know I worked hard to earn my place at the center of attention. What's the big idea? You trying to steal it from me?"

How could he have known to look for such sass and sensitivity in the same package?

"I had to see you." Even to himself, he sounded like a bellows, each word coming out on a puff of breath, but he had to give her what his mother didn't have. "To tell you...I love you."

Vivian nodded and lifted his hand to her mouth. She brushed the back of it with her soft lips. "I love you too."

"I have to get him into surgery right now," Morgan said. The gurney began to move.

Vivian loved him. Carter had so much to live for. Staring up into her face, he drank in the devotion he saw in her eyes. "Viv-i-an, I..." Words crowded his heart, but he hadn't the strength to speak them.

He felt her hand slip away. The bed began to spin.

"I'll wait for you," she said.

Her words echoed off the walls of his mind before the room faded.

Thursday morning, Vivian sat in Miss Hattie's dining room, stirring a stream of honey into her mint tea. Pots and pans clanged in the kitchen on the other side of the wall. Miss Hattie had insisted she didn't need any help and that Vivian should visit with their houseguest.

Carter strolled into the room, his left arm wrapped against his side. The bullet had lodged in the breast muscle. He'd lost a lot of blood before Morgan was able to dig it out. He'd been released from the hospital last evening with the stipulation that he not try to negotiate any stairs or do any lifting for at least a week, which ruled out going back to his apartment above the sheriff's office.

In the meantime, he'd recuperate in a place that would provide him with good meals and care—Miss Hattie's Boardinghouse. Vivian rather liked the arrangement. The broad smile on Carter's whiskered face said he did too.

"Good morning." He greeted Vivian with a lilt in his baritone voice, then stopped across the table from her, wearing a crisp yellow shirt and a pair of black trousers.

"Yes," Vivian said. "How do you feel this morning?"

"Thankful to be alive." He seated himself. "Thankful to be here." His eyes, just as intense as his smile, seemed to be gazing into her soul. He had seen her for who she was and still looked at her.

She didn't look away.

Did he remember what she said to him before Morgan wheeled him to the operating room Sunday night? More importantly, did he remember what he said to her? They'd confessed their love for each other, and although she'd been to the hospital to see him every day since, neither of them had spoken of it. He'd winced with every breath that night. What if the pain and delirium—not his heart—had done the talking?

Vivian unfolded the napkin on her plate. They'd focused on his recovery and on the details of the events that led to his injury. Gilbert and Jon had been in to see him, along with many grateful townspeople. Between the visitors and the medical personnel, she and Carter had not had a moment alone until now, and even this was fleeting. Miss Hattie could waltz into the room at any moment.

"Vivian."

She looked up from the napkin on her lap.

Carter reached across the table and took her hands in his. "I meant what I said the other night."

He remembered. Vivian squeezed his hand. "I did too."

Carter knew her heart, and he'd captured it. Now what?

She'd just opened her mouth to ask when Miss Hattie walked in carrying a platter of fried ham and eggs. Staring at their linked hands, the widow stopped in her tracks. "It seems I still need to work on my timing."

Vivian giggled. "Yes, that would be nice."

Carter let go of her hands, and she folded them in her lap, already missing his warmth.

When he started to stand, Miss Hattie motioned for him to remain seated. "You can be a gentleman another day," she said. Seated at the head of the table, she offered a breakfast blessing full of thanksgiving. Vivian's safe return. Boney and Jesse returning Carter to town in a timely fashion. Morgan's skilled hands. Nell's new baby boy. The bounty on the table.

Vivian's heart and soul echoed every word of praise and even added some of her own, most of which involved Carter.

Between bites of ham and honey-smothered biscuits, Carter relayed what Jon had told him about Leon's checkered past in Kentucky and in several southern states. Leon's cousin, Pickett, hadn't said much, but the ringleader's disgruntled son had plenty to say while waiting to see the judge. Jon and Gilbert had found a considerable amount of money buried under a tree outside the shanty. The portion left after accounting for the train and bank robberies was being wired to Mac's widow and children.

Vivian had just swallowed the last of her orange juice when Carter set his fork on his plate and stared at her. "Do you think you could sit in the parlor with me for a spell?"

"I'd like that." She looked at Miss Hattie.

A quick smile crossed the widow's face. "I suppose a short visit won't hurt him." She wagged her finger at Carter, a gleam in her blue-gray eyes. "Then a good rest before Morgan comes to check the wound."

"Yes ma'am."

Vivian couldn't guarantee how short their visit would be. Right now a lifetime didn't seem long enough.

Carter followed Vivian out of the dining room, giving himself permission to watch her every move. The woman he loved was poetry in motion. He walked with Vivian along the hallway speckled with photographs of Miss Hattie and George. Perhaps this was the pathway to his and Vivian's future.

He stopped outside the parlor, allowing her to enter first. She sashayed into the room and looked over her shoulder at him, the shy smile on her sweet face bathed in sunlight.

Seating herself at the far end of the sofa, she smoothed her burgundy skirt over the bend of her knees. With every step Carter took to the quiet fireplace, he breathed a prayer for the grace and strength to be the man God purposed for Vivian.

He wasn't sure his repaired chest would let him stand long enough to say what he needed, so he seated himself on the hearth and looked at Vivian. "I need to ask you something."

She nodded, her hands clasped and her knuckles white.

As the tick of the mantel clock echoed in the silence, Carter swallowed the lump in his throat. Vivian fiddled with a curl above her ear—something she did when she was nervous. Or impatient?

He straightened, leaning toward her. "Would you still love me if I were just a regular shopkeeper or a miner?"

Her eyes widened. "You're giving up your job as a lawman?"

"God and I are talking about it."

"It's who you are, not what you do, that I love." She leaned forward, pinning him with brown eyes that warmed him clear to his core. "But I believe who you are influences the work you do. Your integrity, your compassion, your sense of justice, your courage, and your reliance on God make you a very good lawman."

Vivian Sinclair was a wise woman, as well as charming and beautiful.

She moistened her lips, and he could no longer resist them. Carter rose from the hearth and closed the distance between them. Vivian stood. Using two fingers, he lifted her chin until her teary gaze met his, then he bent to kiss her.

When he'd summoned enough willpower to end the kiss, she sighed, a soothing salve for his soul. "I can't imagine my life without you as a big part of it, Miss Vivian Sinclair."

She twirled another curl at her ear.

"I thought about waiting until I could get to the jewelry store and propose proper-like," he said, "but I'm not that patient a man." He felt his own eyes misting and knew he had to get his next sentence out before emotion overcame him. "Vivian, will you do me the honor of being my wife?"

"Yes. Yes. Yes." Rising on her toes, Vivian kissed him gently on the mouth. "Carter Alwyn, *you* are a dream come true."

And yet in that moment, he was the one dreaming of the years he'd spend with Vivian as his wife.

Thirty-Two

_____

Saturday morning, Vivian sat with Miss Hattie in the parlor. Two weeks ago today she had fled Leon's hideout, was pursued by Pickett and Elton, and then was rescued by Carter Alwyn. Last week, the distracting deputy proposed marriage, and she accepted. Yesterday, after a week of recuperation in the boardinghouse, Carter returned to his apartment above the sheriff's office. Today, Vivian would plan her wedding and start sewing her gown.

Through the open window, she heard a baby's cry, signaling that Kat was the first of her sisters to arrive at the boardinghouse. Baby Hope wailed from under the miniature parasol of her lace-covered buggy. Kat stopped, lifted the little one into her arms, and hung a quilted bag from her shoulder. Vivian hurried out the door and down the steps. She pushed the buggy to the porch and followed Kat inside the house.

"Thanks, Viv." Kat looked as if she hadn't slept all night, and red lines mapped her brown eyes. Sobbing, Hope kicked her legs and flailed her arms.

"What's the matter with our sweet girl?" Vivian considered taking Hope from her sister, but her inexperience with unhappy babies convinced her to choose the bag instead. She lifted it off Kat's shoulder, then stroked Hope's damp cheek and looked up at her weary sister. "I don't remember ever hearing her cry like this. I've never seen her so upset. Is she sick?"

"Morgan says no. No fever or sore stomach, but she's certainly been out of sorts the past couple of days." Kat sighed. "I picked up the telephone to tell you I wouldn't be able to come, but I had something I needed to show you."

Hattie swished into the entryway, carrying a wet hand towel. "Good morning, dears." She scooped Hope into her arms and rubbed her gnarled fingertip over the infant's bottom gums. "I feel nubs. The poor dear is cutting teeth."

Kat's forehead puckered. "At five months?"

Nodding, Hattie pressed the wet towel to the little mouth. Hope's lips curled over it, her eyes wide, and she began to gnaw on the towel, her cries replaced by the sound of sucking. Hattie leaned her wrinkled cheek against the baby's head, her blue-gray eyes shining. Vivian found it hard to believe she didn't have any children and grandchildren of her own. Some things just didn't make sense.

"I should've known to do that." Kat rubbed her eyes. "Morgan's a doctor. Why didn't he know what was wrong?"

"He's a brilliant surgeon, dear." Hattie tapped Hope's nose with a fingertip. "And you're both new to parenting. Why don't you leave this little angel with me this morning while you go to town with your sisters?"

Kat's shoulders lifted a notch.

"I have plenty of ice. I can round off a piece. That'll help soothe her sore gums. We'll be just fine."

Vivian patted Kat's arm. "You'd probably be better off resting while you can."

Kat shook her head. "I'd rather spend the morning with you, scouring stores for wedding dress materials." She shifted her attention to the contented baby in Hattie's arms. "Are you sure you didn't have other plans?"

"Not a blessed thing more important than this child." Hattie kissed Hope's curly head.

"Thank you. That would be wonderful." Kat suppressed a yawn. "I'll make sure her belly is full before I go."

"Very well then, it's settled. I get some baby time today." Hattie's steps toward the kitchen were light as a ballerina's.

"We may as well wait in the parlor for the other two." Vivian led the way. Settling on one end of the sofa, she laid the quilted baby bag on the table in front of her and looked up at her sister. "You said you had something you wanted to show me?"

"I do." Her voice less than enthusiastic, Kat joined Vivian on the sofa and pulled the bag onto her lap. She reached inside, then paused. "I did this right after Etta turned you down for a job in her shop." She moistened her lips. "But with everything you've been through...well, now I'm not sure it'll be the pleasant surprise I'd hoped it would."

"Surprises are fun." But if Kat was this nervous about whatever she'd done, this revelation may be an exception.

Raising a thin brow, Kat pulled a curled magazine from the bag and handed it to Vivian.

Vivian laid it out flat on her lap. "It's *Harper's Bazar*."

"The September issue." Kat tapped her chin as she was prone to do when nervous.

"You wrote an article about Ida and her business?"

Kat shook her head.

Of course. Her landlady. Kat was probably rethinking the article, concerned about Vivian's sensibilities. "Miss Hattie's involvement with the Women for the Betterment of Cripple Creek." She looked Kat in the eye. "If you included things about the seedier side of Cripple Creek, you needn't worry about my—"

Kat shook her head. An auburn curl swept across her forehead. "The article is about you."

Vivian's mouth went dry, but she managed to respond on a whisper. "Me?" She'd done nothing noteworthy. At least nothing she wanted recorded for all time and eternity. "What?" The word sounded as if it had been squeezed through a sieve.

Kat pointed to the magazine. "Open it."

She wasn't sure she wanted to, but she trusted Kat's judgment, if not her taste in subjects. She opened the cover and studied the first pages. An article on manners. A poem about love. An advertisement for Wilkie Collins's novels. All seemingly harmless.

"Keep going." Kat rolled her finger.

Vivian kept turning the pages until her sister's hand stilled. Vivian's gaze shot to the bold headline: "Premier Eastern Designer Relocated to Cripple Creek!"

She gasped. "You didn't!" It couldn't be her. Sewing clothes for family members did not a fashion designer make. Let alone one considered *premier*.

"I didn't write the headline, and the article I wrote was much smaller than this, but yes, I did write about you."

Pencil sketches of her designs framed paragraphs about her childhood dream of designing clothes for princesses and entertainers. Kat and her editor had also written about the attire Vivian had designed for up-and-coming businesswomen and sang praises for her highly fashionable wedding gowns. Missing was the fact that she'd done all of it for her own sisters.

This had to be a daydream. Vivian blinked, but nothing changed. She met Kat's tender gaze. "This is unbelievable. I can't believe you did this."

"My editor did exaggerate some, but it is true that you're a talented fashion designer from the East and you're now living in Cripple Creek."

"No, I meant this was so…" Her lips quivered. "Sweet of you." Vivian ran her finger over the design for Kat's wedding gown.

"I was trying to help," Kat said. "You really are a creative designer, and you would've eventually been at the top of your field if Etta Ondersma hadn't been too shortsighted to hire you."

Vivian wiped her wet eyes. If sister love were a thread, it would be more binding than any rope out there.

"I just thought the world that reads *Harper's Bazar* should know about your talent."

"I don't know what to say."

"You're not mad at me?"

"Of course not."

"I only hoped the article would help you find work doing what you love to do."

"Thank you." Vivian laid the magazine on the table and pulled Kat into a tight embrace.

She wasn't sure how many women in the Cripple Creek Mining District cared about having their clothing designed and crafted specifically for them. Nor could she say how many women here even read the fashion magazine, but her sister's gesture was priceless.

Forty minutes later, Vivian and her sisters stepped onto the boardwalk
on Bennett Avenue in front of the National Hotel. A landmark of her
deceit, yes, but also a reminder of God's amazing grace and her sisters'
sweet forgiveness.

"I thought we might start at the mercantile on Second," Nell said,
swinging her reticule at her side.

"Then we can check the new one on the other end." Kat's voice had
already gained energy in her brief respite from motherhood.

"Sounds good to me." Vivian strolled up the street between Ida
and Nell. "I just hope someone has what we need."

Ida giggled. "Carter wouldn't care if you wore a flour sack."

"True enough, but I do."

Nell stopped midstride. "It seems only fair that Vivian gets the
dress of her dreams. After all, a premier designer from the East fash-
ioned ours."

They all giggled. Vivian looked up just in time to see a woman on
the boardwalk ahead of them stop, divert her gaze from Vivian, and
bend toward her husband's ear.

Vivian stilled. They weren't the first to stare and whisper at the
sight of her. No doubt many more were nattering behind her back, and
she couldn't blame them. "Perhaps we should cross the street now."

"In the middle of the block?" Ida asked. "Whatever for?" She followed Vivian's gaze up the street. "Oh."

Ida and Nell locked arms with Vivian, and Kat laced her arm
through Nell's.

"We will do no such thing," Ida said. "Hold your head high, sis.
'You're forgiven' has no boundaries."

Vivian blinked back tears, squared her shoulders, and fell into step. Sisterhood. A very strong bond indeed.

By the time Vivian and her sisters had finished their shopping and returned to the boardinghouse, they were all weighed down by paper-wrapped packages. Yards of silk and chiffon. Rolls of lace and ribbon. Hosiery. Even a new pair of white ankle boots, a gift from her sisters.

Hattie met them at the door, her finger pressed to her lips. "Our little prince and princess are slumbering."

Judson stood beside her, drinking from a coffee mug. He studied them and cocked a thick eyebrow. "A successful shopping trip, I see."

"Yes." Nell giggled and kissed him on the cheek.

Vivian felt her face grow warm. In just six weeks and three days, she'd have a husband of her own to kiss on the cheek. She'd liked having Carter close by while he was recuperating. Today was the first day she hadn't seen him since he'd found her up at Ute Pass. Had it really only been twenty-four hours since Tucker took him away in the wagon? Too long.

"Did William behave for you?" Nell asked.

Judson lowered his cup. "Turns out I'm a pretty boring father. My boy slept through most of our time together."

Nell tittered and swatted his shoulder on her way into the parlor. Judson was anything but boring. Vivian followed Nell, and they set the packages on the sofa.

Hattie was untying the strings on a smaller sack when she suddenly twisted toward Vivian. "I can't believe I almost forgot to tell you that Etta Ondersma telephoned for you, Vivian!"

"She did?"

Her landlady nodded, her eyes glimmering. "She did indeed, and she asked that you reply as soon as you returned home."

"My guess is that she received her copy and has seen the error of her ways," Kat said.

Vivian's pulse raced. "You really think that's why she telephoned?"

Hattie motioned toward the kitchen. "Best way to know for sure is to talk to her yourself."

The closer Vivian got to the kitchen, the slower her steps came. The article, even the parts of it that weren't enhanced, didn't change her past. Once Mrs. Ondersma knew the truth about her, the business-woman would change her mind. And Vivian wouldn't blame her. She couldn't expect the widow to risk losing business because of who she employed.

When Vivian finally reached the telephone hanging on the kitchen wall, she stopped and lowered her head. The prayer was quick but intense. If Mrs. Ondersma was actually interested in hiring her, Vivian knew she had a lot of explaining to do. Not the least of which involved making straight the ramblings of a rogue editor who had never even met her.

Please give me the right words, Lord.

She pulled the earpiece from the hook and gave the crank a quick spin. It was strange, talking to one of the girls at the telephone exchange. "Yes, please connect me with Mrs. Ondersma at Etta's Fashions in Victor." Clicks and buzzes followed.

"Hello, Vivian?"

"Yes, Hattie Adams said you telephoned and asked for me."

"I did indeed. I read the article about you in *Harper's Bazar.*" Her voice fairly danced across the words.

"About that, Mrs. Ondersma."

"I had no idea you were so famous."

"I'm not really famous. My sister wrote the article, and an editor who hasn't seen but a couple of my sketches made up the headline."

"I know the writer is your sister, but it's still quite impressive, all of it."

She didn't care that the article was basically a family advertisement? She would care about the rest of it. Vivian drew in a deep breath. "There's more."

"Articles?"

"No, not that. Things have changed for me since I was in your shop. You should know that I—"

"If you're concerned about that Homestead House business, don't be."

Vivian gasped. "You know about that?"

"Carter Alwyn saw some of your sketches and telephoned to recommend that I hire you. He said your talent was what I needed to grow my design business."

Vivian blinked back tears. "And he told you what happened?"

"Yes. He felt I should know, and hear it from someone who knew the truth."

Oh, how she missed that man.

"It's what we do in our future, dear, that decides how important our past truly was."

Vivian wiped a tear from her cheek. "But people talk."

"They do indeed. And I think they'll care more about you being featured in a national magazine than they will about a stint on Myers Avenue that was no longer than a gnat's tail."

Vivian liked this woman and had from the moment she'd stepped out of the back room of her shop wearing bicycle bloomers.

"What do you say to working as a fashion designer and seamstress in my new Cripple Creek shop? The town has grown so much I think it deserves a designer of its own."

"Yes. Thank you!" Vivian jumped up and down. She was being given far more than she deserved.

Thank you, Lord.

THIRTY-THREE

✑

26 October 1897

*V*ivian opened the worn family Bible that lay on the table in front of her. Nearly eight weeks had passed since Carter proposed, and the day of the wedding ceremony had arrived amidst a flurry of activity. Vivian and her sisters had scoured the valley to find fabric and lace that would complement the wedding dress she'd designed. Ida's sister-in-law Willow returned from Colorado Springs, and she and Miss Hattie had joined the sisters in taking turns sewing the dress and rocking babies.

Willow stood in front of a mirror, baby Hope drooling in her arms. Kat sat at one end of the dining room table, arranging a bridal bouquet of purple asters and white daisies. Baby William slept in a bassinet behind Nell, who sat next to Vivian and sipped a cup of tea.

"This was a wonderful idea, Vivian." Ida seated herself across the table and looked down at the oversized Bible.

"I think so too." Vivian turned the gold-trimmed pages to the "Family Records" section. "I thought it would be fun to make the updates together as sisters. A new tradition."

Miss Hattie walked in carrying a tray of deviled eggs and cinnamon rolls. "I'm going to miss having a Sinclair sister living here. Attending a wedding has a way of brightening one's whole year." Blowing a strand of gray hair out of her eye, she set the tray on the table in front of Kat. "And it's been glorious having love floating about the old house again."

Nell looked at Willow, a familiar twinkle in her blue eyes. "You *are* an honorary Sinclair sister, you know."

Miss Hattie brightened. "Oh, that's right!"

Willow met their gaze in the mirror and shook her head. "Don't look at me. I have no intention of carrying on the Sinclair tradition of at least one wedding a year."

"Neither did I." Vivian pressed her finger to her chin and smiled.

Ida passed luncheon plates around the table. "I also know from experience that God's intentions rarely match our own."

Willow turned to face them, her eyes a deeper shade of green. "True enough, but I'm focused on spending time with my parents, and I have a long list of sights I have yet to paint." Her finger traced baby Hope's forehead. "Besides, I've had my turn at love, and the memory of Sam is still too fresh." She directed her attention to the lady of the house. "If you want to talk about second chances at love, Miss Hattie," she said, an eyebrow raised, "I think you're a better candidate."

Miss Hattie pressed her lips together and shook her head. "Perhaps we should turn our attention to the refreshments before we ready ourselves for the ceremony." She set two cinnamon rolls and two deviled eggs on her plate and passed the dishes to Kat.

Nell retrieved the fountain pen off the table and began writing in the Bible.

William Judson Archer 1897, 27 July, a special delivery gift to
Judson and Nellie Jean Archer

Nell turned to the page for recording marriages and looked up at Vivian, her blue eyes glistening. Vivian poised the fountain pen on the line below Ida and Tucker's.

Vivian Dee Sinclair and Carter Alwyn wed 1897, 26 October

She sighed, remembering her journey to this point. *"Thank you, Lord."*

An "amen" chorus echoed off the papered walls.

Two hours later, Vivian stood at the top of the stairs, breathing in the sweet scent of her bridal bouquet. Willow and Miss Hattie watched her from the entryway, each of them holding a baby, while Kat and Nell descended the steps in front of her. Vivian stroked the sky blue satin sash, highlighting the narrow waist of her wedding gown.

"You look gorgeous." Ida cupped Vivian's face. "I couldn't be happier for you."

"Thank you, sis. God is good to shower us with grace and mercy to clothe us in His righteousness."

"And good to send men our way who love us." Ida winked. "You ready to step into your future as Mrs. Carter Alwyn?"

"I've been ready since the day he flung me over his shoulder and hauled me up that mountain."

Ida laughed and then proceeded down the stairs and into the parlor. Vivian followed close behind. At the doorway, she paused and looked upon the other family and friends who had gathered to share in her and Carter's joy. Morgan and Judson stood with their wives. Otis and Naomi Bernard and their four boys. Deputy Jon Ondersma and his wife. Deputy Gilbert Neilson from Victor. A polished Boney Hughes joined Miss Hattie near the window.

Carter stood beside Tucker at the hearth, his hands pressed together in front of him. He looked as though he was praying, but his eyes were wide open, brimming with love and watching her every move as she glided toward him. Toward their future as husband and wife.

"I do." The words escaped her lips before she reached the hearth, and warmth rushed up her neck.

"I do too." Carter's hearty baritone reply gained them a ripple of laughter from the onlookers.

Her brother-in-law cleared his throat, his grin poorly disguised. "Dearly beloved…"

READERS GUIDE

1. Vivian is the *baby* in the Sinclair family and the last of the four sisters to make the move west. One of Vivian's defining characteristics—and her defining struggle—is her natural rebellion. What's good about Vivian's determination to stand on her own two feet? What's bad about it? What emotional state led her to make independence her highest goal?

2. Deputy Carter Alwyn struggles to live up to his father's law enforcement legacy. When in your life have you felt the pressure to perform? Did you eventually discover God's will for you in that circumstance?

3. Vivian's disappearance and the discovery of her association with the brothel create tension between Ida, Kat, and Nell. What are some emotions or situations that often cause friction between siblings? What strategies did the Sinclair sisters use for reconciliation?

4. Under the weight of shame, Vivian feels unlovable and, therefore, doesn't consider herself marriage material. But God brings Carter into her life, and Vivian falls in love with him despite feeling unworthy of his love. Has God ever brought someone into your life who surprised you with an outpouring of grace?

5. The "good people" of Cripple Creek look down on the "other women" and, by association, Vivian. Do you rate some sin worse than others? What does Romans 3:23 and 1 John 1:9 say about God's view of sin?

6. Vivian is influenced by many different people in this book, including, her sisters—Kat, Nell, and Ida; Aunt Alma; Opal; Hattie; and Carter. How does their influence affect her? What qualities do you look for in a mentor?

7. Vivian is descending into a life of secrets, lying to the very people who love her and could help her heal from her mistakes. Often it takes a crisis, hitting rock bottom, before a person recognizes the need for repentance and change. What was the turning point for Vivian? Like Vivian, have you ever faced a crisis that sent you in a new direction, giving you a fresh start?

8. Doc Susie is a historical figure who lived in Cripple Creek at the time this story takes place. Dr. Susan Anderson contracted tuberculosis while in medical school. Still, she returned to Colorado to practice medicine in mining camps. What qualities do you imagine Doc Susie must have possessed that made it possible for her to become a successful female physician in this era?

9. Vivian is updating the records in the family Bible. Is there a family Bible in your household? Is anyone in your family tending to the family tree? What does legacy mean to you?

10. Which of the Sinclair sisters do you identify with most? Feisty, stubborn Kat? Gentle, romantic Nell? Ambitious, determined Ida? Independent, misdirected Vivian? What about that sister draws you? Why?

Mona is available for book club conference calls where she joins your book club for a pre-scheduled fifteen-to-twenty-minute conversation via speakerphone or Skype. When possible, she's happy to add an "in person" visit to a book club in a city she's visiting. For more information, please contact Mona through her website: www.monahodgson.com.

AUTHOR'S NOTE

I don't consider myself a historian by any stretch of the imagination. Instead, I am a writer of historical fiction, who enjoys doing the research involved in delivering a compelling story steeped in history. My historical fiction features actual people, events, and places. *The Bride Wore Blue* characterizes three factions prevalent in Western boom towns like Cripple Creek—outlaws, lawmen, and soiled doves.

In each of the Sinclair Sisters of Cripple Creek novels, you'll meet at least one real-life woman from Cripple Creek history. Doctor Susan Anderson, known as Doc Susie, is the primary real-life woman in *The Bride Wore Blue.* Her portrayal in the story is a fictionalization. Pearl DeVere serves as a second real-life woman from Cripple Creek history. Her portrayal is also fictionalized; however, many of the colorful details of Miss DeVere's death and funeral are gleaned from Mabel Barbee Lee's book *Cripple Creek Days.*

In keeping with my commitment as a storyteller of historical fiction, I played with the actual dates of Susan Anderson's return to Cripple Creek and Pearl DeVere's death to meet the needs of Vivian Sinclair's story.

Harper's Bazar, the magazine I feature in the series, offers a spelling twist. If you're like me, you wanted to add another *a* after the *z,* but until the November 1929 issue, the magazine was spelled with only two *a*'s.

I look forward to our time together in these stories.

May you walk in peace having been justified by faith in the Lord Jesus Christ and rejoice in the hope that is yours because of His redeeming work on the Cross.

MONA HODGSON

ACKNOWLEDGMENTS

Writing is a team sport. Yes, I may be the one pitching the story to you, but many people are involved in creating a home run, which I hope we have done with *The Bride Wore Blue*. Here's a listing of the key players who assisted me.

- My hubby, Bob.
- My agent, Janet Kobobel Grant of Books & Such Literary Agency.
- My critique partner and writing bud, DiAnn Mills.
- My editors, Shannon Hill Marchese and Jessica Barnes.
- The entire WaterBrook Multnomah—Random House team.
- My prayer partners.

A big thank-you to all who are listed, and to all who aren't, who served on the infield and in the outfield.

Dedicated to the Head Coach, Jesus—
the Way, the Truth, and the Life.

ABOUT THE AUTHOR

*M*ona Hodgson is the author of The Sinclair Sisters of Cripple Creek Series as well as dozens of children's books. Mona's writing credits also include hundreds of articles, poems, and short stories in more than fifty different periodicals, including *Focus on the Family, Decision, Clubhouse Jr., Highlights for Children, The Upper Room, The Quiet Hour, Bible Advocate,* and *The Christian Communicator.* Mona speaks at women's retreats, schools, and writers' conferences. She is also a regular columnist on the Bustles and Spurs blog.

Mona and Bob, her husband of forty years, have two grown daughters, two sons-in-law, and a growing gaggle of grandchildren.

To learn more about Mona, to find readers' guides for your book club, or to view her photo album of current day Cripple Creek, visit her website: www.monahodgson.com. You can also find Mona at www.twitter.com/monahodgson and on Facebook at www.facebook.com/Mona Hodgson Author Page.

COMING OCTOBER 2012

TWICE A BRIDE

Book 4 in The Sinclair Sisters of Cripple Creek

1898

attie pressed her lips, covering her mouth, but the giggle escaped anyway. Boney Hughes lay under her kitchen sink, his upper body concealed by the cupboard. His gangly legs sprawled over her linoleum flooring.

Boney scooted out from under the sink and peered up at her. "You think me rappin' my old knuckles on these leaky pipes is funny?"

Unable to stifle her amusement, Hattie nodded. "You look like a..." She fanned herself, trying to regain her composure.

He stood.

"Like a fish out of water."

Boney's winter-white eyebrows arched. "A big old river catfish?"

Giggling, she studied him from his wiry beard to his worn boots. "A smaller fish perhaps, but surely one with a big heart."

"You're still a charmer, Hattie." He hooked his thumbs in his bib overalls. "Wore my best duds for coffee this mornin'. If I knew you planned to put me to work—"

"You would've shown up anyway." She smiled and pulled two mugs from the buffet.

"You know me all too well, Adeline Prudence McFarland...Adams." He said her married name with an air of reverence.

George had died within months of finishing the boardinghouse. He would've relished the ever-changing company the house afforded. Hattie sighed, picturing her late husband leaning against the sink.

"I still miss him too." Boney cleared his throat and looked out the window.

She poured the coffee and set their cups on the kitchen table beside the lemon meringue pie she'd baked that morning.

Boney washed his hands under the running water, then bent to look at the pipes beneath the sink. "Fishy or not, ma'am, I fixed it. Not a single wayward drop." His eyes shining like polished silver, he joined her at the table and gulped his coffee.

Hattie stirred a pinch of cinnamon into her coffee. "You're a good man, Mister Hughes." Bracing her cup with both hands, she sipped and savored the bold warmth as she did the same with the memories. "It's nice to have someone to share coffee and a chat with. The house has been too quiet lately."

"You got spoiled having the Sinclair sisters in the house."

"I surely did." A melancholy softened her tone. She missed witnessing the first hints of affection between the ladies and their gentlemen, the questions, the discoveries, the surrendering of two hearts to become one. Their journeys to the altar. She missed the excitement of the weddings.

She couldn't love those four girls—young women—any more if they were her own daughters. George would have too. Each of them had found a good man and married him. Vivian, the last born and the last to arrive in Cripple Creek, had wed nearly a year ago.

The house had definitely been too quiet these past few months.

Willow Raines Peterson was back in town, and she was as close to being a Sinclair sister as one could get without the blood, but—

Boney cleared his throat, derailing her thoughts and drawing her gaze. Her friend had cut the pie and dished two pieces. "Where'd you go?"

"I was on Tenderfoot Hill, May 30, 1896, watching Kat and Nell wed Morgan and Judson. The next minute at the church, listening to Ida and Tucker's vows. Then in the parlor remembering Vivian and Carter's ceremony. And just now, I was wondering about Willow." She sighed. "Praying she is...content."

"You think she'll marry again?"

"I don't know." Hattie spread a napkin on her lap. "Widows aren't easily convinced."

"Don't I know it." Boney slid a pie plate across the table to her. "You ever miss Missouri?"

She tucked errant gray hairs behind her ear. "I miss the river. Especially during the summer."

He nodded, his mouth full of pie.

"And at times, I miss that girl."

"The one with hair the color of molasses?"

"That's the one." Although she wouldn't have used a pantry item to describe her hair.

"Well, as time would have it, I was fond of that girl and happen to be quite fond of the woman she is today." He scooped another forkful of lemon meringue. "Her cooking ain't half bad either."

"You always were one to flatter the females, Mister Hughes."

"Friends call me Boney." He winked.

The telephone jangled. Hattie lifted herself out of her chair with a *hmph.* Just as well. She'd been dawdling too long on Memory Lane. Some anniversaries of George's death did that to her. Today was a tougher one. She reached the phone, lifted the earpiece, and spoke into the cone. "Hello."

"Miss Hattie, there's a Mr. Harlan Sinclair on the line for you."

"Sinclair?" Oh, the girls' father.

"From New York."

"Yes, thank you."

"Hello, Mrs. Adams!" The line was more scratchy than usual, and he sounded as if he were shouting. "My four daughters have all stayed at your boardinghouse."

"Yes. Delightful girls, each and every one."

"Thank you."

"I've been wishing you'd had more daughters." Her cheeks warmed. *What a thing to say.* "I only meant that I enjoyed having Kat and Nell, Ida, and Vivian here in the house."

"That's what I'm calling about, ma'am."

"About your girls living in my house?" She glanced over at Boney, who was sliding another piece of pie onto his plate. "That's interesting. It's been nearly a year since the last one moved out."

She couldn't be sure but she thought she heard him sigh.

"Mrs. Adams—"

"Begging your pardon, Mr. Sinclair…your girls call me Hattie."

"Very well, Hattie Adams, I need to secure two rooms for the third full week of September."

This was September 9, the second Friday. Hattie opened her mouth.

"Week after next." Mr. Sinclair's words were clipped. "I expect I'll need at least one of the rooms, perhaps both, for a month or more."

She thought to ask why he didn't plan to take his lodging in one of his daughters' homes, but the man clearly wasn't given to chatter. But then costly long distance rates from New York wouldn't invite windy conversations. Still...she wondered if his daughters knew he was no longer in Paris.

"Do you have two rooms available for that week?"

"I do, and they're now reserved for you."

"Very well. Until then."

After a click, the static on the line fell silent. Hattie shivered, staring at the phone for a moment. The girls had obviously inherited their warmth from their mother. She returned to the table and regarded Boney, a man with a very warm heart. "That was Mr. Sinclair."

"Father to our Sinclair sisters?"

"The very one." She scooped a generous bite of pie. "Mr. Sinclair will arrive in Cripple Creek in about ten days, week after next. And he's bringing a guest."

"He's bringing a friend with him?"

"He let two rooms. He didn't say who would fill them."

"Perhaps it's the girls' aunt coming with him."

"Yes, of course. That's probably who it is. Aunt Alma." The prospect made her smile.

Alma Shindlebower could brighten a room any day. Perfect!

Hattie raised her cup as if she were toasting her grand inspiration. The lively Alma Shindlebower was just what her friend Boney needed in his life. Willow might not be ready for a match, but those two were long overdue. And soon the Sinclair family would fill her home again.

August 1865

When Maren Jensen arrived in America nearly two years ago from Denmark, she was surprised to find that Thursday quickly became her favorite day of the week—the day the quilting circle met at her employer's farm. She could barely work a needle before immigrating, and she had little interest in textiles, but she loved the company of women who gathered.

Elsa Brantenberg, her employer, sat in a rocker by the window. A log cabin quilt top draped her lap and spilled onto the braided rug at her feet. Maren sat in a wooden chair on the other side of Mary Lou Kerr and her mother-in-law, Irene, thumbing through a stack of colorful squares. She'd planned to tell her friend Adeline about the drifter called "Wooly" who showed up at the farm yesterday, but they hadn't had a moment alone this morning.

Mrs. Brantenberg folded her hands over her quilting and looked across the room to where Adeline pulled thread through an appliqué. "I believe it's your turn to ask God's blessing upon our time together, Adeline." She cocked her head and grinned. "I mean to say, *Miss Hattie*."

Maren raised an eyebrow and wondered if the new nickname Mrs. Brantenberg's four-year-old granddaughter, Weibke, had assigned Adeline this morning was going to stick. The fifteen-year-old Adeline wasn't content with a simple summer bonnet, not when she had her ailing grandmother's closet to draw from. Today she wore a green straw hat with a wide brim and feathers that had made quite an impression on the little girl.

"Yes ma'am," Hattie said, smiling.

Mrs. Brantenberg folded her hands and bowed her head. "Don't forget to thank God for our newest member, dear."

The activity in the room stilled. Without being too obvious, Maren tried to sneak a glance at Augusta Milburn. The newcomer sat on a settee beside her sister Inez, a flower basket quilt top spread over their laps.

Augusta appeared solemn as she pulled a handkerchief from a pocket in her skirt and pressed the cloth against the wet tracks on her face. "Perhaps I shouldn't have come."

"Unsinnig." Mrs. Brantenberg crossed the room and captured Augusta's hand. "That's nonsense, dear. You are among friends here."

Colonel Milburn had not joined his bride in the four months that had passed since the South surrendered.

"It can take a man awhile to travel if he was deep in the south." Maren had come to appreciate Mrs. Brantenberg's voice of reason. "Dear, his regiment could've been sent west to fight in the Indian wars."

Augusta shook her head, squaring her shoulders. "The last word from him…" Her words were slow and heavily weighted. "His regiment was in Georgia."

"In one of the last battles?" Mrs. Brantenberg looked toward Inez, who nodded. "You've written to the Department of War?"

"I did." Augusta looked at the handkerchief in her lap, her index finger tracing an embroidered letter. "They have not responded."

Inez and Augusta had lost their beloved father a short time ago, and now there was a good chance Augusta would never see her husband again, either. Maren brushed a tear from her own face. Most of the women in the circle were doing the same thing, or shuffling and clearing their throats. Mrs. Weber, one of the women who rode in on the Kerr's wagon, lost her son in the same battle. Mary Lou Kerr's husband had come home missing a foot. And now Colonel Milburn was missing. Mrs. Brantenberg was one of the more fortunate ones; her son-in-law had survived the war and returned home. His regiment had been sent to the Arizona Territory, and he returned home yesterday—welcomed, or not.

Mrs. Weber pressed a hand to her long neck. "Here in this quilting circle, dear, none of us are alone. Not in our sorrows, nor in our triumphs."

Go back *to the* beginning

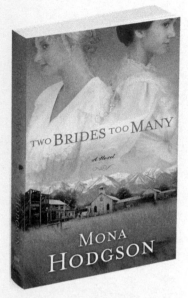

Two sisters,
Two missing misters.

Kat and Nell Sinclair are headed west—away from the manicured lawns of Maine to the boisterous, booming mining town of Cripple Creek, Colorado, to start new lives for themselves as mail-order brides. But when they arrive, neither fiancé is there, leaving both sisters questioning their dreams and the hope for true love.

Ida wants a career,
not a husband.
Her sisters—and God—
have other plans.

Ida Sinclair joins her sisters Kat and Nell in Cripple Creek. As the business-savvy Sinclair sister, Ida has never wanted to settle down. Instead of love, she craves success. But while searching for one, she just might find the other.

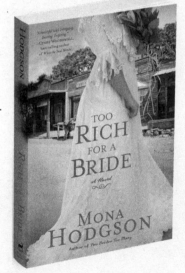

Read an excerpt from these books and more on
WaterBrookMultnomah.com!